A DANCE TO WAKE A DRAGON

A NOVEL

RICHARD PRATT

A Dance to Wake a Dragon

By Richard Pratt

Trade Paper: 978-988-8904-27-3
Digital: 978-988-8904-26-6

© 2025 Richard Pratt

FICTION

EB228

All rights reserved. No part of this book may be reproduced in material form, by any means, whether graphic, electronic, mechanical or other, including photocopying or information storage, in whole or in part. May not be used to prepare other publications without written permission from the publisher except in the case of brief quotations embodied in critical articles or reviews. For information contact info@earnshawbooks.com

Published in Hong Kong by Earnshaw Books Ltd.

PART 1

Chapter One

When a dancer runs through a forest, swaying and stepping, skipping and leaping, is she running or dancing? When a dancer runs through a forest for no reason, and no one is looking, except maybe a small, foxlike dog who runs with her, and her heart tells her to spin and to shimmy, is she dancing, then?

And so Shengli came dancing-running through the even snow, down the path through the bamboo forest, slipping and sliding and sometimes, sighting a pile of fluffier stuff for a soft landing, jumping into the snowdrifts and rolling out of them in a single movement. A laugh and a lunge and a pause to lift up her arms and to sing out to the silent, silvery, woodland world. Boken, her best friend, was having a little difficulty keeping up. Boken liked to run ahead of Shengli, not flump around behind her trying to deal with belly-depth snow and then negotiate the slippy bits where his four paws would take on minds of their own and argue about which way they should slide. He was hoping Shengli would practise her crash landing in a minute, and he'd have a chance to organize himself, shake the snow out of his fur and to discipline his mutinous feet.

"Aaaaahhhkarash-landingggg!" There it was. Shengli had

spied a nice deep drift and accelerating down the slope, she launched into a classic swallow dive and plunged far into the deep, white, pillow, pile of still-fresh snow. After pausing for just a moment to savor the sensation of being face and shoulders submerged, she pulled herself out and turned back to look for Boken. "Come on, Boken, lazy hound!"

Boken responded with a twitch of his ears and a slightly haughty sniff before returning to the minor matter of sorting out which bits of his doggy world were still under control and which needed attention. He was golden brown all over with upright, triangular ears, a nicely pointy snout, and a bushy tail. And no, despite appearances, he was not a fox. Although sometimes people would tease Shengli about her 'fox-friend', he was just a brown dog who looked, admittedly, a little bit like a fox.

"Are you ready now?" Shengli asked him. Boken looked back and spoke. Or rather, he didn't actually speak because, of course, dogs can't speak in the same sort of kind of way that people speak: their faces and mouths and so on are just the wrong shape for that. And things are just the shape they are. But Shengli knew that Boken was speaking to her and she understood him. If she asked him a question, he would respond with a twitch of the nose or a twinkle in the eyes, his ears would turn one way or the other, or independently, and he would pull one corner of his mouth one way or another, his snout would nudge, or his head would cock at one or another angle or however you like in some doggy way and, with his face and fur and features, he would speak to her.

Yes, he responded, now that you've quite finished and you've remembered that I'm rather small by comparison with yourself, and this snow is rather deep in some parts and that you sometimes seem to forget these small logistical elements, I am now fully composed and am quite ready to continue our journey back home. I concede that I'm a little frustrated that I cannot, as I would prefer, bound ahead, scouting the way and checking back occasionally to see you trying to keep up as is the case when conditions favor the four-footed over your poor, deprived, bipedal self but as long as this wretched white stuff covers the ground I will have to accept that circumstances are, hopefully temporarily, disadvantageous to a canine of modest dimensions. Please lead on and I will putter behind to the best of my ability. Boken really did say all that. Although he didn't actually say it but it was, one might put it, written all over his face and Shengli could understand him perfectly well.

"All right, you pompous puppy. We'll take it easy from here. I want to keep an eye out for Shonan and Durfin anyway and I can't do that while watching the ground in front of me. I think they'll be back soon. They've been over at their Grandpa's house for a couple of days and if I see them before they see me, we could ambush them. So, let's go quietly from here!"

Boken signaled his approval. Although a serious-minded dog, he was rather fond of practical jokes and especially if they were at the expense of the twins. They teased him often enough so it was always good to get one back on them. Shonan was a bit more sensitive but her brother, Durfin, was a clot at times and seeing him face first in the snow would make this a good day.

Shengli set herself into 'prowler' mode. That meant looking left and right, shoulders hunched, knees bent, hands out front as if feeling her way in the dark. Which wasn't really necessary given that it was bright daytime but if you were going to do 'prowler' you had to do it right. She checked the pose, wriggled with it a little, and wondered if 'prowler' needed a bit more hunching? Meanwhile, Boken started a puppyish dance with his eyebrows, ears and nose. But for once, Shengli wasn't looking. There was nothing for it: he let go with a little 'yap'.

"Hush, you dopey dog! This is an ambuuuuu..."

Well, thought Boken. I was trying to tell you I could smell them but if you won't pay attention. Shonan and Durfin appeared suddenly, launching out of the forest, armed with snowballs and, with the advantage of the higher ground, came crashing down on Shengli and Boken. The melee ensued. Shengli landed a fistful of fresh snow slap in Durfin's face but it was hard when you were facing up the slope and she was soon on her back, with Shonan sitting on her chest, fully in control. It was a rare victory for Shonan and she felt inclined to enjoy it for a moment or two.

Boken, wrapped up in Durfin's arms and being held upside down, was in no position to assist. If it hadn't been for the snow, then that clumsy potato would never have caught him, dammit.

Peace was declared and the four friends stomped through the snow back down to the village. The little houses were neat and tidy around the frozen pond. The villagers had worked together to take turns sweeping the snow away from the paths and for all that the winter had been hard going, the smoke from their efficient fireplaces winding from the chimneys twisted like the sharp edged paths that, in turn, spoke of the care that the householders took in looking after things, just as the orderly rows of winter greens in the vegetable plots gave the sense that, even though the non-arrival of spring meant something was clearly very wrong, in this little corner of Tianya at least, those matters that could be handled locally were being well-managed.

The group separated just before reaching the pond. Shonan and Durfin lived in one of the larger cottages in the second row back from the pond and Shengli lived with her father in one of the smaller homes that looked out over the pond. The cottages around the pond had the pleasant advantage of looking out over the water and on summer evenings, this tended to be where the villagers would gather to sit together and while away the hours.

These homes were smaller though and for families that were a bit larger, like Durfin and Shonan's, where they lived with both parents and a younger sister and brother, the second-row houses were larger and so more suitable. That, of course, was how the balance came: smaller houses had nicer views, those with larger houses accepted that in return for more space, you gave way on the nice view. Shengli kicked off as much snow as she could on the doorframe and then pushed noisily into the cottage.

After the bright sun on the snow, the dark indoors, lit only by light from the small fire, meant that her eyes didn't quite adjust at first but she announced herself in her usual way,

"Ho, Ba! We're back! Boken has been a total lump so we didn't get that far in the end but I found these," and she emptied her pockets of the mushrooms she had found while they were out walking.

"There's still no sign of any bamboo shoots or anything else but I'll have another wander later. Oh! Hello, Old Tam, I'm sorry I didn't see you."

As her eyes adapted to the cozy, if dark, interior, she became aware for the first time that Old Tam was sitting in the corner by the fire, nursing a cup of her father's home-made mulberry wine that had most likely been taken from the little earthenware jug propped up at the edge of the hearth, warming by some faintly glowing embers. Immediately adjusting her manner to one more appropriate for a visit by her family's old and beloved friend, and her own teacher and mentor, not to mention the man who was in a sense the 'father' of the village, she dusted herself down, walked over, and accepted the two-handed greeting that Old Tam extended.

"How are you, Dear Shengli?" he asked. "It is a while since you came to visit and to talk with me and, dare I mention it, read with me a little?"

Shengli shuffled slightly and, pulling her sleeves over her hands, picked up the wine jug and topped up Old Tam's cup. He smiled. He didn't really mind that she hadn't been round, except that truthfully, he just enjoyed her company. He had known Shengli since, well, before she was born in that he had been close to her father and mother since they themselves were children. He enjoyed taking the time to encourage her occasional interest in reading, and to talk with her about books and the ways of the ancients, but he was happy to wait for her to come round when she felt like it. His view, that he didn't trouble to share, was that there was no point trying to teach anybody anything; you could only help someone to learn. Which of course meant that someone had to want to learn before they could be taught. Looking at things that way, in fact, Shengli was a long way ahead of the children in the city even though she didn't go to an actual school, as such, and only turned up to Old Tam's cottage when she felt like it. But when she was there, she learned more in a short time than the city children learned in months just because she wanted to be there.

But she didn't know any of this. She knew little of how things were in a big city like Lungdou, or even a small town like Quiczu. Indeed, the idea that you had no choice but to go to school, even if you weren't quite in the mood and would rather go for a wander in the forest with your best friend, or your joint second-best friends, would have confused her more than anything. They sat in silence and felt at peace. After as long as it was, Old Tam was the first to speak.

"Shengli," he said, and there was something in his voice that told her they were about to have a different sort of conversation from normal.

"Yes, Old Tam."

"Do you still practise the dance?"

"Why yes, of course. Every day. Slowly, like mother taught me, and never all of it in one go. So, some days I do the first sequence and then other days the middle or third sequences."

"Could you do it all for real?"

"Of course!"

"I'm afraid you're going to have to."

Earlier that day, weary from the all the study and anxiety, Old Tam had placed his astrolabe carefully back on its rest and he had looked out into the snow-filled forest beyond, certain of his next move. Every calculation had led him to the same conclusion and there was no longer any doubt in his mind. The dragon lay beneath and would not come above unless the dance was performed at Zamai. Spring was now two months overdue. The forest and fields were still draped in snow and the novelty of that had very much long worn off. Forests in the winter time are pretty, for sure, but without the spring there is no new life. The flowers will not bud, the crops cannot be planted, the animals will not reemerge from their winter homes and the cycle of seasons will not turn. Spring was sometimes late, but this was different. It was now clear beyond doubt that the Li dragon, the ruler of rivers and rain, seas and seasons, points of the compass and patterns of the clouds and skies, the Li dragon that descended each Autumn to shorten the days and bring the winter, and who reascended each Spring to direct the new cycle, had not risen. It was still. It lay beneath.

This had, he knew, happened before. The ancients had seen it and they knew, that dragons being dragons, they could need encouraging. Even the Yu dragon, the dragon of order and balance, of government and law, could have off-days. And dragon days being of indeterminate length they could last a while. And when the Yu dragon was inattentive, that was when wars and chaos among the different creatures of Tianya could bring so much misery. It had, thankfully, been a long while since the Yu dragon had been distracted but who knew if the time might come again? Old Tam hoped that if it came, it would be well after he himself had fallen asleep for the last time: he still remembered the wars in the days of the current King's grandfather. He'd been a young man then but had seen things that haunted him still.

He made a point of playing his lute every day as a help to the Yu dragon to stay alert. Then, of course there was the Jiao dragon. The Earth dragon who needed, by contrast, to be kept at peace. Restlessness by that old thing meant the moving of mountains, the diversion of rivers, landslides and tumbling buildings. It was understandable that the creature might need to shift from time to time. Old Tam had difficulty sitting still himself; but tenderness to the earth and easing the 'itch' that came from poor management of the forests and fields would help the Jiao dragon relax and the creatures of Tianya could shuffle around on his lumpy body, going about their business, like fleas on a dog's back without too much disturbance.

Finally, there were the Mang dragons. The little dragons. They couldn't do much harm, and as long as they were left alone, they tended to do their own thing, playing and joking around with each other and only occasionally causing a little mischief to the creatures of Tianya by teasing or playing tricks just to pass the time. Their role was to ensure that the beauty of randomness remained in Tianya and that every attempt to bring about order and organization would have an occasional bit of a muddle thrown in. When Old Tam was playing his lute, for example, and found his fingers taking him off on a little moment of improvization, he knew that a Mang dragon was tickling him.

But dragons were, well, not human obviously, but they could be forgetful or distracted, or else just plain lazy. Tianya needed everyone to be working and keeping things tidy for matters to remain in equilibrium and it looked as though the Li dragon had chosen to lie beneath, was not in a mood to rise and, while this was amusing when reflecting on the playful and perhaps naughty character of dragons, it was a living nightmare for the creatures of Tianya as without the spinning and swirling of the Li dragon in the skies above, spring would not come.

And before long that would be the end of all that was good: the end of flowers, and foods, and fun; the exhaustion of winter stores, and for time to be too long before the planting of new crops, and then hungry times ahead. Above all, there would be no signal to the animals in the changing season to resume the cycle and so no cubs or chicks, kits or tadpoles, calves or hatchlings, foals, kids, leverets or any baby creatures would be born as their mothers would instead lift their noses, or twitch their whiskers, or fluff their feathers, or shuffle their gills, and conclude that the time wasn't right for new life and however much their hearts told them different, the spring wasn't here and the wait would have to go on.

But the ancients had understood this and had learned there was a way, when the Li dragon was sluggish, to bring him back above. And that was the dance. The dance that was performed at Zamai. The dance performed at the point where the primary dragon lines intersected, under the temple of Zamai, around which the city of Lungdou had grown and there, articulating, through the dance, the critical vibrations in the fluence, the Li dragon's veins would be aroused and curious, and he would emerge and dance again above Tianya and the cycle of seasons would resume.

The only problem was that no one believed in any of this these days. The Dance Academy over in Lungdou had long given up training new dancers and no one knew the dance anymore. Except Shengli, of course, but, love her dearly as he did, Old Tam had to concede that she was, only thirteen years old, and a bit silly, and she could hardly be expected to take on such grave affairs. So Old Tam just spoke of village matters with Shengli while her Ba brought their supper. It was a fine meal and typical of the kind of food they had at this time of year: winter greens, some pickles, mushrooms, beans, and barley. Everyone was ready for a bit of a change and some seasonal spring vegetables, and all were feeling the effect of the stocks of dried and winter foods running down, but it was still a wholesome and tasty dinner. The talk, as happened increasingly often in the village these days, turned to dragons, and in particular the Li dragon and the problem of his still lying beneath.

"And so you see," Old Tam started to conclude, after sharing his thoughts, "I'm convinced that the dance has to be performed at Zamai, with the spells embroidered in the dancing shoes and, since your mother died, and the Academy has decayed, I think it may be true that you are the only person left who knows the dance."

There was a pause, and then Shengli asked, "But why at Zamai? Why can't I do it here?".

"Because that is where the fluence must be revitalised."

"I'm sorry, I know you've told me before, but I don't really understand what the fluence is."

Old Tam smiled and, not for the first time, explained gently.

"You know how when your Ba plants his beans, they know how to grow, all by themselves, as long as he's panted them in good soil?"

"And with a proper mulch...", the normally quiet Ba interjected,

"And with a proper mulch. But then, the bean somehow grows, and knows how to grow, all by itself?"

"Ye-e-es", replied Shengli, who'd been expecting something

a bit more fancy in a conversation about the mysterious fluence than talk about beans.

"Well, the force that through that bean plant that drives that bean to flower, and then create new beans, is fluence. And for the time that that bean is growing, it is like a dragon vein itself for the small, but strong enough, fluence that it channels. The force that drives the bean, is the same force that drives all the moving and changing things, the turning of the days, the seasons, and everything in the world."

"Do I have fluence?"

"You most certainly do!"

"Then why do I have to go to Zamai to do the dance if the fluence is everywhere?"

"Well, firstly, it isn't everywhere, it has to travel through veins. That's the structure. The world is made into a living world by fluence that moves within the structure that is underneath everything. Without the structure, the fluence would spill out everywhere and become weak. When it is channelled in a structure, it moves strongly. Like when water runs through a pipe. When the fluence runs up the beanstalk, it is channelled. And that is just enough fluence for the bean plant. But to turn the seasons, then that needs a major channel, a big pipe, if you like, for a lot of fluence, and that means the primary veins. The Li dragon is the guardian of the primary veins in the lower ennea, and don't worry about what that means for now, and to revitalise both of those veins at the same time, since we can't know which of the two veins the dragon will be lying in, the only place it can work is Zamai."

Shengli didn't respond immediately and there was a period of silence. The wind outside was gentle but strong enough to catch the edges of the little cottage wall and to make a low whistling sound; the fire crackled in the grate, and a small gurgling noise muttered briefly from Old Tam's stomach as his supper engaged with the business of digestion.

———∞———

"But that would mean traveling to Lungdou. I've never even been on the north side of the forest. And I don't know anything about it. What about the other dancers? Didn't they have children? Didn't they teach the dance to anyone?"

At this point, Old Tam looked over at Shengli's Ba and raised his eyebrows as if asking a question. Ba sighed, but nodded. "Yes, she ought to know. I should have told her before but you know, I didn't like to think of all that."

Old Tam looked back at Shengli, sitting across the table from him on her little stool. She still looked like a little girl to him but maybe that was only because he had grown so used to seeing her that way. In the light from the fire, he could see her mother in her features. The same slightly turned up nose, the same similar, intelligent and inquisitive eyes and the same slightly rebellious air that had caused all the trouble back then. She even seemed to wear the beads in her hair in the same patterns as her mother did. And he began to explain how Shengli's mother had been forced to leave the Academy because she had argued with the Dama and was determined to marry Shengli's father.

The rules in the Academy in those days were strict. The Dancers were forbidden from marrying. The idea was that they were 'married' to the Dance, to the Academy and to the Dama, but Shengli's mother was not the type of spirited young woman to live under that regime for long. Although it had been a huge privilege to be accepted into the Academy, to be chosen by seekers from the court, who in those days traveled to all the towns and villages to find girls with the potential to train for this vital role, she always pined for life back in the village, and especially her childhood sweetheart, Shengli's Ba. In the end, she tried to escape, but she was caught and brought back and then she tried misbehaving on purpose to get herself expelled. It was all, at the time, a source of shame to the village, but everyone loved the family so much it was all soon forgotten. Old Tam had made a big difference then, telling everyone that it was never in the minds of the ancients for the system to stand in the way of love and joy between young people.

Shortly afterward, the old King died, the current King's father succeeded him and brought with him the new age of engines and the rejection of the ways of the ancients. No one believed in the dance anymore and it didn't seem to matter, after all. By the time Shengli's mother died peacefully in her sleep, for no reason that anyone could see and with no apparent cause, no one cared about any of that stuff anymore anyway. It was only for playfulness and exercise in her life in the village that she had continued to practise the dance and for a bit of fun, had taught it to Shengli. But for niggling reasons that she couldn't explain in words, she had always been careful to insist they never danced the whole sequence and that they never used the spells.

"And," continued Old Tam, "so as far as anyone knows, there is no one alive now who knows the dance. Since the old Dama died and the new age launched, the Academy has just been used for show dancing and, really, just as a way of collecting money but mostly it has just given up and the last I heard, the Academy was falling into decay. Some of the old dancers are presumably still alive, of a similar age perhaps to what your mother would be if she had lived, although she was the youngest then, but there is no reason to suppose that they taught anyone the dance and the reality is that age catches up with all of us. Perhaps there is someone who could teach a youngster the dance from memory but how long would that take? And how much longer can we wait? And do they, in any case, have the spells? You still have them, of course?"

"Yes, of course."

And Shengli rose from her stool and walked over to the small desk by the wall where there was the only picture of her mother, a drawing made of her by Shonan and Durfin's mother, her own childhood friend. Reaching behind the picture she felt for the little key that was kept lodged in the frame and finding it, she unlocked the desk drawer. There, reaching to the back of the drawer that, in the way that drawers do, seemed to have become filled up with things that no one knew where to put, she pulled out the two embroidered insoles, one for the left foot and one for the right foot, that were her greatest treasure.

"Here they are. I haven't taken them out of the drawer for a long time. I know they're fairly fragile and I don't want to damage them."

"Can you still make out the nüshu?"

"Yes. I've always kept them in the drawer so the light won't fade the writing."

"Have you ever danced on them?"

"Of course not. And anyway, my shoes were always too small."

"What about now?"

"I don't know. It's been ages since I last took them out. And then only to make sure that I could still trace out the nüshu with my fingers and to say the words a bit. I like doing that sometimes. They feel nice to say."

"Perhaps we should see if things have changed a bit? Why not find your dancing shoes and let's try them?"

Shengli closed the drawer behind her and turned to fetch her dancing shoes from her little bedroom at the back of the cottage. They were always out and easy to find as she made sure to practise every day.

"Are these the right size for you now?" asked Old Tam.

"Yes, Lele made them for me only last month or so. They fit perfectly."

"Put the soles in."

Shengli suddenly felt her heart racing. For all that the little cottage was toasty warm from the fire and the thick walls were protecting them from the winter weather outside, she felt goosebumps on her skin. She looked over at her father. His face showed a mixture of emotions. He hadn't said anything all this time but he had been watching and listening in his close way. Now he looked on as Shengli gently handled the embroidered insoles, mostly white but with red writing in the secret script known only to the women of Tianya and now, apart from the rumors about the nuns at the priory on the Eastpoint Island, and who knew if they were true, mostly forgotten by all except for a few old ladies and perhaps just one or two younger women who had grown up around it in the more remote villages, as had Shengli. She took the left shoe in her left hand, the corresponding insole in her right and slid it in.

It was a perfect fit.

Chapter Two

Shengli took her thoughts, the dancing shoes and the soles and went quietly into her bedroom, closing the door behind her, leaving Old Tam and Ba together in the soft orange glow of the fading embers. Her father was first to speak.

"Old Tam, is this really going to be necessary? Shengli is so young. And Lungdou is, well, you know what it is. Or what it has become. Especially since the new age. And I have to tell you, old friend, if anything happened to her I would..."

"Don't say it. I know. But I can't see any alternative. I've sent letters to those of the old ways with whom I can still make contact. Many haven't replied and I don't know what that means: some may be dead. We can't any of us have long left and I don't know if there are any younger learners, or maybe they have just given up on the ancients also and think, like everyone else, that it is just silly old-fashioned nonsense. Those that have replied have come to the same conclusion but they are in despair. But look outside! Count the days! Hibernating animals must already be starving in their sleep. That means the bumblebees may not survive. Think about what that means! Imagine: the Li dragon rises in another month or so? And there's no guarantee of that. We humans might get through for a bit longer but what about them? And what about our old friends, the bears? They can manage torpor for up to six months but we have had snow on the ground for nearly that long already."

"I know, I know. Don't forget that I'm a village man through and through. I understand the seasons. For once, you old thing, you don't need to be my teacher. But in the name of all the dragons, why Shengli?"

"Because for all our knowledge, and amid the wonder of the age of engines, alive in the arrogance and confidence of our bold age of discovery and invention, I find that all my learning, everything I believe, and every effort I have made to understand and to look for solutions to this crisis, they all point to the same conclusion. The fate of Tianya rests on the shoulders, and in the dancing shoes, of a thirteen year old girl."

"I can't bear the thought of her in Lungdou," her father said. "She doesn't even know that they eat creatures there. How will she deal with that? Or will she get the taste for it herself? And I don't mind going to prison for this, of course not, I've done it before and you know I'd do it again; it was just about me, but the exile is still imposed on me and if I enter the city and am identified, well, maybe no one will care anymore about a crime against the Dance Academy over twenty years ago but then, maybe they will. And how can I look after Shengli if I'm arrested and jailed?"

"You won't need to go. Indeed, you mustn't."

"Don't be ridiculous! My daughter, on the road, traveling to Lungdou of all places! Of course, I must go. Sometimes I wonder if all that calculating hasn't done some damage to that old brain of yours."

"I reached out to a friend. A very special friend. I cannot tell you who. He has promised to send his son, a fine warrior, to escort Shengli. I'm hoping he'll be here tomorrow. His name is Renzi. If you are satisfied that he will be a fitting escort, will you drop your opposition? And I will go myself, of course. I have no reason to fear the guards and if the noise of the engines causes this old head to fall off, then it won't be before its time."

That last remark, and the twinkling smile of the old man was enough to lighten Ba's thoughts. Old Tam rose to leave and the two men embraced before he stepped out through the little doorway into the dark, snowy night.

The hour was late and Ba was going to have to work this through in his own mind. He missed Shengli's mother every day but sometimes the hurt was of a different kind and especially when it was about Shengli. Some kinds of loneliness he could manage. In practical terms, the pair of them got by and, you could say, they did better than most and in any case, the village meant they were surrounded by good friends. But the depth of isolation that came on him when trying to work out how best to influence and raise his daughter, who had been so close to her mother and who was so like her, could leave him feeling like all his insides were being scooped out with a rake by some invisible monster. He trusted Old Tam and would, if this Renzi was someone he felt would keep her safe, end up agreeing. But it was hard to bear.

But what was Shengli going to say? She would, he knew, make her own mind up and then, just like her mother, if she had a firm opinion, then nothing anyone could say, not Old Tam himself, not anyone, would persuade her. And what if she refused, said, "I'm not going."?

She refused.

The next morning, conversation had gone round in circles a bit and Old Tam and Ba, who now found themselves allies, were again, as many times before faced with the immovable object that was Shengli when she didn't want to do something.

They were all three sitting outside the little cottage, breathing clouds of mist out into the frosty air. Without anyone saying so, it had felt better to get out of the close confines of the cozy but suddenly claustrophobic little home. They were sitting on the wooden benches that were so often the gathering point for villagers and visitors for debates and discussions. More usually the topics for analysis would be important matters such as recipes for mulberry wine or the best mulch for pea plants but at that moment, though, in the minds of the two adults, there was a combination of fear for the future of Tianya and parental anxiety.

In the mind of the girl, there was a deep irritation that they seemed to have made their minds up together, talking after she had gone to bed the night before and for that reason she was not inclined to cooperate. Just yet.

Old Tam broke the silence and said, "Your father has agreed that if Renzi is, as I promise you he is, a reliable and secure escort, then he will lift his objection to your going. You know the situation, you know how much we have to fear if Spring is delayed much longer, and it won't even be that difficult a journey. There is an engine that runs now from Quiczu to Lungdou so even though I'm still not myself so sure in my heart about these things, there is some advantage as what used to be two or three days across mountain paths is now half a day riding in a sort of wagon on rails. It might even be quite interesting. So all we have to do is to follow the path through the forest to Quiczu and if things go smoothly, we'll be back in a couple of days. I'll be with you the whole time, we can do some reading together in the evenings and after you've done the dance, and the Li dragon has risen, it will be spring in the forest and..."

"They were cruel to mother." Shengli blurted out. "They exiled Ba and they eat creatures."

Old Tam and Ba looked at each other. Ba spoke, "I didn't

realize you knew that."

"Oh, of course I knew. Stop treating me like a little girl who doesn't know anything. Durfin told me. They kill creatures and eat them. They burn the bodies and then they eat them. Everybody knows. And you want me to go there? You think they'll eat me? And you don't care about that?"

"They don't eat people, actually."

"What's the difference? So they won't eat me. But what about Boken, then? He's not a person but he's a creature, too. And if you think I'm spending even one day without Boken to talk to when he's my whole world then you're really crazy and those calculations have addled your brain, Old Tam, and you too, Ba, even if you don't do a lot of calculating…maybe, whatever it is, it's contagious."

Curled up behind Shengli's feet, Boken allowed himself a discreet doggy smile. It was nice to feel appreciated and this business of eating creatures was indeed a little unnerving. He'd heard that actually dogs were generally exempted but if people were prepared to eat pigs or lambs or whatever, it didn't suggest a healthy environment for a quadruped of any sort. In the general balance of things, there were those animals who were required to eat meat, including, after all, small, foxlike dogs, and the Yu dragon organized things to keep that in balance. But when people start eating creatures well, that was a whole different thing. It wasn't necessary and surely it would throw everything out of equilibrium?

The three humans and one dog went quiet and to keep things calm, looked out with intense interest on the pond that they had all lived alongside for their entire lives and which, being frozen solid, wasn't doing anything at this moment that it hadn't been doing for the past several months. But when the argument had reached a pass like this, it was hard to look at each other and instead, careful examination of a point of view in about the middle of the ice seemed to be compelling for all of them. The little village, lying on the far side of the forest from the town of Quiczu, accessible only by an old track through the bamboo forest and in so many ways isolated and simple, had been Shengli's whole world.

Old Tam had seen much, too much, but the more he had seen, the more he had concluded that the village was where he wanted to be. Ba had been caught up in the trouble in Lungdou all those years before, and it had only convinced him that any answer he needed could be found around the pond, or in the forest or worked out while pottering in the vegetable plots. The villagers would earn a little from selling forest produce such as fungus and medicinal herbs, and those examples of their beadwork that they were prepared to trade, keeping the best for themselves, and the peddlers came by every now and then with the kind of useful commodities that were a nuisance to try and make yourself. There was the courier who carried letters and small packets by pony but otherwise, the general feeling in the village was that they had it pretty good and didn't need much else.

Shengli had never felt any need to question this worldview. But suddenly she felt that she did want to say something.

"Maybe you're wrong. Maybe all that stuff about the ancients is rubbish, just like they say in Lungdou. Why has it all rotten away if it isn't rubbish? I think it's rubbish. I'm not going to Lungdou, or anywhere, and I don't believe in the dragons, or any nonsense and I totally don't believe in your old rubbish and Boken and I are going to go and…and, and we're just going, that's all."

And they stood up together and the little girl and her foxlike dog companion crunched off through the snow and up into the forest. By the time they returned, it was already dusk. The two friends had made sure to visit some of their special places and they had ended up in a small clearing that was the spot that they tended to go to when the mood was somber. They made themselves a small fire so they could spend a moment more time by themselves. Shengli needed to speak with Boken and by their little campfire she could look into the crackling twigs and keep some warmth so it wasn't necessary to go back to the village before she was ready. This way she could really be honest about her feelings.

As always, Boken spoke plain good sense and he seemed to give her answers that in an odd way, she felt she would have come to herself eventually. In a funny way, he seemed to know what thoughts she was coming to but hadn't quite got to yet. Of course, she didn't think that the learning she had grown up with was all rubbish. Everything she loved and made her who she was, was wrapped up in the worldview of Old Tam, her Ba, and all the people of the village.

Unlike, Durfin, she didn't feel a hankering to taste the world beyond the forest and she wasn't drawn to learn more about the engines or the new ways. Her instinct on the whole was more to feel defensive for her own territory and community. But now that was exactly what was under threat. Shengli missed her mother. She used to think that that the pain would ease with time but if anything it just got worse. When, on that horrible day when her Ba had woken her and taken her in to see the beautiful and silent form, to see the cold, waxy, but perfect whatever that looked simply like her mother in the most peaceful sleep ever, and he had explained to her that she was dead, and what that meant, and she had wept with every last ounce of her being until she could weep no more, and then there was an even deeper sadness that seemed beyond something as feeble as just crying.

She would always be grateful to her Ba for taking her into

that room and showing her, and giving her that opportunity to understand what death looked like. He had explained to her once, later, that he had been unsure if it was best, wondering if it would only hurt her more, and then he had decided that she should see the deep stillness her mother had found and that it would help. He had been right. But it turned out that now, even five years on, she seemed to need her mother more, and it was a different, in some ways a more painful type of grief. It was a kind of hollow or void; a space that couldn't be filled but that had outsides that were pushing in, even if they couldn't, because the hole had a kind of force to it. As she closed her eyes and thought back to the dancing, to the walks collecting mushrooms and shoots, to funny stories of childhood adventures with Shonan and Durfin's own mother, to baking days and learning nüshu together, she knew that the spirit that had been transferred to her was one that would never abandon the stories and the dance. Perhaps they had given up on it in the city and maybe the engines were amazing things but Shengli knew that if her mother was here, they would make the journey together and they would dance at Zamai until they were dizzy or until their feet bled or they collapsed into each other's arms in exhaustion or until whatever it took to call the Li dragon, to save Tianya and to bring spring back to the forest.

And that is what would happen. She would be dancing and her mother would be right there with her, in her heart. So it was that she and Boken returned to the little cottage with heads full of questions about how, where, and what needed to be done to get to Zamai and to do the dance but no longer any doubt at all about why or whether.

They leaned against the little door and entered in more measured fashion than the previous evening, Shengli fingering her hair beads as she did when in one of her more thoughtful moods. Moving more slowly, and coming in from the yolky, crepuscular winter light, there was no similar moment of adjustment and she saw straightaway that there was a stranger at the table, seated one place further away from the fire, and thereby from the wine jug, than Old Tam who was, properly, in his familiar spot.

The stranger was youthful but an adult. His features were more sharply defined than those of the men Shengli had grown up around, his nose and chin more prominent, his brow more forward. He had dark and wavy shoulder length hair and his face was unshaven but still perhaps a week away from becoming a full beard. He was dressed in the conventional clothes of a traveler in the district: a cape with a full hood over a tunic of thick material, a checkered scarf that would have been knotted round his neck but which now hung untied over his shoulders and a broad belt around his waist. There was a small pack on the table to one side and a walking staff, looking as though it was cut from fresh bamboo and so improvised for this day's journey, leaning on the wall behind him. As soon as Shengli had seen him, she felt that he had already been watching her. His eyes settled on her face in a watchful but not threatening way and did not flicker or look away. They were soft, amber-brown and perhaps not so unusual in color but seemed somehow to be lit from behind. A trick of the light no doubt, caused by the candle on the table and the early evening fire that was sparking and taking hold. Shengli closed the door behind her and as she did so, the stranger's face broke into a warm and broad smile.

"Shengli," said Old Tam, in a soft voice, "this is Renzi."

For all that he could appear stern and perhaps even a little scary, Renzi was also funny and it wasn't long before he and Shengli were laughing together as he told her a story about a rabbit being chased by a wolf and who slapped the wolf in the face with his hind legs as he scuttled down his hole. Renzi's face as he mimicked the wolf, smacked in the nose by the hind feet of a rabbit, had her laughing out loud. Boken also seemed to feel attached to Renzi in a way that he didn't normally connect with humans other than Shengli. After sniffing around him, he nodded back to Shengli: there's something about this fellow that I like. Can't put my paw on it but he just seems to be a good sort.

Anyone that was all right by Boken was all right by Shengli that was for sure. And Ba also felt that here was a man he could trust to protect his little girl on this journey. He was clearly physically and athletically impressive and would deter unwelcome attention on the road, and if Old Tam vouched for his character, then that would do for him also. It seemed they were set.

"What about Shonan and Durfin?" asked Shengli.

"What about them?" Old Tam asked back, first to respond.

"Well, they're my friends and they're both going on all the time about wanting to see the other side of the forest. They're both a bit mad for engines, even though they've never seen one, and so it would be nice for them to get the chance to visit Quiczu at least. Durfin can be a bit of a dope but Shonan keeps him in line. If Renzi is with us, we'll be fine and if I go all the way to Lungdou, and they don't, they'll be kind of upset and probably a bit funny with me afterwards. If their mother and father agree, which really means if their mother agrees, which she will if Old Tam says it is all right, then if it is so safe and all right for me, surely it would be for them? And we'd have more fun and be safer anyway because we'd look out for each other and for all sorts of reasons they just have to come as well. Or at least I have to ask them."

It was a hard argument to refuse. With so much optimism around since the arrival of the splendid Renzi and with Shengli's clear-headed sense of purpose since her conversation with Boken in the forest, it was as if everyone had forgotten the anxieties of the morning. Old Tam nodded, Renzi smiled his lovely big smile and raised his hands, palms upwards as if to say, "The more the merrier," and Ba was, in his quiet way, clearly glad of the idea of sharing the difficulty of separation with fellow villagers. Although it was starting to get late and Shonan and Durfin might already have turned in for the night, Shengli crashed out of the cottage and raced around to the second-row shouting, "Nan-nan, Fin-fin! Nan-nan, Fin-fin! Engines! Lungdou! Renzi!" and more until the whole village was stepping to the doors of their cottages to see what the fuss was about and Shonan and Durfin appeared, definitely looking like they had just gone to bed but hadn't yet quite fallen asleep and Shengli poured out everything about the dance, about the Li dragon, Zamai, Renzi, and about the plan.

Ba, Old Tam and the gentle Renzi themselves then walked around to the second row and before long, all the adults were sat around the kitchen table in the larger cottage and although there was, as there always is with adults, a lot of talking and a lot of pointing out why and how things could go wrong, the mood was buoyed by the presence of Renzi and there was such a deep trust for Old Tam and affection for Ba and Shengli that it was impossible that in the end Shonan and Durfin would not be joining the trip.

It wasn't long at all before the talk was of details, packing, monies, and all the rest of it and one of the good things about being thirteen was that you could cheerfully ignore all that and could instead talk of all the exciting things you were going to see and do and so everyone talked and talked until it really was time to sleep and Renzi stayed at Shonan and Durfin's overnight where there was more room and he curled up peacefully on the rug before the dying fire.

Shengli went home, and as she calmed down from the excitement, she took out the soles and traced the nüshu with her finger. The words didn't make much sense to her really and perhaps they weren't meant to. They were, after all, not to be spoken but to be activated by the dance. They were regular words but the order didn't work out and they didn't seem to connect together in any logical way but there was a nice sound when you spoke them and, for Shengli, it was also a way of hearing her mother's voice as she traced the curving lines. She had never herself found it easy to remember how to write nüshu and it was on her list of things to do one day but her mother had taught her a bit about these spells at least and so she could make out the sounds. She wrapped them carefully in soft material and put them in a little cloth bag on a cord that she could hang around her neck. They were fragile and although replicas could perhaps be made, there was no reason to suppose that it was as simple as that. These were from the Academy, from the old days. There may be no others left. With her pack carefully organized and Boken long asleep on her bed, Shengli finally shuffled under the blankets and closed her eyes. The journey would begin tomorrow and now was time for sleep.

Chapter Three

"How do we know we're not wasting our time?"

The others all looked at Durfin. It was typical of him to come over all stodgy and negative. It sometimes seemed that unless something was his idea then he had to find fault with it.

Shengli felt her blood rising and was about to say something sharp when Old Tam raised his hand,

"Durfin is right. He has a point."

From all staring at Durfin with confused faces, eyes all turned with even greater astonishment to goggle at Old Tam. Whether they were amazed at the thought of Durfin being right about something, or Old Tam suggesting the old ways might be a waste of time, it was hard to tell but either way, it was a bit surprising to say the least.

"If we turn up at Zamai and Shengli performs the dance for the first time and for some reason we can't know, whether she has a step slightly out of time or there is a mistake in the nüshu or whatever, and nothing happens, we might just end up being the people who killed all faith in the old ways. I'm afraid that I cannot die thinking that through carelessness, I put Shengli in a position where, because we had not prepared, she and I, were responsible for, if you like, proving that the learning of the ancients is indeed nonsense just like the engineers say."

"So what do you suggest? I should do the dance now?"

"Dear Shengli", the elderly sage spoke gently, "I think that is exactly what I am suggesting."

Suddenly the mood of adventure, the high spirits of a party of friends packing and chattering about the days ahead, the mixture between anticipation of a change of routine and uncertainty about leaving the familiar, shifted to a realization that this was deadly serious. To everyone's surprise, Ba spoke next.

"Then it must be done properly. It will need to be up at the way-block in the forest. That is the only place near here where two dragon-lines intersect. They aren't primary lines obviously, otherwise Zamai would be here after all, but the only way we will know if the dance is correct is if Shengli can inspire a response from one of the Mang dragons by dancing on an intersection of secondary lines."

Old Tam looked at Ba. He saw, perhaps for the first time, how the old learning would survive his own death. Ba was no scholar, he didn't trouble with calculations; he was a villager who tended his vegetable plot, took his turn in minding the shared grounds, carved beads with sensitivity and dexterity, and brewed the best mulberry wine in the area. But he was also always the man who would step in when there was a dispute, who would say the right word at the right time to calm someone down when, as would happen even in a peaceful little place like this, someone got upset. His words weren't eloquent but they always had some kind of truth. Perhaps because they weren't eloquent. The old learning was only partly about the calculations and the texts. Those things were important. Essential, even. But the lessons of those calculations and texts were the same. And Ba, with his care for his neighbors, his sensitivity to the changing patterns of the forest and the seasons, his responsiveness to the wants and moods of others, his simple personal needs and his knowledge of when and how to act: he was the essence of Halteres-lore. Simplicity, compassion, patience in the service of balance.

Old Tam felt a kind of peace. He knew he didn't have long but with men like Ba in the forest, the old learning would be well. If only his old friend, Lord Kang, were here to see it. It wasn't going to happen but one last evening of talk with that dear friend, in his garden at Lungdou, that perfect spot, discussing the Halteres-lore and sharing their love of learning and Old Tam would be ready to say goodbye. And if only he could be there to be able to explain to poor old Kang, who was after all in the thick of it in the city, that the learning lived on out here in the forest, in the form of villagers like Ba, well, that would be a final gift to his old soulmate. He nodded over at Ba, who nodded back.

Quietly, Ba explained to Renzi about the way-block, which was a large, flattish boulder-like piece of natural iron that rested deep in the forest, and which sat precisely on the point of intersection of two secondary dragon lines. It lay about an hour's walk away. The others had all been there many times but usually for picnics or play or just because it made a good point a useful distance away to walk to and then turn around and walk back. The decision was made that only the travel party should go. It would be false if there was some kind of support from others that would not be there at Zamai and so the three youngsters, Old Tam, and Renzi, lined up their packs and left them neatly inside the little cottage. Boken had decided against carrying any luggage. There were some advantages to being a dog. Shengli took out her dancing shoes and tucked them into her belt, and checked the insoles were still hanging around her neck. She wanted to keep her hands free when walking through the snow.

Nobody thought about it. Nobody said anything. Somehow

everybody seemed to know. The path only allowed single file and Shengli set off in front with Boken, as always, traveling four times as far as everyone else by taking a few steps ahead, turning and trotting back to check on Shengli, and then bouncing ahead again, battling with the snow as he had done all through this long winter.

Renzi came next. His job was to protect Shengli and whether it mattered or not in this local place, he placed himself right there behind her. The twins muddled behind him and Old Tam brought up the rear. Renzi and Old Tam had picked up sticks of bamboo to act as makeshift staffs but the children were so used to coming and going on the paths around the village they didn't feel the need. In a few moments, as the path twisted away through the tall lines of dark green, they were already out of sight to Ba and the other villagers who stayed watching from outside their cottages until long after there was nothing left to see other than the lines of the bamboos, the snow, the footprints and the rest of the timeless scene of the village on the edge of the forest.

The way-block was an oddity in the forest. It was, in simple terms, just a huge lump of iron. A large flattish piece of iron, about the size of a bed that would fit two of the children. Not quite square but nearly. It was a thing of mystery and curiosity that had given rise to as many theories to explain how it got to be there as there had been people who had passed by and wondered at the fact of a large lump of naturally occurring iron in the middle of a forest. It had the rough surface of a regular sort of rock but close up, one soon realized that it was indeed iron that had melted on the surface and then cooled, leaving the pitted surface that you saw now. In the past, there were some early people who had removed sections and must have worked them in the days before iron-making was more understood, but once the learning had established that the way-block was on the intersection of secondary dragon lines, it was generally felt best to leave it alone. In the summer, it got rather hot and for that reason, it made a great place for a picnic as one could literally fry mushrooms or heat a pan on the surface but that was about the limit anyone would consider in terms of interfering with it.

Anyone seeing it for the first time, as Renzi was now doing, was astonished at such a remarkable object. "Did it fall from the sky? Was it made by some ancient people? How in the name of all the dragons did it get here?"

"No one knows", Old Tam replied. "What we do know that it is almost all iron with some nickel and traces of cobalt. Actually, what's interesting is..."

But attention had already shifted to Shengli who had put on her dancing shoes with the nüshu insoles and was standing totally still, her eyes closed as she ran through the dance in her mind. Ever since she had first been taught the moves, it had always been necessary to keep the three sequences separate. Who knew if the dance, if performed in full, might not upset something in the vibrations of the dragons? This was actually going to be the first time she had performed all three sequences together, one after the other.

She stepped up onto the way-block. It was uneven, and a hard and unforgiving surface for a dancer, but it was just about flat enough and Shengli wasn't going to do this unless she was right on the point where the vibrations would run out along the dragon lines. And she and her mother had, in more playful times, run through the sequences just about everywhere they went so this wasn't too strange. A village girl doesn't need a perfect surface to dance.

Eyes closed, she dropped her chin to her chest, pushed her hands down straight by her sides and then straight up as high as they would go. A moment, a heartbeat, and then the dance. A sequence of pulsing moves that beat against the air and pulled and pushed the vibrations. Hands reaching for, and stirring, and throwing out waves of fluence; knees bending, shoulders arching and contracting, rising and falling through all the levels of space around her; pinches and snaps at different points in the vertical plane that was the focus of the first sequence. Shengli threw her head forward and her long hair, all in slender braids, cascaded forwards through a perfect arc, her beads catching sparkles in the sunlight; a flick of her shoulders and it span first in one direction and then in the other. And then the transition to the second sequence. The second sequence played through the horizontal planes. Here is where Shengli's feet began to work, shimmying sideways, backwards and forwards, knees bent, arms out at angles, pumping the energy, driving the vibrations along the four dragon lines that radiated out from the way-block. And then the spins.

Dizzying to the watchers, stunning and compelling as Shengli span as low as she could go, crouching down near the rugged surface of the block; then springing up to spin through each level, punching out the vibrations horizontally. And then the transition to the third sequence. The footwork. The spells. The dragons should have been alerted by the vibrations along the horizontal and vertical planes, fluence rippling along the four lines, pulsing in the rhythms identified by the ancients and studied and practised for generations since. The flow should have been activated so now came the critical, climactic sequence and the message of the spells; words embroidered in the language of nüshu, the secret language of the women in whose wisdom the spells were entrusted. Words that would be activated with pulses from the footwork in the dance. Words that would then spiral out along the dragon lines, tickling and teasing the dragons who, in the lore of the ancients, would be called and would appear, first as spindly clouds, spinning arms of gases, different colors for each of the four dragons: yellow for Yu; green for Li; red for Jiao, and blue for the little Mang dragons. With the dance would come at first a kind of misty gathering which would then form into a swirling vortex of cloud matter gradually, before one's eyes, solidifying into a dragon who would, so said the ancients, blink and at the surprise of having crossed over into the world of dust, disappear instantly.

Everyone present knew this. Everyone present was watching for the first hint, the first wisp of the mist. Old Tam had a spent a lifetime practising and studying the lore of the ancients. No one, not even Lord Kang, knew better how it was written. For all of his long days he had known what would happen and what it would look like should it ever be necessary to call a dragon. He was ready.

The others were no less prepared. Shengli pulsed and pushed, her feet arched and stamped into the hard iron block and she rolled the balls of her feet on the insoles and in the final, crescendo-move of the third sequence, reached her arms up above her, spread them wide, palms up and then in an instant, pulled herself into the smallest ball possible. The dance was done.

And nothing had happened.

There was silence. Shengli stepped gently down from the block. Her feet were sore from dancing on the lumpy iron. She looked briefly at the others and then turned quietly and walked off into the forest. Boken followed her in grave mood. Renzi started to follow but Old Tam put out his hand to indicate he should stay.

"There is no need. She is safe hereabouts and she knows this place like her own home."

And then there was silence. Maybe a minute, maybe a little

more, but in a moment like that of course it can feel much longer. The only sound was the shuffling of breeze in the tops of the bamboos. The winter forest was quiet anyway without the calls of birds in spring or the scuttling of small animals, fattening up after hibernation, but without the excited voices of the twins or Shengli chattering away to Boken or Old Tam musing philosophically it was less like an absence of noise and more like a presence of silence.

It was broken by the aged scholar,

"Perhaps there was a step that wasn't quite right? Perhaps over the years, some mistake has crept in and it is no longer the dance? We may have to accept that when Shengli comes back we will just have to go home. I'm sorry for being a foolish old philosopher and causing all this trouble for everybody."

That this statement itself indicated a surrender of all the learning to which he had devoted his life and which defined his very soul was left unsaid. They sat around awkwardly, the silence broken by a quiet, cautious, but thoughtful little voice.

"Old Tam, shouldn't we have been doing something?"

"Dear Shonan, what are you saying? You don't know the dance so what can you do?"

"Well," Shonan started, hesitantly, and she twirled her hair beads a little as she tried to find the words, "what happened in the old days at Zamai? Did everyone just stand around feeling awkward and useless or did they do anything? Maybe we are the problem? Maybe we should have been doing something?"

"Well, there would have been the King. And the musicianers." Ol Tam replied.

"Well maybe that's something we need to think about?" she answered. "Maybe they weren't just watching? Maybe they did something useful, too? What was it they did?"

Old Tam stared at her. Of course! How could he have been so

stupid? The drums and music must have exercised the ether as well. In all the talk of the dance, and all the years of Shengli and her mother practising around the village, he had never given a thought to the role of the musicianers. Or the King. What did the King do? In the texts it would refer to the King as being "in accordance". He'd always assumed that meant "in agreement". But what of the sense of being 'in harmony'? Was the King participating in some way? Some musical way? It made sense of course.

"Shonan, you clever, clever girl, you bright button, you fabulous and brilliant spark of wonderfulness! That's it. We need musicianers to play out the rhythm, and we need someone to represent the King and to beat time. Shengli has the rhythm in her head and the time deep in her heart so she has never needed it but it is part of the dance. Of course, of course! How could I have been so stupid! Poor Shengli. I'm such an idiot -- oh, I hope she's not too upset. We must make drums or some sort of -- quick: find some bamboos, nice thick sections that will make a good noise if you knock them. Membranophones are going to be too hard to organize now but idiophones should have the same effect...I suggest percussion rather than concussion as being easier to control for novices."

"Old Tam, you're losing me" Durfin never minded admitting he didn't understand something. Everyone assumed he was stupid anyway so it wasn't as if he had anything to hide. Even if he pretended to know what Old Tam was on about, no one would believe him. That was just what being Durfin was about, or so it seemed.

"Like a kagul, or, or, or a huiringa, or a takuapu, or like an ekwe: that would be the type of thing -- a teponaztli, a resonating chamber with..."

With an air of amusement and an authoritative voice, Renzi

spoke, "He means get a thick section of bamboo and a smaller, more solid stick. We'll use my knife to cut a slit in the thick, hollow section of bamboo and then you just hit it with the smaller, harder stick."

"Thank you, Renzi," said Durfin, "Why didn't he just say so?"

And with smiles of relief, they dispersed to rummage in the forest around the way-block and it wasn't long before they had the simple materials needed and Renzi whittled slits on one side and they started to experiment with the sounds that could be made, striking the bamboo section in different ways and with different actions. Renzi carved horizontal cuts down one side of his bamboo and he found that he could scrape on one side and strike on the other and then everyone wanted that on their bits of bamboo as well. The sense of being busy and the simple joy of hitting something and making a noise soon had them buzzing with happiness and faces full of smiles. Old Tam, having decided that he would try and represent the King's role, was himself experimenting with different conducting styles: florid hand movements, strictly beating time with a twig, slapping one hand into the other. In his analytic way, he was experimenting but he looked a little comical with his serious expression and hands waving to some imaginary music.

Shengli watched from the edge of the clearing. She had talked it through with Boken and walked back to rejoin the group. She had failed, but she had tried. She had nothing left to give. She knew that that had been the dance as her mother had taught her. She had obviously done it wrong but she didn't know how she could find out how to do it right. They would just have to find a way to tough out the winter and the wait for the Li dragon. She couldn't save Tianya and she couldn't be her mother. She would have to work out how to deal with that but right now she wanted to go home and have a cry and to see her Ba. It hurt to see the twins messing around and Renzi amusing them with his knife and who knows what Old Tam was up to, flapping his hands around like that but why should she blame them? She was the one who had failed and why should anyone else feel bad?

She cleared her throat to be heard over the ridiculous clattering of the sticks, "Can we go home now?"

Everybody froze and looked at Shengli. Their arms dropped to their sides, chunks of bamboo and makeshift batons hanging loosely from their fingers.

"I'd like to go home. I'm very sorry but I just want to go home."

"Shengli," Old Tam spoke, with his kindly tone. "We have an idea. Or rather, Shonan had an idea. We think the problem was us. We didn't serve the vibrations by accompanying your dance with the rhythm. We probably got in the way and certainly we didn't contribute. That's what all this is about." He gestured, a little sheepishly, with his makeshift baton at the others, with their chunks of bamboo. He shuffled a bit and looked sort of awkward. Everyone knew he had a sense of fun but he was still a grave old scholar and being caught pretending to conduct an imaginary band with a floppy piece of twig seemed a bit dubious under the circumstances.

"I'm tired." said Shengli, "my feet hurt."

"Please, Shengli, let us try." It was Shonan speaking. "We really think we can help. I hated watching you on your own with all that and I knew it was wrong. I felt really awful. We're your friends, we know there is something wrong and we think we have an idea to try and make it work. We really want to share this with you. Please."

Shengli had determined that she would not cry until she got home. She had wanted to cry in the forest with Boken but she had just felt too empty. Then she felt she wanted to rejoin the group so that they could get back to the village because she knew that when she got home, she would find her Ba and then it would all come out and the feeling that she had failed Tianya, failed her village and most of all failed her mother would have time and place to come out, and crying would be all right then just like it always was. She had been sort of all right at that point and in a way, seeing them messing about in what she thought was just the usual silliness had made it easier. She had felt hurt and let down that they could play around when she felt the way that she did but being annoyed at them worked against her feeling of upset. She didn't feel so guilty when it looked like they had just reverted to playtime so quickly.

But then Shonan, quiet, sensible little Shonan took away the one thing that made her feel she could control how and when she would deal with her feelings and that one thing was her idea that, apart from Boken, she was after all on her own. She burst into tears. Shonan ran over and hugged her. Old Tam shuffled on the spot, shifting his weight from one foot to the other. Renzi found a critical point on his bamboo instrument that needed some attention from his knife and he focused on a totally unnecessary refinement to one of the notches he had already carved perfectly. Durfin looked confused. Only Boken understood that this was cause for celebration and he spun around the two girls yapping cheerfully. Eventually, Shengli smeared the tears across her face and coughed a little.

"All right. You'd better explain. What are we going to do? And Old Tam went through the idea and of course it all made total sense. Shengli had felt there was something missing. She had performed a dance without music. And when you pointed that out, it was obvious that it was just wrong.

She knew the music of course; she knew it like the sound of her own heartbeat. Her mother used to tap it out with two fingers in the palm of her hand or beat a wooden spoon on the side of the mixing bowl or just click her tongue. She knew it so well that since her mother died, she had just let it play in her head while she practised the dance. It was just different rhythm patterns really. You could beat it out on anything.

There were three patterns that could be played in different combinations, by different people at the same time if you liked, or you could just play one of the patterns and then switch to one of the others if you got bored. The tempo was really important though. It had to be the right speed for the dance. Too fast and Shengli wouldn't be able to complete the sequences; too slow and momentum would be lost and the vibrations wouldn't catch. So Shengli taught them the three patterns.

Shonan, as you might expect, got them straight away. Durfin was rather slower and it was agreed that he would just learn one and stick with it throughout. Renzi picked it up quite quickly but he had a tendency to add little flourishes of his own and that wasn't helpful as it would throw the others out of time so he had to be told to stick to the thing. Old Tam would play the part of the King and that meant that he would keep the tempo and he found that if he just kept saying, "Mulberry-mulberry-mulberry-wine" to himself then it would work. Everyone agreed that he should continue with the makeshift bamboo baton. Not because anyone thought it made much of a difference but he looked so funny with his beard swaying left and right and the twig waving about that it made everyone smile and that kept them all going.

"Shengli, do you think we're ready?" asked Old Tam.

"I'm sure you are." she replied. "If Durfin just sticks to the first pattern and Renzi can resist the temptation to make up new bits then I think Shonan can switch between the patterns to keep it interesting. You just keep thinking about that mulberry wine -- and it had better be my Ba's that you're thinking about!"

"Of course! It is the best and I only ever drink anyone else's just to be polite!"

"All right," she said and then paused before whispering, "Let's call a dragon."

The three percussionists placed themselves on three sides of the way-block, Old Tam at the fourth. They all faced inwards. Boken sat himself in front of Old Tam. Not being equipped with the opposable thumbs required to grasp the sticks, he'd conceded that the drumming was best left to hominids and he would contribute by thumping his tail in time with Old Tam's conducting. There was a pause.

"How shall we start?" Durfin, again, with the obvious question that everyone else was thinking but was too shy to say. Shengli thought for a moment before answering,

"If Old Tam says his mulberry wine rhythm twice through, then you all start the patterns and don't you all worry about me. I'll start when it feels right. I don't know about stopping but I guess when I make the ball at the end you lot just stop hitting or whatever. Please just stick to doing what we've agreed. Don't change in response to anything I do. If I go faster or slower, that is still in relation to the music, whatever you do, don't speed up or slow down. Got that?"

They all nodded. They set themselves. Old Tam recited his mulberry wine poem twice and the three drummers began, the hollow knocking of the bamboo tubes making warm 'bock' sounds that rang more clearly as a result of the adjustments Renzi had made with his knife. Old Tam had not concentrated so hard since he sat the royal exams as a young man and he was surprised to find how grateful he was to Boken for that steady 'thwump,' thwump,' thwump' of the bushy tail beating on the floor by his feet, keeping him in time.

They all started on pattern one and then first Shonan and

after that Renzi started to shift between the two other patterns but Durfin stayed solid on the first and that proved to be a help to all of them. It started to feel like a unit; as if there was actually only one person playing a complicated pattern instead of three of them playing different but, in themselves, relatively simple patterns. Shengli was watching them with a smile on her face. She started to feel a rising sense of confidence and power. Her young friends, her wise mentor, and her strong protector were round her, pushing and driving the rhythm and lifting her own heart and spirit in a way that was new. She had danced the sequences every day since she could remember and doing so was how she felt whole and real and how she felt close to her mother. But this was new. She allowed her eyes to close, dropped her chin, pushed her hands first down and then up to the starting form. That pause. That heartbeat

And she began. And at that moment, Old Tam had forgotten everything. He had forgotten the learning, he had forgotten the texts, he had forgotten the calculations. He had forgotten the scripts and the lore. It felt like he had forgotten his own name. He just kept beating the twig and chanting in his head "mulberry-mulberry-mulberry-wine; mulberry-mulberry-mulberry wine..." feeling the solid and supportive beat of Boken's tail as it brushed his leg, striking the ground by his feet.

Durfin knew what was needed. Solid. Stick to the first pattern. Keep it true, keep it straight, keep it secure. Shengli needs me, Shonan needs me, Renzi needs me. Don't mess up, you potato. Keep it solid. Concentrate. Keep it solid. Faithful and true. Faithful and true.

Shonan moved between the patterns. Allowing some kind of inner voice to tell her when to switch. She was dancing with Shengli. All her life she had loved but also watched and envied Shengli who had this thing with her mother that she herself had never been able to share: Shengli was the dancer, and she was Shengli's friend. Now, she was the leader of Shengli's group. The musicianer. In it together. Together.

A rush of familiarity had flooded through their new friend, the strange, handsome, lean and pointed hunter. We run in time, his heart told him; we are one. Watch the leader, watch Old Tam, keep the time. Follow but play your own part. Eyes on the leader, you know who you are. Stay alert; you are active; you are poised; you are disciplined. Disciplined.

And slowly, as they drew deep into the music and played their parts, they began to see it. First there were signs of a thickening of the air in places, a pulsing of the space around them and then strands of thicker air, refracting the light and then starting to move, in anticlockwise pulses around the dancer, coalescing into a more visible, gaseous substance.

Shengli then kicked into the second sequence, and the gassy form span more firmly, thickening into a mist, a fog, an increasingly concentrated smoke. A smoke that took on a color. From transparent to translucent; gray mist to blue-gray smoke; thicker, a clearer form. A curved cylinder, a tube; from gray-blue to blue, to blue with specks of gold. A cylinder, a cylinder with four little offshoots, no, limbs. A tube, no, one end thickening up and filling, one end thinning; yes, a head and a tail. Limbs, yes, legs, four claws to each. A head, a face! Little horns. Blue, they were blue, and scales became clear; little flecks of gold and red but blue, absolutely blue, the blue of a Mang dragon.

Shengli's feet snapped into the third sequence. Durfin drove on: solid, solid. Old Tam beat time, his head empty of all else. Shonan exulted in the joy of sharing; Renzi kept his eyes on the leader: discipline, discipline. And there it was. Undeniably, unarguably, completely and utterly a beautiful, shiny, perfect little Mang dragon spinning in the air above Shengli, above the meeting of the secondary dragon lines until he seemed to jolt awake, to shoot upwards to the vertical: a line of blue, gold and red and at the top of it, a face that looked down with eyes wide like glass bowls, shiny and moist and totally, splendidly, astonished at what had happened. He twisted like a corkscrew, flipped over and disappeared head first, abruptly, into the way-block right down through the point between Shengli's feet and in an instant, and with a last flick of his tail squirting into the seemingly impenetrable iron block he was gone. Shengli completed the sequence, finished with the ball, concentrated right on the spot where the dragon had shot through the iron block and then, as Old Tam dropped his shoulders and let his arms hang by his sides, they all rested.

Chapter Four

The first day on the journey through the forest to Quiczu had gone smoothly. Although they had of course brought supplies, they were all good woodsfolk and they foraged along the way, so they only had small packs. Shengli, of course, had the insoles in the small cloth bag on a cord that she hung around her neck and kept inside her shirt. Otherwise, they didn't really have anything you might call valuables. They carried some small monies for expenses in the city and Old Tam had given those to Renzi for safekeeping, apart from some little pieces for the children. What he called 'emergency monies', but no one could really imagine what kind of emergency could be handled with such small sums of cash.

They kept the order that they had already established: Shengli and Boken in front, Renzi behind, then the twins and, bringing up the rear, walking with a new vigor that he seemed to have found from somewhere, Old Tam. Quiczu was a day's hike away through the forest but with the snow and the later start in the day, they were planning to make an overnight camp. This also fitted with the plan to catch an engine in Quiczu and although the information might be out of date, the last word they had had was that the engine left each day at noon and to miss it would mean staying overnight in the town. That was to be avoided if possible. They had their monies but they would be needed in Lungdou and they were all much more used to, and at home with, a makeshift camp in the forest anyway.

The air in the greenwood was crisp and fresh and it puffed out from one's nose and mouth in little clouds. The clean snow was unbroken apart from occasional animal tracks: little spiky bird's feet, trails of small mice and voles and every now and then, the padded paw of something larger.

At one point they heard a swishing sound coming towards them that they all recognized as Gan, the woodsman, drawing a stand of bamboo behind him to deposit at the wayside where villagers would come and collect it later, leaving bundles of food, jugs of wine and other conveniences for him in repayment. Gan wasn't solitary; he was perfectly happy to meet and chat, indeed, he was usually very happy for the diversion and could fill a couple of hours quite easily exercising the voice that didn't get much use the rest of time, but nor was he inclined to sit around waiting for anyone to turn up and nor did the villagers always feel like waiting around by the wayside for him so this little arrangement had developed for the convenience of all.

"Ho, Gan!" Called out Shengli. Like all the villagers, she knew him, and was known by him, even if they met, as a result of their paths crossing by chance in the forest, maybe only once every couple of years.

"Ho, Shengli! And Boken! And twins! And Old Tam! And a new friend. Hello to you, Sir!"

"Hello, Gan," Old Tam spoke, "How're things".

"The winter has gone on too long" the woodsman replied, "but I don't suppose that is just for me. What are you lot up to?"

Old Tam held out his hand to stay Shengli who was about to

answer. "This is a good friend of ours, Renzi. He's been visiting but he must go to Lungdou and so we are seeing him to Quiczu and the engines."

"Ah, well rather you than me. Those places have never appealed. The more people go to those places, the more ignorant they seem to become. It seems the farther you go, the less you know. The stupidest people I meet are travelers."

"The only people you meet are travelers," laughed Durfin.

"Well, I guess so. And very proud they tend to be as well. We had someone come through here the other day, I don't know when, before the winter anyway, and all he could talk about was how 'backward' everything was. How I needed this and how I needed that and how he would be reporting to the King's Councilmen about how the forest could be, what was the word, I can't remember, it was a strange word talking about a forest... that's it, I think, it was 'developed'. Tell me, Old Tam, what development can you have in a forest that is already older than any of us know? How did the forest get developed? We weren't none of us around back then. Seems to me that if you want a forest to develop, you have to do nothing. And then everything you need to do, gets done!"

Old Tam laughed and smiled. "Too true, Gan, too true. One wishes for a world where people enjoy their food, are content with their clothes, satisfied with their homes and take pleasure in their customs and stories. Perhaps if there were nowhere to go to, then we wouldn't need engines to take us and if your business was simple enough, we wouldn't need to try so hard to remember everything. And if there were nothing to fight for, no one would manufacture weapons for fighting. And here we are, off to Quiczu to put our friend on an engine. It looks like we are becoming part of the problem."

"Oh, I wouldn't take too much notice of me. You don't get

much lower down the social scale than me. What do I know?"

Old Tam looked at him thoughtfully and after a pause, spoke gently, "The streams flow into the sea because it is lower than they are, my friend. One day, I rather imagine, we will all be wondering where it went wrong and why we didn't study your example more carefully."

"Away with you, mysterious old man. It's been good to chat but I'd like to get this load down the slope before it gets dark and I guess you'll be wanting to push on. Overnighting in the forest? Are you aiming for the scoop?"

"That's right"

"Then safe travels and remember, deal with things before they happen, and you'll never have any worries!" The two laughed and Gan picked up the trunk of the largest of the bundle of bamboo stems, rested it on a cloth pad on his shoulder and hauled the load of branches behind him. He had his hatchet tucked into a home-made wooden bracket that hung from his tattered, but still functional, belt and a gourd of, perhaps, some of the mulberry wine that he enjoyed as much as anybody and which would hopefully be topped up from the jug left for him by the way-side in exchange for the wood. For the travelers, it was a useful reminder to push on for the hollow before dark. With the snow making it hard going it would be a couple of hours at least and the light was starting to fade.

They reached the place they called the 'scoop' a little after dusk. As its name suggested, this was a patch of ground in the forest that looked as if it had actually been scooped out by a spoon. There was a sharp edge to the north, where the giant spoon would have entered the earth and then a kind of scrape as if the spoon was pulled out of the ground at an angle. This made it a good place for an overnight camp as there was shelter against the winds from the north but sun during the day and, ordinarily, the ground wouldn't stay wet too long from rain. Even in this snowy winter, the northern edge of the hollow provided protection and the snow had drifted away from what shelter there was. A fire would kindle more easily without battling the cold north wind and for everyone, it was just cozier to feel the vertical surface of the scoop behind you while being able to look out at the clearing in front which opened up gently, ensuring a good view of any approaching strangers.

Renzi took the lead organizing the fire and building the cleared snow into useful walls to add a little extra shelter. He didn't need to be in charge as any one of them would have known exactly how to go about setting up for a night in the forest in the middle of winter but there was no denying that he was biggest and strongest, and he was quick and efficient at a time when no one wanted to be standing around for long.

Soon, with a nice fire burning, their bivouac shelters laid out and vegetable stew heating gently in a pot hanging from a tripod over the comforting flames, the travelers were settled in a circle and were feeling that special and unimprovable richness of good companionship amid warmth and comfort when the world outside, or just beyond, is cold and inhospitable. Old Tam was especially lively. His eyes sparkled in the firelight and he was unstoppable in his chatter. He had stories and jokes and he switched from teasing Shengli about her friendship with Boken to serious questions to Renzi about life in the mountains to the north and west of the forest. Renzi must have spent some time in that mysterious region and Old Tam was as curious as ever for new knowledge and learning. How were the relations between bears and wolves governed? How had the creatures of the mountains responded when men started to dig black stones from out of the mountains in order to fuel the engines? Was it true that the men had literally hollowed out one of the mountains near to

Lungdou? How did it remain standing? And how did the Jiao dragon react? The news of landslides and avalanches as the red lord of the earth chafed at the hewing out of minerals was very much what Old Tam would have anticipated, but what form did it take? Renzi answered everything patiently, his honey-colored eyes again glowing with that trick of the firelight. Tam chattered away. How he remembered the days of the wars, when the Yu dragon had slept and men and creatures had been consumed by a kind of madness as they harmed each other and themselves for reasons no one could remember and maybe no reasons at all.

Old Tam had been caught up in the fighting and the three children and Renzi listened silently as he described seeing a good friend die beside him and how he was forced to leave the body and flee for his own safety and he had never been able to forget or forgive himself, even though he knew there was nothing he could have done, and his rational self told him his feelings made no sense, that he survived but his friend perished. But then he lightened the mood and told stories of his childhood. How his own teacher, whom he mimicked in such a style that the children were laughing out loud, would chase him around the village when he hadn't done his exercises. It had never really occurred to the youngsters that Old Tam had ever been anything other than a bearded veteran.

Finally he grew serious again. "These are troubled times but not like before. Not like the wars. That was terrible but in a way, it was a familiar terrible. There had been wars before and we all guessed that the Yu dragon would sleep again one day and there'd be disorder again but it was part of the pattern of things. The new disturbance worries me in a different way. How can you put back what you take from out of the mountains? How long did it take the forest to establish and what will it take to restore it if it is destroyed? If people get used to wanting more all the time, how will they know when they have enough, and if they never feel that they have enough, what will that mean? If we create a world of engines and products by taking from nature, does that mean that nature will gradually reduce? Maybe we will reduce nature to the point that people can no longer survive and that will be our own fault, and we will deserve it, but how much damage will we do to all the rest of existence?"

"But we'll make it all right, won't we?" asked Shengli.

Old Tam looked through the fire glow at the faces of the three children; he saw the calm focus in the face of Renzi and smiled as his eyes fell on the already sleeping Boken. Remembering the meeting with Gan earlier, being reminded that there really were good ways after all, and they could be rediscovered, feeling the fellowship and optimism of his companions and thinking again of that moment when he saw the little Mang dragon, when focusing on the words "mulberry-mulberry-mulberry-wine" had thrown all thoughts out of his head and he had found every element of his being directed to that single task and the sensation of power that he had felt...it all gave him a sense of optimism that he hadn't felt in a long time.

"Yes, Dear Shengli. I really think you will."

They woke with the first light and set about bundling up their simple gear. Old Tam wasn't around but that was no surprise. He was well known for being out and about before the sun rose and there were his morning exercises and probably some calculations to occupy him. Breakfast was a more immediate priority than worrying about the whereabouts of an aging but worldly and experienced scholar. Mushrooms and cakes made from ground barley fried in nut oil had everyone warming up and ready for the day but it was starting to be a bit of a nuisance that the antique philosopher was still off on his ramble. They kept some breakfast back for him and then packed up, leaving the scoop looking, apart from disturbance to the snow, as if no one had been there. Finally, Renzi suggested he see if he could find the old chap and hurry him along a bit. It would hardly be much of a task for a tracker given the footprints in the snow and it really would be better to be on their way given that Quiczu was going to be a bit of a challenge for lots of reasons and they would need to be sure of being at the mounting bay for the engine in plenty of time.

Talk of the engine stirred Durfin although he tried hard not to show his excitement. He was more than aware that Shengli and others from the village were fairly hostile in their attitudes towards the new ways although Shonan was a little bit fascinated as well. Just sometimes they'd let conversation between the two of them drift off into speculation about a life that was not limited by the boundaries of the village or the distance one could walk and still be back before it got dark. It was all very well to love the village, as he did, but it could, in all honesty, be a bit boring at times. It didn't seem to bother the grown-ups with their mulberry wine, beadwork, and seemingly endless interest in mulch, and Shengli was different anyway, but he and Shonan couldn't help wondering if there might not be a bit more out there. Durfin knew he could never win an argument with Shengli, let alone Old Tam, so he never spoke this out loud except to his sister, but here was Renzi, who seemed to have been around a lot, and sometimes the peddlers would chat about Quiczu and the changes and well, at least today he would get to see an engine and then he could decide for himself.

His thoughts were interrupted by the surprising but unmistakable sound of a wolf howling followed, a moment later, later by Renzi's voice calling out, "Shengli, twins, quick, here." They raced towards the voice, following at the same time the twin lines of footprints, the old man and the young tracker. The older man's footprints a little softer around their edges with new fallen snow; Renzi's tracks crisp and clean.

Weaving between the bamboos they were almost right onto Renzi before they saw him and then they froze. He was kneeling on the ground, with his head bowed, in tribute to the still, silent person of their familiar old friend, playmate, mentor, teacher, guide, entertainer, and guardian. Old Tam was seated crossed legged, with the backs of his hands resting on his knees, settled in the meditation position that they would often see him using when they might turn up at his hut unexpectedly and then tiptoe away. But instead of the slow breathing they were used to hearing there was total stillness; instead of the passion, the twinkle, that Old Tam still had even when sitting with his eyes half-closed, there was cold and gray. The three youngsters ran towards the old man, but it was clear before they reached him that there was nothing anyone could do.

Shengli had seen death close up before of course but the twins had not. It didn't matter. Nothing could have prepared any of them and grief washed through them like a wave of ice-cold water. They fell and stumbled around the still figure and threw themselves at it with embraces only to recoil at the shock of the rigor mortis that had taken hold in a body only known to them before now as filled with warmth and life. They went down on their knees also, unconsciously imitating Renzi, and simply wailed with shock, loss and despair. The friendly forest had never felt so chilled or the white of the snow so colorless.

Frost had gathered on Old Tam's beard; his lips were blue and his skin hung slack from his face. Stillness in the old man was no surprise; coldness was different. But he was dignified. His back straight and his head upright and around his frozen, cyanose lips there was not a smile but a look, perhaps, of quiet satisfaction in a job well done. That job was a life. A life lived in honor and in the service of learning and for the love of his village, of nature, and of all creatures, but for his dear friends most especially. As the shock abated and the tough reality began to kick in, all four found voice, soft and difficult to speak but all of them knowing that it they had to be strong together and find the right thing to do.

Shengli spoke first. "We'll have to take him back to the village. My Ba will handle things. Maybe one of us go back and get the villagers?"

Durfin next. "Of course. You go. You'd better have Renzi go with you as he's committed to protecting you. Shonan and I will be fine here. We'll wait."

"No", Shengli argued back, "you two go. I can stay with Old Tam and if Renzi is supposed to stay with me then that's all right but I don't really need looking after in the forest. Me and Boken are always out. It wasn't because of the forest that Renzi is here."

"But if I go, they'll just think I'm being a clot as usual and they won't believe me. Not about something so important. You have to go. Or Renzi. He's oldest after all."

And so on until Renzi spoke. "If Old Tam was advising us, what would he say?"

"That's easy," said Shengli, "he'd say…", and she tried to mimic Old Tam's' voice Why are you fussing about a dead old philosopher when there's business to be done and a dragon to be called.' "

"Do you remember what he said last night?" asked Shonan. "He said so much. I've never known him so talkative. I think that's it, Durfin. I think he made a decision. Do you remember how, when Shengli asked if 'we'd' make it all right, he said, 'Yes, you, not we, you.' He meant not himself. He knew he wasn't coming. And look, he's set himself in the meditation pose and it is like he has chosen to die here, like this. He would have known the risks, at his age, of being out in the forest in these conditions at that time. He knew his time was coming and I think he decided that it was now. Especially now that he knew he could go, leaving you to look after everything he cared about."

"But that's ridiculous! Old Tam, commit suicide, never!" Shengli was outraged.

"Not commit suicide." interjected Renzi, "But rather, choose the timing and manner of a death that he saw coming. That isn't suicide."

There was silence. To see Old Tam, one could almost hear his voice saying that no, he wouldn't be coming on the rest of the trip, the time had come, the work had passed to others and the proper thing was for him to take a seat in the forest and to feed back to nature. What they started to contemplate was a decision that would have seemed unimaginable a few moments earlier. To prepare a forest burial for Old Tam and to continue the journey to Zamai without him, not reporting his death until they returned.

Quietly they set about the business of preparing a shallow grave amid the bamboo. It was not the custom of the forest people to build great tombs or stand up stones where the bodies lay. It was the teaching of the ancients that within each form, animal or plant, is the essence of new life and for that reason a burial place is nothing more than a temporary way-station while the natural processes work through. With that idea, one feels that in reality, everything, all matter and all living things, have existed since the beginning of time and will exist until the end of time. It makes no sense to speak of life after death for the forest people since it is rather more a case of life through death. This isn't consolation or a kind of trick to make you feel better. The pain is just as hard as anyone could imagine whatever the philosophy might be and Shengli had now lost her mother and her dearest adult friend, a figure as close to her as any relative. But the ritual surrounding the handling of death was low-key, plain and simple. A dignified matter but no more than a laying of the body in the ground, patting down the earth and sharing stories with each other about how the person who was now ready to feed into life in another form had brought meaning into their own days.

Old Tam had been through this many times in his long life as he watched his many friends and family each take their turn and he would not have expected, and certainly would not have wanted, anything different now that the circle had come round to him. Indeed, as Renzi believed and Shengli was beginning to suspect, he had seen his death coming and he had planned to leave the trail at this point and in this way. Some of his remarks of the night before made sense seen like this. He had set them on their way and then withdrawn for them to finish the task. It was a good end for a good man. Returning to the scoop they collected their few belongings. It would now be a challenge to reach Quiczu before noon but they all needed to be busy and being busy in a cause that Old Tam had entrusted to them was a good way of moving forward.

Renzi asked for attention. "I know you haven't known me for long and you don't know anything about me really but my father was a long and dear friend of Old Tam's as was his father before him. I cannot fail Old Tam because to do so would be to fail my father and all my family. In the community I come from, we believe that we remember someone by being what it is that that individual wanted you to be. As my way to remember Old Tam, I want to be the protector and guardian that he wanted me to be when he contacted my father and asked for help in this expedition. To do that I need you to trust me. Are you willing to accept me as pack leader for the rest of this journey, except for the time of the actual dance? I pledge to do whatever it takes to keep all of you safe and to serve the cause that Old Tam left for us with all my ability. I must tell you, I have limited experience partnering with young people like yourselves."

It seemed natural for Shengli to respond. "Of course. If Old Tam trusted you then so do we. We know we are only children and can't do this on our own. We need you to take the lead and you can trust us to be careful and sensible and you will see no difference between us than you would with whatever companions are more familiar to you. "

"Then you will be fine young humans, indeed! Let us start on our march and try to make Quiczu in time for the noon engine. It will stretch our monies to find a place to stay overnight there. In Lungdou, I can call on a friend to help us but until we get there we are relying on our own resources. The days ahead will be hard for us all but in different ways. I am familiar with the cities but I am not familiar with caring for young people. You are not familiar with the cities and you will have to trust me even though I am still almost a stranger to you. We will have to accept some hardship, I am sure, and we will have to stay alert. If I am to be leader, you must keep your eyes on me and hold to the discipline of the pack. Do you all understand?" They all nodded. Boken perked his ears. He felt a stirring in his soul of something he had forgotten. Loyalty to Shengli was his entire existence but he found it easy to combine that loyalty with fealty to the leader.

"Then let us march." This time Renzi went ahead. Long, loping strides meant the children had to work hard to keep up but they didn't complain. They were village children and they knew that sometimes you'd be cold and sometimes you'd be tired and sometimes you'd have to keep going with something even though you felt like you wanted to give up through discomfort. Shengli found herself thinking how only the evening before last, warm with the success in calling the Mang dragon and contemplating the departure on the morrow, she had been in her cottage, cozy with the constant fire, with all that was certain and familiar around her: Old Tam near the wine jug, Ba managing things in his quiet way and Boken checking over at her and sharing her thoughts. In just a day she had lost her mentor, felt her heart break in a new place while it still hadn't mended, if it ever would, from the old wound, and entrusted herself to a near stranger to accompany her, and her friends, to places that she had always secretly feared.

Shonan and Durfin, she knew, had a quiet desire to see Quiczu and city life. By contrast, she was, in truth, a bit scared. In the village she was the livewire, the dancer, the happy character that everyone brightened to see. In that little world, she was safe and she flourished. She was quicker and smarter than the other children, even though she didn't ask for teaching very often, and she was more skilled at the things the villagers valued. In the city she might just be nobody at all. What did you have to do there to be the best at everything? And what does it feel like for people to see that you are confused and lost when everyone is used to your being capable and clever? All this thinking was causing her to drop behind. She put her head down, concentrated on her feet and picked up the pace again. After undulating gently for most of the way, the path took a steep rise. Earlier peoples had cut out steps but with the snow and ice they were slippery and it became an even greater challenge to keep up with Renzi who would seem to skip up three or four steps and then look back, see he was in danger of losing them and then wait while they came up behind.

It was particularly difficult for Boken as the steps were high for his smaller stature and in places, Renzi lifted him up and carried him in his arms. This stretch had them puffing and regardless of the cold, breaking out in sweats under their heavy felt winter clothing. More than once, there seemed to be a final ridge that as soon as you got to it, gave way to a slight dip and then another slope upwards that had been invisible up to then. It was as they were approaching one more such apparent ridge when Renzi bounded away opening up a further gap than before now. He reached the crest and lay Boken down gently before turning.

"Quiczu!" And he pointed down the other side of the slope. This gave them all an extra burst of energy and it became a race to see who could be first of the three children to see the town they had heard about all their lives. Durfin won on this occasion but the two girls were close behind. The bamboo covered slope fell away from them before, about half way to the plain, giving way to tea fields and then, as the land leveled, vegetable plots and barley fields. The first houses appeared in little clusters at intersections between tracks but the concentration of buildings built up as they got closer to the river. The river could be seen leading towards the town from the west and although cloud and mist reduced visibility, one could make out the shapes of the western mountains beyond. The river widened as it approached the town but took a meander just as it came near and the central district had developed around that bend, with a bridge at the narrowest point as the meander turned back, after which the river widened again and set off on its final journey to the sea, only a few miles to the east but hidden from their view by the line of forest that curved in to protect the town. They would descend the slope with that forest to their right and the opening plain and the river valley to their left and ahead. The town itself was built up mainly on the north side of the river, centered on the crossing point at the eastern end of the meander. To the disappointment of the children, it was almost invisible beneath a cloud of fog and mist, darker and grayer than the woodland mist they knew from home. Still, the excitement of the unfamiliar spurred them on as

A DANCE TO WAKE A DRAGON

well as the knowledge that if they were to meet their deadline of noon, they needed to push ahead with still at least an hour's march to the river crossing and not much more time than that available before the sun reached its zenith.

Chapter Five

The hardest thing of all was the smell. That rotten egg smell that Renzi explained was from the burning of coal, the 'black stones' of which Old Tam had been speaking the night before. Then there was the stench of decaying refuse that gathered by the street edges and the piles of dung left by the horses, the press of bodies in the more crowded alleys and worst of all, the smell of burning flesh coming from street-side peddlers who stood over charcoal fires and held chunks of cut animal to the embers. Renzi assured them they would get used to it and that after a day or two they wouldn't notice any more but in a way that was not reassuring. Did one want to get used to all this? Sitting around a fire at home was a nice smell: they used charcoal, of course, but it made a homely smell. Here, the burning coal that Renzi explained boiled water for the steam engines made an acrid, biting smoke. The air seemed to carry dirt that stuck to your face. All their eyes were stinging and they noticed some of the townspeople were wearing goggles and masks. People walked in a different way to village people: quicker and with their heads down. They had their hair tied up, under scarves and hats, and didn't wear beads. The children soon gave up on their instinctive habit of offering a greeting to each person they saw coming towards them. Not only was it just silly when there were so many, the reactions they got were either indifference or really not very friendly looking. And in any case, you really had to watch where you put your feet with the splashing, slushy mud on the uneven roadway and the horse carts and occasional steam-wagons.

The first time the children saw a steam-wagon they felt a mix of thrill and disappointment. An engine! Even Shengli was excited to see one, at last. But it was a dirty, smelly, noisy thing. It had three wheels, a small one at the front and two larger ones towards the back so in some ways it was like a regular three-wheeled cart. There were various pipes twisting around a kind of cylinder that stood vertically in the middle, and a chimney that came out of that, shumping out wads of smoke or steam or whatever. There were a couple of mechanical arms going up and down and seated behind all the metal mechanics, on a wooden seat, was an engineer wearing goggles, a hat with earflaps down and tied under his chin, a face mask against the smoke and big leather boots. The engine was towing a wagon that was piled with coal and everything was coated in black dust. After seeing two or three go by, staring in wonder gave way to staying alert not to get caught up in some dreadful way by the mechanics or simply trapped underneath and presumably squashed horribly.

Quiczu had grown on the back of trade built around timber from the forests to the south and west and coal and other deposits extracted from the mountains to the east. There was also rich farmland in the floodplains around the river. Goods would at one time be taken up the river to the estuary and then by sea to Lungdou and elsewhere but, since construction of the railway, much of that commerce had shifted from the riverside wharves to the mounting bays where the engines would rest and the wagons would be loaded up. Buildings followed the style of the region being made of brick faced with plaster and perhaps they had looked bright and clean when new but they were grubby from the coal dirt and so the general color was gray to black. Roof tiles arched away and upwards in the usual fashion but eaves didn't extend out as far as in the village; instead, streetfront buildings had verandahs under roof extensions, held up by slender pillars. Everywhere, the snow had turned to dirty mush. The noise was something new to the forest-raised youngsters as well. The engines would make a pushing, shoving kind of sound and sometimes there would be a screech of a whistle. Voices were louder than in the village and sometimes they would walk past a building that was lit inside by what must be some sort of very strong flame.

"Renzi, what makes that light?" asked Shonan.

"It is made by burning a kind of gas that engineers can produce from the coal. It is remarkable really. Most of the buildings you see with it are taverns, where people go to drink wine and buy meals cooked by someone else but they say that one day, there will be gas lighting in every home. In Lungdou, it is already in some of the streets, from the tops of poles. I have to admit it is convenient at night time to walk around the city without having to carry a light of your own but as with all these things, one wonders where or how it will end? I like the lights. I don't like the engines. Well, in a moment we will be at the mounting bays and then we will have to spend some monies to buy tickets and you will see the railway engine and that is the most powerful moving engine yet. It can pull a whole chain of wagons, some for people, with seats, some for goods and so on. Amazing, when you think about it, and we have to admit, useful to us now as we would have a much harder job getting to Lungdou otherwise but again, it must be throwing all manner of things out of balance. The mounting bay is just around this corner. It will be crowded there and you must keep your eyes on me at all times. Got that?"

They all nodded and Boken pressed close to Shengli. The turn took them into an open space and on the other side, a more ornate building than any they had seen yet. There was a central tower, with a fancy, scalloped design and a domed pinnacle, tiled roofs extended each side. The scalloped design continued around the eaves that curved up and, as in all the larger buildings in the town, there were roof extensions out over a verandah supported by pillars.

Renzi led them to a doorway in the middle and then, leaning through a hole in the wall, he had some sort of conversation, pulled his head back, turned and joined the children.

"It's fine. We are still in time and I have tickets for us. We won't be here long. Follow me."

And he led them through one of the wings of the building, stepping between and over people who had settled on the floor, spreading out their legs and their luggage to create an obstacle course that the children skipped around nimbly and Boken took as a personal challenge, jumping and shimmying as necessary. At the other end of the building was a great opening out to the mounting bay itself and there, waiting, was the engine. It looked like a jar laid on its side; lined by slats of wood but with black metal at both ends, and a tall chimney one would think of as the front. There was a platform at the back where two men in the by-now familiar goggles, ear-flapped hat and face-mask were biding their time as the engine was still. All along the mounting bay, people were hauling themselves and their bags into wagons. There were clutches of people flustering around individuals, some red-faced and tearful, who-knew-why, others red-faced and sweaty from moving boxes and bundles of who-knew-what. The noise was messy and confusing but Renzi pushed through, the three youngsters and Boken kept their eyes tight on him and he led them to one of the wagons, which were simply like covered horse carts but with flanged wheels, resting on rails.

"Here we are." said Renzi, "We're in this one. Any seat, just get in and try to make yourselves comfortable." And they climbed into a kind of little room with benches down two sides, sat down and looked at each other nervously.

"You'll find it strange at first." he explained. "The engine will pull us along maybe twice or three times as fast as the fastest you've ever run. That is a strange thing. But like everything, you'll get used to it pretty quickly. It is noisy and smelly like all the new things but seeing the world outside move by while you sit still is quite fun, I have to admit. Any minute now, there'll be a kind of a jolt as the engine starts up and we are pulled along. Be ready for it: the first time it's quite a surprise."

Renzi's confident handling of the situation and their own growing familiarity with the noise and dirt meant that gradually, they were starting to feel more at ease and were not even too unsettled by the bumping that came when the engine started up.

And indeed, it was funny to see the world moving while they sat still and after all the horror of dealing with Old Tam's death, the demands of the fast march through the forest and then the stress and confusion of their first encounter with city life, they were glad to embrace the novelty and before long were laughing and pointing out of the open spaces between the roof supports to the wagon. They were pressing on to Lungdou and the worst must be over.

And finally they arrived in the city as the evening light was starting to fade. The sulfuric air, the noise and the clamor of people and objects were less of a shock after Quiczu but it was all on a larger scale. They pressed through the crowds outside the mounting bay until Shonan suddenly let out a scream. A man sitting on the streetside had pushed his hand out towards her, palm up and had done it so suddenly and shockingly that all the tension that had built up over this overwhelming day flooded in on her.

Renzi seized her and immediately placed himself between her and the figure on the ground. The man was barely recognizable as a person; his hair had matted into a thicket of snake-like fronds, his face was blackened with coal dust and dirt, and his mouth had only a few teeth and they were bent and twisted. Whatever his clothes had once been, they were no longer, and rather than a person dressed in tatty garments, it seemed more that were looking at an animated bundle of dirty waste rags that was reaching out towards them.

"Spare some monies, miss; no harm, mister; spare some monies? I'm hungry." Renzi wrapped his long arms around the two girls and signaled to Durfin and Boken to keep close. He guided them forcefully through the crowds and towards a less densely packed street.

"Renzi," Shengli spoke, "I have a couple of barley cakes in my bag left over from this morning. Perhaps I could give them to that man?"

"Not now, Shengli"

"But he's hungry"

"Yes, but keep your barley cakes for yourself."

"But I'm not hungry and he is."

"That isn't how it works in the city. Stay close and we'll talk about it later."

For a moment Shengli resented Renzi. He had made her feel like a little child and that stung. The dusk continued to fall and they turned down a street that had the lights on poles that Renzi had described. They gave out a murky glow that didn't so much illuminate the night as reveal the fuggy nature of the air. People in the street were transformed into shadowy, blurred specters, their outlines lost in the shifting shades of yellowy-gray. Closer to and farther from the light-poles they became more and less visible as they moved through the nebulous gloom. A steam-wagon clattered down the street, the mechanical arms heard before they were seen, the airy whistle calling with a kind of fuzzy sound that only added to the sense of unreality, the dreamlike state that the confusion to the senses was creating in the minds of the youngsters.

After a turn down one street, and then another, and another, until they had no sense of where they were, feeling that they were being carried through some kind of sleepworld, where sights and sounds were muffled into non-reality, Renzi stopped and knocked on a door. Rather than answer in the normal way, a panel opened at head height to an adult and a face peered out.

"Hey, Renzi! It's yourself!"

The door swung open and the stranger and Renzi embraced.

"Good to see you again, Tongman! As you can see, I have a party with me and I need to get them to Jiong's place soon. They, and I, are tired. Would you be able to take us there in your wagon? I'd love to take a bit of time then to catch up as well as we're probably going to need a friend or two over the coming days."

"Renzi, my man, I should say 'no' just to punish you for staying away so long but no matter how long it is, you will always have the best of me whenever you need it. Come on in and wait by the fire while I go and get the old girl steamed up."

The red-faced, burly man embraced Renzi and the two exchanged looks before Tongman stepped outside to attend to the wagon that he had meant, confusingly, when speaking of the 'old girl'. The party entered the little building and with five new bodies in the small space, it felt very full. There was a plain wooden table by the wall with two white enamel plates on it showing leftovers from a supper: a chunk of bread on one and a few vegetables on the side of the other. A mug of the same material still held a little wine, perhaps taken from the stone jar that stood by the paraffin lamp, which gave off an amber bloom. Otherwise, the room was rather bare, with grubby whitewashed walls and a chair by the small stove in the corner. You wouldn't have called it cozy and with so little room, Renzi encouraged the two girls to sit down and said that he and Durfin would stand. Shengli and Shonan woud normally have protested at this well-meant but unwelcome, and inaccurate, suggestion that they were weaker than Durfin, but they were so tired that they couldn't be bothered. Boken was glad that no one thought it strange for him to curl up in front of the stove. He was due a warm-through.

They waited in silence until Tongman returned and ushered them back outside to where his steam-wagon was waiting, and he helped them climb up into the cart at the back. In the same day, they had had their first experience of a railway engine, gas-lit streets and now a steam wagon. Not to mention dealing with the death of a dear friend. They were practically numb with exhaustion and as the wagon clanged into life and set off, they simply shut down their own senses to the experience and waited for whatever was coming next.

Next was in fact crossing the Great Bridge, over the river that runs through Lungdou to the sea, as it falls from the western mountains and across the plains to join the natural harbor that was Lungdou's historic source of contact with the outside world. In the lightless early evening there was nothing to see but still, the knowledge that they had crossed to the northern bank, and into the ancient city where the royal palace, the hall of Zamai, and the historic colleges and garrisons were situated stirred a little interest in the group only, once again, for that to be mixed with the general sense of disappointment at how grubby, dark and just smoky everything was.

If this was the ancient seat of Kings, the center of learning and culture, the incredible city, then it was just looking a bit drab right now. Finally they stopped, Renzi bundled them into another building, one that had a kind of desk at the entrance, there was more talking and then they were led up some stairs and into a room where there were three beds. "You'll have to share I'm afraid. There isn't enough monies for anything different. I'll be in this room here, on the other side of this wall. I'm going to catch up a bit with Tongman but we'll just be downstairs. I suggest you get yourselves some sleep as soon as possible."

The children didn't care about sharing a room. They slept anywhere and when camping no one had ever given any thought to who was sleeping alongside whom. Nor did they need any encouragement to get to sleep. For all that this was their first ever night in a city, or a guesthouse, they had no feeling or energy left for excitement or curiosity. They climbed into the creaky beds fully clothed and were asleep within minutes.

Shengli was first to wake the next morning and she nudged Boken. "Come on puppy. Let's go and see this city. I'm hungry as well so maybe we can find some breakfast and bring it back for the others." Boken stirred and shook himself in that corkscrew way whereby he started with a shimmy of the shoulders that then seemed to spiral down to his fluffy tail. Right-ho: let's see if Lungdou is ready for us.

The air was clearer in the morning and it was easier to see how this was a different place to Quiczu. The old houses mostly had yellow walls: whether painted yellow in anticipation of the staining from the sulfurous smoke or just a happy accident made no difference. Most of the buildings had bright red, tiled roofs and window frames and the doors tended to match. Unlike the south side of the river, where streets had followed straight lines and all Shengli could later remember of that walk was repeatedly turning at right angles, the alleys of the north side snaked and twisted. Looking down the bend of such an alley, Shengli realized she could only see a short way in front and a short way behind. The buildings on both sides were as close together as perhaps two people stretching their arms out and three people walking side by side. Whenever a pair of people approached them, she would press herself against a wall to let them go by. Peddlers and porters with handcarts and carrying poles hunkered down and pushed through: it was your job to get out of the way or risk getting whacked by a box of cabbages or a cartload of cooking pots. They turned into an alley that seemed to be especially for stalls selling fruits and vegetables. The bright colors of the produce were uplifting and joyful. Carrots and cabbages, mangosteens and turnips, lettuce and fresh herbs, persimmons and pomelos; oranges and aubergines, giant squashes and tiny little peas, stripy watermelons and bright red tomatoes, tamarinds, figs, jackfruit, kumquats, and the king of them all, the majestic durian. All these rich fruits shipped from the islands to the west and south where it seemed the winter never reached: mysterious domains, still part of Tianya but swayed by the spirit dragons of the seas, rather than those of the mainland, and known only to the majority of the mainland people by the wondrous seeming foods and other good stuffs carried across the sea, borne on the hoys and luggers of the island people, and unloaded at the harbor each day.

The market was an assault on the senses that had been so dulled by the smog and gloom of the evening before. There were flower stalls whose fragrance was released as Boken's bushy tail brushed against the blooms. The spice stalls had sacks of powders and seedpods, opened at the top and rolled back, revealing perfectly sculpted cones of produce. There was a pickle stall with glass jars lined up, each containing green, red and yellow chopped radishes and mustard greens spiced with seeds and sauces. A mushroom stall reposed with dried, earthy fungi of many types in sacks and boxes. Shengli was a village girl so there was nothing unfamiliar about fresh produce but the profusion was splendid and her heart soared.

The alleyway continued to turn and the scene changed. Instead of rich looking, healthful and vigorous fruit and proud vegetables, there was suddenly a scene of such awful cruelty and desolation that Shengli rocked back in shock. From stall after stall was hanging the flesh of dead animals. Whole corpses of small lambs, rabbits, partridges, and quail were suspended from S-shaped metal hooks. Men with white aprons, bespattered with blood, stood behind the tables at work with terrifying cleavers, hacking away at the remains of bodies, now nothing but random hunks of flesh from who knew what sorrowful creature. So this was what they meant when they talked of the city-folk eating creatures! Shengli retched in disgust. She looked at Boken who seemed to say, I know. It is out of balance. This is the truth of people who eat creatures. When there is no necessity for them to do so as there is for the likes of us dogs.

But she could not ignore it. She had to face the reality and she determined that she would walk down the alley, witnessing the depth to which humanity could descend and so acquire some sort of wisdom about people. "Come on, Boken." she whispered, "I have to understand this." And they walked together down the middle of the narrow alleyway, as far from each side as they could be. The stench of dead creatures mingled with sadness at the thought of the lives sacrificed so needlessly.

Shengli, like the others of the village and the woodsfolk generally, had never thought to eat a creature. It just wasn't their way, and looking at the portly, red-faced men behind the stalls, with their sour expressions and clothing stained by the entrails of little pigs, proud oxen, and chirpy chickens, she could not see how the creature-eating people were any better off for living this way. It was with relief that they reached the end of the alley and a junction of six such lanes where a sundial stood on a pillar. Coming from one of them was the much happier fragrance of fresh barley cakes on a griddle and with a smile, Shengli skipped towards that stand and felt for the few monies she had in her pocket. She bought two for each of herself, the twins and Renzi and shared half of the one she ate now with Boken. "Don't worry, Boken. I hated that market but I do know that you are a dog. I'll talk with Renzi about how to ensure you get your rabbit since you can't go hunting for yourself here in the city. For now, whatever I eat, I share with you." Boken's warm eyes gave a comforting response. It's all right, Shengli, old girl. I know these aren't normal days and I'm not sure rabbit would taste right if I hadn't caught it for myself anyway. Frankly, some of that stuff hanging back there looked a little stale. You don't have to worry about me. I'll muddle on through.

A little farther on there was a tower. A tapering cylinder, a slender cone, topped off by a little platform where there was an ornate cupola with the same kind of scalloped pattern that they had seen at the mounting bays and a bare flagstaff poking out of the top. Round the outside of the cone wound a staircase and it looked like you could walk up to the top and look down on the city from a higher position. This was irresistible to Shengli, and she tucked the bag of barley cakes into her belt and jog-walked towards the tower, which stood in another little space, at the other end of the barley-cake alley from the sundial square.

The two friends ran up the steps and were soon on the platform at the top. Shorter of breath than they would have expected after such a quick burst of exercise, they nonetheless enjoyed a flush of elation at the novelty of being high up and looking down on the red rooftops of the old city of Lungdou. There were the winding old alleys and the sundial they had just seen. Circling round the platform they could see the battlements of the garrisons and the slender towers of the College of Learning. There was the Royal Palace: smaller than Shengli had expected but a palace nonetheless, with the gold leaf glinting in the morning light and one more turn and there: the soul of Lungdou. The reason for the choice of this site as the capital city and home of Kings. Zamai. The intersection of the primary dragon lines. The circular building surrounded by smaller, crescent shaped halls with the cross cut into the dome of the roof marking the exact tracks of the lines themselves. Zamai. Which meant the collection of buildings just beyond, with the low roofs, with scattered trees and surrounded by a wall with buttresses must be the Dance Academy.

Shengli looked down on it all. She could do this.

The two of them raced back to the guesthouse. For a village girl used to finding her way in the bamboo forest there was no danger of getting lost in a city with all its landmarks and curiosities. And in any case, there was always Boken's nose if her own instincts failed her. They bounded up the stairs and burst into the room where the twins were sitting on one of the beds and Renzi was on another. "We've seen the dead creatures being sold for people to eat and we've walked all over and we've been up a tower and we've seen the palace and the garrison and the college and, of course, Zamai and we've got barley cakes for breakfast and..."

"Never do that again, Shengli." Renzi growled. His face was graver than she had seen it before.

"Never do what?" She replied, genuinely confused.

"Go off without telling me where you are going or without being accompanied by me."

"But we were just walking about outside and what's wrong with that? And me and Boken, we're always going out, what's the matter? I thought you'd like some breakfast: they're better than I expected. Not as good as ours at home but really not too bad at all when you consider they were made by city people, here you go...", and she passed around the cakes.

"You are under my command," said Renzi, "you accepted my leadership, and you must do as I say. My duty is to keep you safe, and I cannot do that if you do not accept discipline."

The three youngsters looked at Renzi and saw that his eyes had seemingly narrowed as he stared at Shengli. The corners of his mouth had pulled back but not in the smile that had warmed them when they first met him or that had reassured them on the trail in the forest. From feeling confident and in command, streetwise in the city, facing down the horrors of the flesh market and being first to see Zamai and being the bringer of breakfast, Shengli was made to feel like she had been irresponsible and childish.

"Sorry, Renzi." Shengli mumbled. But she wasn't. The all munched on the cakes silently but somehow, they didn't taste so good now.

"After breakfast, we need to get ready for going to Zamai." snapped Renzi. "You kids are dirty from the trip and if you turn up like this, you might get turned away and we'll get nowhere. I'll arrange for some hot water and soap to be sent up and we can get on with a cleanup."

The mood she was in, Shengli was not at all impressed by the idea that they, fresh from the forest, should be thought dirty by the city people who, as far as she could see, lived in unutterable squalor. Even the air was dirty. The others were more surprised than anything.

"Do city people look down on country people?" asked

Shonan.

"Yes." said Renzi, "They do."

"But in the name of all the dragons, why?" the usually quiet girl blurted out. "They live in this dirty place, all squashed up, there is rubbish everywhere, and they eat creatures. They're just disgusting and cruel and they're stupid because they lost the learning and we saw a Mang dragon so we know it isn't all rubbish and even if we hadn't seen a dragon we'd still know because Old Tam told us and that would be good enough for me so even if the Mang dragon never came I'd still believe because he was Old Tam and..."

There was no stopping the tears. And then Shengli followed and Durfin next and all three were feeling small, a long way from home and bereft of the wisdom and compassion of their old teacher. They cried with huge gulping sounds, tears smeared and smudged through the grimy faces and they felt lonely, vulnerable and dependent.

Boken climbed up onto Shengli's lap and nuzzled her reassuringly. Renzi was not so lacking compassion that he couldn't wait a little and then he went out to organize some hot water and soap which came up in a large earthenware jug with a basin of the same rough ceramic. He then quietly withdrew and left the three of them, in their own way, to put the outburst of tearfulness behind them and to organize the cleanup with Durfin politely staring out of the window for as long as it took for the girls to get ready and then taking his turn, while the girls settled in to straightening out each other's braids and hair-beads, which is the kind of task that takes your mind off things and cheers you up whatever. Before long they were spruced up, the dust and grime of the journeys in the wagons had been washed off, and some of the resentment they had started to feel towards the city, towards Renzi and towards everything that wasn't their old village was ebbing away. They knocked on Renzi's door and called that they were ready and they lined up to set off to Zamai. He looked them up and down and nodded his approval.

"Shengli, you'd better give me the insoles."

"That's all right, Renzi," she said, "I have them safe."

"Give them to me.", he almost barked.

"It's fine, they're here, safe. I won't lose them. They have power, that is mine to look after, and I can keep them safe."

"No, Shengli, you accepted my leadership and that is an order. The insoles have power, my family are under threat and you cannot be allowed to risk losing that power through carelessness like you showed this morning."

"I don't know about your family and I want to know more and I'm sorry about whatever it is but I will not part with the insoles and I don't see how they will make any difference to anything and I need them for the dance and I won't let go of them to anybody. I'm sorry. I will stay very close to you and you will not need to worry. But I will not give you the soles."

"Before we leave, I need to see someone. I will be back very soon. Wait here and do not move. Do not move. Do you understand?"

They nodded and as he left, they looked at each other uncertainly. Shengli put her hand to the cord round her neck and felt that the little bag with the two insoles was still there.

PART 2

A DANCE TO WAKE A DRAGON

Chapter Six

Durfin took a bite from one of the barley cakes and chewed for a moment before trying to say something. His voice was muffled by speaking with a mouthful of breakfast but he was only asking the question that was on all their minds.

"Shengli, what is going on?"

"I don't know, Durfin. But I know that the soles are important and that I have to carry them. I can't hand them over to anyone," Shengli said

"But Old Tam trusted Renzi. Shouldn't we?" he asked, with only a small number of crumbs escaping.

"Old Tam isn't here now. And since we've been in Lungdou, something is different. I don't know; it's like the Renzi in the forest and the Renzi in the city are two different creatures."

"But he's big and his job is to protect us." Durfin went on. "Perhaps it is better if he carries the soles? What if something bad happened? Like, a thief or something, who tried to rob you? Wouldn't it be better if Renzi had them? You're only small and you couldn't fight anyone if you had to and he's, you know…"

Shonan cut in, "Shut up, Durfin. If Shengli doesn't want to hand over the soles to anyone, then that's all right. Who'd steal them anyway? Only someone who knew what they were. To anyone else they just look like, well, shoe insoles. Who would steal them? Especially here where nobody seems to know anything about anything and they probably think that even shoes are old fashioned and you should have steam engines tied to your feet instead of shoes and you'd probably like that better as well because you're just as bad as everyone here."

"Shut up, yourself." Durfin shot back, with a further small explosion of barley cake debris. "You just sit there doing nothing all the time." he said, "I'm just worried. If Renzi is angry with Shengli because he thinks she doesn't trust him, then is that a good thing? Of course not. What do you know about anything, anyway?"

"You shut up." Shonan snapped. "You're just so stupid sometimes and we're here to help not…"

"No, you shut up, you're just…" was the best Durfin had in reply.

"Both of you shut up!" Shengli screamed.

She'd been used to the twins bickering all her life. They were her best friends and she was used to it. But right now she wondered if having them here was helping. She couldn't think with them quarreling and she couldn't hear or see if Boken was trying to say anything, and she was beginning to feel frightened but she wasn't sure why. She got up and walked over to the window. The early sunlight had dimmed and a fog was settling. Lungdou was by the coast and mists were naturally part of the character of the city and many of the old songs and poems would refer to how the air could change suddenly as a sea fret rolled in. The way that would be described, especially in the sing-song ways of the ancients, it would sound magical and mysterious. Tales of the Kings and the court, the dancers and dragons of the classical ages always seemed to be viewed through a soft focus of time and draped in veils of gossamer and fascination.

Nowadays, with the smoke and dust of the engines this had become more of a sticky fug that you could feel on your skin and that scraped on the back of your throat. And now the brightness of the early morning was giving way as the gloom descended and clouded in on the streets. Shengli turned back from the window and spoke to the twins.

"Right, we've got to remember why we're here and what we have to do. Renzi is here to help us but he can't do the dance, only I can do that, and although when we're on the road we listen to him and follow his instructions, overall, the fact is that this is about a task that I have to do, and I need you two to help me and the best way you can do that is for us to stick together. All I want is for us to get to Zamai today, for me to do the dance and one way or another get on the road back home as soon as possible and then the spring will come to the forest and everything will be just like it should be. Are we agreed?"

The twins stood up and bounced over to Shengli and all three had a big hug. Boken skipped and yapped around them, delighted to see that spirits were back and they all then fell on him and started a tickle-torture of his belly and his ears that was both marvelous and horrible at the same time and he wriggled to escape from them while not trying too hard to get away and the relief of the moment set them all laughing and then the door burst open. Renzi stood there with Tongman.

"Shengli, we need to talk. Tongman here confirms he can find a buyer for the soles that will bring enough monies for us to secure safety for your village and my clan, to buy and secure food supplies until the spring comes and things return to normal. The situation is getting very serious in the mountains and we need to act immediately. I need you to hand over the soles. The lives of my family are under threat and your village cannot survive much longer either without supplies brought in from outside. We have very little time and we are lucky that Tongman has been able to find a trader who has a fascination with old things and will give us good monies."

"What are you talking about?" she snapped back, "I need the soles to do the dance!"

"Shengli, that is superstition. We have real needs right now that can be solved with monies."

"But we're here because Old Tam…"

"We're here because Old Tam knew the situation was desperate both for your village and for my pack in the mountains."

"Your what?"

"My family, I mean. They're going to die without new supplies and we can get them with the monies from selling your insoles."

"But we saw the Mang dragon! You were there!"

"An illusion, Shengli. When people dance and make music, and the energy and mood among them is strong, they can believe they see anything. There is no scientific basis for the theory of dragons and this is the age of engines. We need supplies in the mountains and in the village, we need monies for that and you have something that will get us those monies. Old Tam cared for your people and mine, this is what he would have wanted."

"No!"

"Give me the soles and stop being a selfish little girl who doesn't understand the ways of the world." Renzi made a little signal to Tongman and the two of them took a step forward. The children took a step back towards the window. Boken snapped and barked, Renzi snarled and growled; Shengli was shouting, the twins were shouting and Tongman stepped beside Renzi and cracked his knuckles. Boken jumped up at Tongman, biting and snapping and he, startled, took a step to the side leaving a gap between the men and the door.

Shengli dived for it and darted out of the room, Boken wriggled through the gap behind her and the two of them bounded down the corridor and the stairs. Back in the room Shonan and Durfin grabbed at Renzi and Tongman and pulled at their shirts and hair, delaying them for a few moments before a firm slap from Tongman sent Durfin reeling back across the room and Shonan was wrestled to the ground by Renzi and the two men rushed out of the room, shutting and locking the door behind them before setting off in pursuit of Shengli and Boken.

Shengli clattered down the stairs with no real idea of where she was running to other than to get away from Renzi at that moment. There was no plan but the instinct to run was strong and whatever threat Renzi seemed suddenly to have become would surely be less dangerous in the busy streets where there were people around. And maybe after a little time, the moment would calm and they could try and work out what was going on. And who was Tongman and why did he seem so important now?

She and Boken pushed out of the door and onto the street and hesitated. Which way to run? And then she thought of Durfin and Shonan. She turned for a moment, thinking to go back for her friends but she heard the voices of Renzi and Tongman as they came bounding down the wooden staircase. Boken nipped at her ankle and his eyes drilled into her with as clear a message as ever: we have to run. The twins will be fine. It's you he wants. Get out of here. Come this way. Run!

He turned and darted away and round the corner into another street. The smog had fully settled now and even with only a few steps, it was hard to breathe. Shengli felt her chest tightening with the thick, sticky air, and she froze. A steam-wagon came up from behind and passed them: the noise of the metal parts, the rattle of the wheels on the hard road surface and the guffing of the steam seemed to close in on her from behind like it was the engine pursuing her, not Renzi and Tongman. She felt a surge of panic rise in her as the engine approached, only for it to pass by and for the noise to diminish as it went on its way, unaware of Shengli and uninterested in her. Boken barked at her: come on. Come on. And then clear voices. Renzi shouting to Tongman: "you go down there -- I'll try this way!"

"Boken," Shengli whispered, "I don't think I can outrun Renzi." Come on old girl, let's try down here. Boken pleaded at her with his eyes and signaled another turn. This would be the best hope. The alleys and snickleways of Lungdou created a muddle and a maze and they could lose their pursuers in the fog. They sprinted down the little lane as it bent when Shengli saw a deep doorway and pulling up, she pressed her back into the space and gave a little whistle to Boken to join her. She wanted to see if they were being followed before running heedlessly into who knew what trouble. But what they saw was how Renzi paused at the head of the alley, dropped to the ground in a crouch and, closing his eyes, sniffed sharply and cocked his head a little as he listened. He had the trace he needed.

Not running now but loping in a long stride, knees bent, his head and shoulders forward he called gently, "Shengli, why are you running? We need to work together. Shengli!"

Shengli and Boken shot out from the doorway and further down the lane towards a little stone bridge over a small stream, a tributary of the great river. Boken yapped: not over the bridge. We'll wade across. "What? Why?" Just do as I say. We must confuse the scent... Boken led the way to the side of the stream. It was a filthy channel of stagnant water. Green film lay across the top; waste and refuse had gathered along the banks. The stench was enough to make Shengli gag. Boken looked up at her with eyes screaming: pick me up -- it is too deep for me. Come on! This will lose him. Shengli could hardly bear the thought of stepping into that foul soup, but Boken knew something that she didn't and he was sharp and clear in his thinking. She picked him up, counted to three super-quickly, and stepped into the stream.

Scum attached to her ankles, and she squirmed at the sensation of the silty and slimy creek bottom but it was only three or four paces and she was out the other side. She put Boken down, pressed herself into the wall of one of the greasy yellow buildings and looked back. She heard Renzi before she saw him. Calling, "Shengli! Shengli!" And then she could make him out at the stream bank, by the bridge, looking left and right. He dropped down to the ground again, and sniffed, and looked puzzled. Shengli pressed against the building and staying in the darkness under the eaves of the stunted little houses, she and Boken sidled along the wall and turned again and into a slightly larger street, with some steam-wagons parked along the pavement edge.

One of the wagons had a body like a long wooden barrel laid on its side. The wheels were bright red and almost glowed in the gloom. The two lamps at the front were like the protruding eyes of a giant frog, and the chimney reached straight up with a little crown on the top. It seemed cleaner and more cared for than the other engines they had seen so far, with shiny brass bands and decorations. On the seat the operator had left his long coat and his driving helmet: a leather skullcap with ear flaps and a huge pair of goggles. Next to this was a pile of blankets and animal skins. Shengli recoiled at the thought of clothing made out of creature skins but she also had an idea. She signaled to Boken and stepped up onto the wagon. She pulled the long, leather coat over her arms and, shivering at the thought of the poor animal whose body it came from, wrapped up her braids and then pulled the driving helmet over her face and the goggles over her eyes. She gathered up Boken and wrapped him up inside the huge coat and, with just his nose poking out, he flattened himself against her front and held on tight as she drew the belt around them both. The grubby glass in the goggles meant she could hardly see a thing now but she felt confident in this disguise. Renzi wouldn't be far behind even if clever Boken had thrown him off the trail for the moment and she couldn't run all day. She needed to find a busy place and to disappear in a crowd as someone else. Taking a deep breath she tried to imagine herself as a fat, pompous, engine operator. She put her feet at ten to two, held her shoulders back, thrust her Boken-padded stomach out and she set off up the street waddling like a penguin.

Meanwhile, Shonan and Durfin shouted and screamed and banged their fists at the door but it had been locked and either no one heard or whoever was out there was ignoring them. They sat on the edge of one of the beds, feeling hopeless and useless and each one trying hard not to be the one to start crying as they both felt very much like doing. Shonan stood up and went over to the window. It opened fairly easily and she looked down into the street below. It was two storeys down to the ground but there was a drainpipe just slightly to the side of the window.

"I'm going to try going out of the window, Durfin. We can't just sit here."

"Do you think you can do it?"

"Yes. There's a pipe here that to be honest, is going to be no harder climbing than anything we do back in the forest. Easier, really. We can both do this. Let me go first and then wait for me to get to the ground before you start because we can't know how strong it is."

With that, she sat herself on the window ledge, facing into the room, then stood up slowly with her back still towards the outside but facing inwards. She reached with her right hand for the drainpipe that was just on her fingertips. She shuffled right to the edge of the ledge when suddenly some paint flaked away from under her feet and she slipped, her right foot falling into mid-air. She grabbed at the pipe with her hand and swung freely for a moment before getting a good grip, feet together around the pipe and both hands holding tight. She looked over at Durfin leaning out of the window and gave him a big grin, "No problem!" Her determined face and reassuring smile lifted his spirits and he watched her edging down the side of the building hand over hand, as she kept saying to herself "Three points of contact; three points of contact..." over and over again.

" Be careful!" Durfin whispered. She didn't look up. She was focused.

Leaning out of the window he smiled encouragement and started to think about his own climb. It should be okay; he'd need to put his right hand there and...and leaning out and focused on planning his next move, he never heard the key turn in the lock or the soft steps across the room or the slow breathing or the little creak in the floorboards or any of the other tiny signals that there was someone else in the room behind him who approached quietly but purposefully to the point where a hand reached out and grabbed his shoulder. His heart missed a beat, everything inside him froze for a moment and then he turned his head to face a stranger. A small man, but still larger than himself and with knotty, wiry arms, and legs and fingers like little knives that dug into his shoulder, who pulled him roughly round and took hold of him by both arms. "Where do you think you are going, young mister?"

Durfin tried to twist his head and screamed down, "Shonan!! Shonan! Find help! There's..."

But he could say no more as a strong claw-like hand closed over his face, gagging him and disgusting him with a greasy, slimy smear of dirt and sweat.

"Back into the room, little hero, back into the room." said the croaky voice of the innkeeper, Jiong.

Durfin was pulled back towards the bed and shoved down firmly. "My friend says you've got something that he wants. That he says was promised to him." Durfin said nothing. He didn't know what was going on. He didn't understand how things had turned like this or why or what any of it meant. He couldn't say anything because he didn't know what to say but he wouldn't say anything because whatever was going on, this man was on the other side of whatever side Shengli was now on and Durfin thought he couldn't do much but at the very least he knew that he could do stubborn and he could do silent.

So that is what he did.

"All right, little hero." said the grubby man. "Perhaps we'll just wait a while and see if you feel a little more talkative then. Just for now, shall we say for your own safety, why don't we put in place a little reassurance that nothing silly will happen? Shall we?"

And taking one hand off Durfin, he undid his leather belt from his waistband then wrapping it around below both elbows, used it to strap Durfin's arms to his side. With the buckle at the back, there was no way that Durfin could reach to undo the belt. The man let go of him and Durfin slid back along the bed to sit with his back to the wall. A prisoner.

"Since you don't want to say anything, I guess that will do for now. I'll just sit here. There will be some friends come along later who can help us solve this little situation in a tidy way so don't you worry. We could try and get on? You look a bit of a scrawny kid who could do with a spot of breakfast. Why don't I organize us something nice to eat and we could see about being a bit sociable?"

Durfin just stared back at him, still. Whatever happened next, Shonan had got away, Shengli had got away, and they would find someone or get some sort of help or even if not, they were out of this danger and it was just him. The belt around his arms was tight and he could feel numbness coming on in his arms and hands but he could ignore that. He could wait.

Down in the street, Shonan knew something was wrong but Durfin had said to run and get help. With no Old Tam, no Shengli, and Renzi turning, there was no one to ask what to do. So be it. She looked up and down the street and seeing no sign of danger either way she turned right and started to run.

Just a few streets away, Shengli had got used to her new identity and waddled down the street feeling very confident in her disguise. She had entered a busier part of town, with market stalls, and people coming and going, and while she didn't quite know what she was going to do, she felt safe for the moment with Boken pressed to her tummy, cozy and warm in the big coat and leather helmet. There was no sign of Renzi just yet and all she could think was to try and find someone who looked to be in some sort of authority.

Feeling tired from the chase in the thick, sticky air and with the weight of the coat and Boken, she sat down on a barrel that had been left by a pile of old packing stuff. The now familiar grime clung to people as they shuffled to and fro. The traces of snow that lingered at the street side and on the rooftops were all black from coal dust and smoke and it was hard to think of it as snow at all. Did you just get used to the dirt? Maybe that was the way of things everywhere. Maybe the city people would find the village confusing?

She smiled at the thought of the village and she watched the faces of the people passing by, none of whom seemed to notice the begoggled, portly, off-duty wagon-driver sitting on an upended barrel by a pile of old boxes. She imagined that many of them must have been from the forest or mountains once but who had moved to the city on the promise of a better life. Like that old man there, pushing that cart; or that younger looking man with the moustache who looked like he'd just forgotten something or that young mother with what were maybe baby twins, or else she was someone who looked after other people's children? Or what about that youngster, running this way, stopping and looking around? What was…wait! Shengli pulled off the helmet and goggles and cried out, "Shonan! Shonan! Over here!"

Shonan rushed over and shrieked with relief. "Oh thank the dragons, you're here!"

"Yes, yes, I put on this disguise, what do you think of it? And so I managed to lose Renzi. Where's Durfin?"

"He's at the inn; he can't leave. He's trapped. I don't know what happened but I know he is trapped. Shengli, what are we going to do? We need to find someone who can help us?"

"I know. I thought we could try the Court maybe? Maybe someone there remembers Old Tam?"

"What's happened to Renzi? I can't believe what happened."

"No, me neither. But whatever it is, it isn't safe for us."

And just then Boken made a little yap sound from inside the coat. Shengli loosed the belt and opened up and pulled him out and he spoke to her with his eyes: He's near. I can smell him. And if I can smell him, then he can smell us. "What do you mean?" Shengli, I don't know why or how but he's not like a man. He can smell and track and hunt and hear and no man has skills like that. Men are clumsy and slow; he's not. And then he stopped, twitched and with a sudden movement fixed his gaze in the direction of one of the market stalls in the middle-distance. Shengli followed his eyes and saw, locked onto her own, the amber-yellow points that saw right through her. Renzi.

He leaned forward and started to walk towards her. She pulled off the huge coat so she could run but already she knew she could never out-pace him. She was backing away, pulling Shonan with her and Boken, little Boken, stepped forward and started barking furiously. Louder than she had ever heard him before: a rasping, snapping bark and the fur on his back stood up. He turned back and looked at Shengli: get away! Get away!

Renzi's walk stretched out into a slow run and his shoulders dropped, his arms stretched out and then fell to the ground. As he did so, he shook off his old cloak and the things of men and stretched forward, his back long and his legs reaching out. His jaw thrust out and the familiar features exaggerated; the strong, athletic body shook itself and fur was fluffed out, a tail unfurled, and Renzi's form shifted to show the alert ears and proud features of the warden of the mountains. Pulling back the corners of his mouth, throwing his head back, Renzi, the wolf-prince, let out a howl of defiance and he began to run towards them in an easy canter, his level back hardly moving and the smooth and elegant stride making it seem that he was floating across the surface of the grubby street as the clumsy, fearful, townspeople screamed and panicked and fell over themselves and each other, crying, "Wolf! Wolf!"

Shengli fell back, screaming, into the pile of boxes and barrels. Shonan fell with her. They tried to stand but slipped again, stumbling over the waste and refuse that had gathered at the street corner. Boken stood his ground, barking furiously, as Renzi padded towards them and then stood, only a few yards away, and fixed those yellow eyes on Boken. He raised his shoulders and cocked his head a little as if to say, 'Are you sure, little brother? Are you sure?'

Time seemed to stand still as Shengli and Shonan looked on, chilled with anxiety, and Boken stared back at Renzi, looking so small and vulnerable but not giving ground. Renzi's eye seemed to show that, regretfully, the time had come. He hunched back and summoned up the power of the wolf-prince preparing to pounce.

Then there was a sound like an explosion of air released; a sound familiar from the engines, from the fire and steam of the new age, and something smashed into Renzi's side and with a howl of pain he was thrown off his feet. He struggled to stand and yet something was sticking out from his fur. The same explosion, another thud into Renzi and he fell again and as he did he let out another cry, more human. From across the street a Constable approached. His crossbow reloaded and held at his waist, ready to fire again. As he approached Renzi, through the smog and mist, the wolf-prince resolved again into human form, naked and with two crossbow bolts buried in his back. Renzi lay in the slime and slush of the dirty city street, now as a naked man, face down in the grime, and as the Constable stood over him a crowd of city-folk started to gather to stare and then the noise and chatter began.

Shengli crept forward and she and Boken embraced. "Brave, brave little dog! Oh, Boken, Boken!" Tears welled up, but Boken looked her straight in the eye: we're not safe here. Come. While there is this confusion.

And Shengli, Shonan and Boken sneaked away behind the garbage and through the fog and left their old protector-turned-enemy, the wolf-prince, Renzi, naked and dead and surrounded by the mocking clamor, the pointing jeers and triumphant snorts of city folk who moments earlier had fled in fear and screams at the sight of the warden of the mountains himself, brought down by a shot from a mechanical device.

Chapter Seven

In the crowd between the market stalls stood Tongman. He turned and disappeared into the shadows. Renzi was dead but the little girl still carried the magic soles and wasn't it altogether nicer, after all, not to have to share? There'd have to be a cut for Jiong back at the inn but he didn't know what was at stake and he wouldn't know that his slice would only be a small fraction of the takings. One of the children had been missing from the group, which maybe meant there was one still back at the inn. In any case, that would be where they'd go next. And after that?

To Zamai? It was time to get back to the Dama and update her on events. This chasing and brawling in the streets was getting vulgar and risky. Better, perhaps, to let them come to him?

Back at the inn, Jiong was sitting watching Durfin while eating a sandwich made of a slice of salty, fried animal flesh, and some soft bread. "You sure you don't want some? No hard feelings or anything. Your friend has got something that my friend wants and me, I'm just trying to make ends meet, you know? No need for us to be hostile. It's just business. Here, try some of this..." He put together a second sandwich for Durfin and took it over and held it up to him. Up to now Durfin hadn't said a thing but this time he flexed his arms to show how he was still bound by the belt.

"Fair enough." Jiong got up and locked the door and put the key in his pocket and then walked over and closed the window.

"I don't suppose you'll get very far. I admit I don't feel right tying up a kid like you. Here you go." And he removed the belt from Durfin who immediately felt a surge of relief as he rubbed his arms to get the blood back into his hands.

"What's all this about?" Durfin blurted out. I don't know anything. Shengli is the smart one. Shonan is clever too. Everyone knows I'm a bit of a clot but if no one ever tells me anything how am I supposed to understand?"

Jiong looked closely at Durfin and after a pause, he smiled a soft smile. "You and me both. This is my inn and getting monies these days ain't easy and then you've got the likes of Tongman and Renzi with plans and schemes and if I'm lucky I'll get a bit of a cut, no questions asked. But this business, I don't know. Your friend has something they want. And I was supposed to keep you and the other girl who was still here..."

"...that was my sister, Shonan."

"Your sister, yes, keep you both here while they went after the other one. They'll have something to say when they come back and find one of them got away."

Durfin hesitated. He didn't want to get too sociable like this. On the other hand, Jiong had already taken the belt off and he didn't seem too bad. Maybe he could be smart about this?

"Who is Renzi? We thought he was protecting us. He was supposed to look after us."

Jiong laughed. "I think that was the idea! To look after you, all right."

Durfin looked confused and Jiong smiled. "Don't worry. All it will take is for your friend to hand over whatever it is and then

we'll all want to get you out of here and on your way home on the first engine. No one wants anyone to get hurt. Renzi is a solid fellow but there is trouble in the mountains and his first loyalty is to that, not me, not you, or anyone else. The key is finding ways that your interests align, right? He needs monies for that. I need monies just to keep my head above water. Tongman owes monies to some people who aren't very nice at all, no indeed, not very nice at all. You want to get out of here and get home. If what I want, and what Renzi wants, and what Tongman wants, and what you want are all lined up, and we can all get what we want well, that's just reasonable, ain't it? Here, have a sandwich..."
He handed Durfin the sticky pieces of bread with the bit of flesh pressed between. Durfin took it and looked at it feeling a bit unsure. This was creature flesh, right? But city people ate it all the time and he had to be honest, it smelt really rather excellent. Kind of salty and maybe a bit greasy, but not like nut oil, better.

"Go on -- won't kill you. Look, I'll take half see, nothing wrong with it. We've got this bit of business to get through. No reason for any suspicion." And he tore the sandwich in half, took a share and pushed it into his mouth. He smiled a great big open smile that showed the white bread and pinky flesh turning over in his mouth until he forced it down with a swallow. "Cracking, that. Go on then. Look, it hasn't killed me."

Durfin lifted the sandwich to his mouth and took a small bite. He chewed cautiously and then started to feel the sensation of the new flavor and texture. He'd never tasted anything so good. He closed his eyes and turned the flesh over in his mouth. It was sort of savory and salty but sweet as well and a kind of smokiness that reminded him of sitting round camp fires in the forest but there was also a richness that he hadn't tasted before. Although the greasiness was really noticeable. it was still crispy. He pushed the rest of the sandwich in and chewed it greedily and as he looked up he found himself smiling at Jiong and a dribble of the fat slipped out of the corner of his mouth. Someone tried the door and rattled the handle. Jiong winked at Durfin and got up to unlock it.

"We'll soon have all this sorted." He opened the door and instead of Renzi or Tongman he saw Shengli, Shonan, and Boken. They looked in and their eyes went from him to Durfin, sitting on the bed, his mouth full of the flesh sandwich, shiny fat on his chin and the remains of the smile he had just shared with Jiong still showing. The girls looked hard at Durfin as the reality of what he had done started to become clear.

In the silence, Jiong spoke first, "What? Where's Renzi? Tongman?"

"Renzi's dead." answered Shengli. "He was shot by a Constable. I don't know about Tongman. And if you don't get out of here and leave us alone, Shonan will run for a Constable and you'll never catch her. She can really run fast. Shonan, go and find one of the Constables"

"Wait, wait. No trouble. I'm nobody. Renzi dead? Constables? That's me out. And you too. You get out of my inn now and you were never here, understand? Oh dragons, oh no, the Dama, Tongman...you just get out..." He was turning his hands over and over each other and the corner of one of his eyes started twitching.

Shengli started. "The Dama? What's the Dama got to do...?"

"Oh my, oh dragons, oh my...you just get out, will you? Old Jiong doesn't want any trouble. Just trying to get some monies together. 'Ain't that so, little hero? Eh? We were getting on all right, weren't we, eh? Come on now? What has the Dama got to do with all this? Oh, nothing, nothing, nobody, I didn't say anything, just old Jiong's nonsense. Go on, out of here before there's trouble, go...go"

"Come on, Shengli," said Shonan, "I think that's our best move. Let's try and get to the Court or the Academy. It can't be good if we stay here. Tongman is still out there somewhere and if he comes back here we'll be back where we started. Come on!"

The two girls stepped into the room and started to gather together their few things. Shonan made a face at Durfin and he followed them. Jiong stepped out into the corridor and looked left and right and then when they had picked up their little packs he hurried them down the stairs into the street. "You was never here, and that's fine by me? Got it? And if you see Tongman, stay out of his way. And if I see him, as I will, I don't doubt at all, I'll say you tricked me. That's no matter. He thinks I'm an idiot anyway. Not always a bad thing that!" He winked at Durfin, "Take care, little hero." He looked left and right again and then pulled back inside and closed the door on the children.

"Durfin, did you eat creature?" Shonan looked at him hard.

"I-I had to. I had to. He forced me."

"Come on, you two." interrupted Shengli. "There's no time for that now. Let's think. Tongman's going to come here and he's going to learn we have left. He'll be looking for two girls, a boy and a little dog. We need to be smart and to split up, so we aren't so easy to find. We need to get to the Academy, but we mustn't go anything like a direct route. It isn't far from here, we saw it this morning from the tower, but I think we should go away from it first, then turn back after a few hours so that if Tongman is looking for us, or anyone he has helping him, they get confused. What do you think?"

The twins nodded. Boken looked up, That's my girl!

"How about this," she continued' "Boken and I will go and cross the river back to the south side and maybe you two go towards to the docks. That's down there, the opposite way from here to the Academy. Then, when the sun starts to go down and we have a bit of cover as the daylight drops we turn back and aim to meet at the main gate of the Dance Academy at sunset? It's easy to find and if I were Tongman, I'd think about waiting at Zamai for me to come and do the dance so we don't want to go there straightaway. That is, if he has any clue why we're here but that's what I'm thinking. Try not to be noticed and don't act suspicious in any way, like you think someone might be following you."

The plan made sense and it felt like they were taking control after having either been led by adults or just reacting to events. Strangely, given the awful things she had just witnessed with Renzi, Shengli felt more comfortable and calm than at any time since they left the village. It was clear what had to happen: she had to get to the Academy with the twins so she could do the dance while they made the rhythms and then they had to get out of Lungdou. 'When it looks like the goal can't be reached, think about the steps, not the goal'. That sounded like something she'd heard before, the kind of thing Old Tam might have said. Maybe it was him? It seemed appropriate right now. Next steps: get away from this place, keep out of sight for a few hours and then meet up again.

"Let's do it," she said, with renewed confidence.

The twins nodded back and turned to walk away down the lane and in the general direction of the docks. Shengli swung her pack onto her shoulders, nodded at Boken and they went the other way, more generally towards the center of the old city and then aiming for the bridge back over to the south side.

It felt like a relief, all of a sudden, just to be her and Boken, and she looked down at the little dog and smiled. "I love you, Boken. You are so brave and when you faced wolf-Renzi, I don't know, I just can't believe it except, of course, I can believe it 'cos it's exactly what I knew you'd be like but then it is still amazing and I can't, you know..." He smiled with his eyes and ears and told her, now, now! Less of that. Come on, let's find a place we can lie low for a bit. I could go for a snack if we see anything suitable. It's been a bit of a day so far! She laughed and they picked up the pace.

The busier streets led to the old bridge and the crossing over to the south side, away from old Lungdou, the Palace and the Academy, and presumably wherever Tongman was searching for them. They walked over the bridge, dodging the crowds of city folk as they pressed ahead, half going one way and half the other, heads down and coats and collars pulled up against the sharp breeze that ran up from the broad water below. Shengli looked down at the dark, sliding expanse of brown-gray river and began to feel her mood change.

For a moment, just then, she had felt the elation of survival from the chase, her exhilaration at Boken's bravery, and then the sense of control that came from making decisions about what to do next and directing the twins. But something about the faces of the city folk and the flatness of the river started to slow her down. At the end of the bridge, taking a small staircase down, they were able to enter a riverside park, a grubby and tired-looking park that you entered through a broken, rusting gate.

Scrap paper, and other litter, rolled in the breeze, and the coal-dust flecked snow banked up at the path edges. But it was quiet at least, and while the workers and shoppers and travelers and busy men and women pushed backwards and forwards across the bridge above, Shengli and Boken looked for a spot out of the direct wind where they could pass an hour or so. There were flowerbeds and trees but without Spring, all that was on show were crusty, frosty patches of bare, gray, earth, speckled with traces of ice and frozen sludge, and spindly black branches like gnarled and crooked fingers reaching into the soupy sky. There was a playground with swings, a roundabout, and a slide that had maybe been a place of laughter and fun at one time but with the winter and the neglect, paint was flaking off, colors had faded, and one of the swings hung broken, its chain flapping in the breeze and slapping tinnily into the steel frame.

They weren't the only life in the park. There were crows and jackdaws in the trees and the whistling of the wind in the branches would be answered with the strangled cawing of the unlovely but at least living birds. The residue of dead leaves from the long-past autumn picked up in the breeze and mixed with the litter: scraps of paper, packaging from foods, an old, green bottle, and an abandoned, broken umbrella, spiny and twisted. Beside them, as they walked, the snuff-colored river slid slowly toward the sea. Ahead, they saw the promise of at least some shelter. A small pavilion with curled eaves and a stone seat. That would have to do.

Shengli sat down and shuffled as she tried to adjust to the cold surface. Boken climbed up onto her lap and they huddled for warmth and the little dog rested his snout on her arm and closed his eyes. Within a moment she could sense how his breathing had slowed and she felt a little moment of envy that he was able to sleep while she all she could do was to try to shelter from the worst of the cold and wait until it was time to brave the city streets again and hope to meet the twins at the Dance Academy. And in this chill place, amid the browns and grays, to the sound of the jackdaws and crows, and with the shapes of the tangled twigs and branches silhouetted against the colorless sky, she felt tears start to come and she could not help a choking sound as she gasped and, for all that she hated weeping and wanted to be strong, she let out a silent cry of grief.

First, for Old Tam, who she needed so badly right now. Then for Renzi. She needed to understand how that dignified hero-figure whom she had so trusted had turned on her; how he was wolf-become-man or man-become-wolf and how, in either case, even though he had become her enemy, he was still finer and more splendid than anything or anyone in the scrappy street where he had died, brought down by a device that gave killing power to a man who in no sense was his equal.

And then Durfin, his face greedy at the taste of a creature's flesh. Her heart tore at this last, almost the worst of all. Old Tam's death came, as she could see now, when he chose for it. He was ready and it came at the end of a long life that had been lived well. Renzi was a mystery but he hadn't been her friend for long. But Durfin was part of her, almost. And suddenly he felt like a stranger. The cold air chilled her tears against her cheeks, and she used her free hand to rub her face and as she looked up, through her moistened eyes, the clouds and the pattern of the branches beyond the upturned eaves of the pavilion blurred, and it seemed like little rainbows formed. She rubbed again but the effect only grew. Gently, but steadily, however much she blinked or rubbed, the rainbow effect in the sky grew clearer and sharper to the point where it formed into a rose shape, a sunburst figure of colored lights. The effect of the colors on the drab, winter scene was like waking up from a deep sleep.

She closed her eyes, unsure whether to believe what she was seeing, and heard a gentle voice speak in tones soft and strange; she opened her eyes again and saw, from within the rainbow there rose, at first, a face and then the body of, yes, it was she, she, the lady. Slender and tall, her delicate features shrouded in flowing waves of white that fell from a modest crown. White drapery and ribbons fluttered from her shoulders and blurred her willowy figure; locks of her shiny black hair caught the breeze and fluttered and played across and behind her oval face. Her arched eyebrows curved down a thin nose to a mouth that held a gentle smile, a smile that said, "Everything is going to be all right," and made you believe it. One hand was held before her in a gesture of blessing, reassurance and protection. In the other, she held a small flask, fragile and long-necked. She looked down and her eyes rested on the little girl and the sleeping dog and she poured a drop of liquid from the flask. It landed softy on Shengli's cheek and mixed with her tears.

Shengli whispered, "Who are you...?"

"They call me 'The One Who Sees Cries.'"

"You saw me crying?"

"Not quite." the figure smiled, "That's not quite how it is. I see the cries. When a creature of the world of dust is in anguish, even if there is no sound or there are no tears, I see it. Of all the creatures, of whatever type, I see when there is pain. Even if the cries are silent I see them. And there are many. So very, very many. There is so much and the greater tragedy is that so much of it is so easy to avoid but the world of dust is in confusion. And I see all the cries and I try to answer and bring comfort but sometimes it is hard for people to see me or hear me. The world of dust is so noisy both on the outside and on the inside."

"On the inside?"

"How much of the noise that shuts me out is from inside the heads of people? How much of the noise you hear all the time is from inside you? And how much from outside you? How often can you really hear nothing, really nothing, or so little at least that there is room for another voice to be heard?"

"Sometimes, sometimes when I'm back in the forest and when it is really, really quiet and I'm just there on my own, or with Boken, if he's sleeping or just being quiet himself, I forget to think and..."

"Yes, go on..."

"...and then it seems like well, not a voice really, not like someone speaking, but kind of like little answers or something come...like a voice, but not a voice."

"Shengli, there is so much suffering. And you are suffering. You have had terrible trials and now you have a great task to perform."

"I'm so tired. Really, I am. I'm only a little girl and I'm scared and I know why it has to be me but I wish it wasn't me and why can't it be someone else?"

"There is no answer to that, Shengli, my dear. It is how things have come to be. And you are blessed. You have the gift your mother gave you that you can use now to raise the Li dragon and bring an end to this winter and all the hardship that we see around us."

"What about Renzi? Can you help me to understand that?"

"You will understand. But not yet. But you can know that he was motivated by love, too, even if it led him to a terrible misunderstanding. The noises in the city were too loud outside of him as were the noises inside him, noises from the love that was driving him. Feel for him, Shengli."

"I do."

"I shall go now. There are so many cries and there are some that come where there is space for me to answer. It is only chance, accident, fortune, that brought this great duty to you but it is a duty you must love for the gift you can bring and the suffering you can lift from all of Tianya. From all the creatures and all the people and for the oneness and togetherness of all living things that feel pain. In all we do, Shengli, we are blessed if we can use our gifts to reduce pain in the world. You are blessed with the gift of the dance and you will use it and you will relieve suffering and there will be joy, and hearts will lift, and the seasons will turn and the confusion in men that leads to so much of what you see in Lungdou and that troubles you so much, that will have its answer through dance, through the spring, and through your love."

"Will you come next time I cry?"

"Shengli, I am in you. There is no me that is not you. You made me and I am in you, for you, and by your side just as I am in everyone and for everyone and by everyone and there in all creatures that can feel pain. There is nothing outside the world of dust, Shengli. It is all there is, it is all there is, it is all there is…"

And as the voice faded, the image dulled and disappeared, and Shengli blinked and saw again the sludgy brown river, the cracked pillars of the pavilion, the grimy soot-spotted snow-slush and the black and buckled branches of the leafless trees. Boken stirred. "Boken, Boken, are you awake?" Well, I suppose I am now, old girl. How are we doing? It seems darkish. I guess sunset can't be far off. Perhaps we should toddle off over to the vicinity of the Academy and try and catch up with those two? "Boken, have you ever seen the One Who Sees Cries?" Boken looked at her, twitched an ear, wrinkled his nose and shuffled a whisker. It was all the answer she needed. The two friends stood up, stretched and shook off the stiffness from being still for however long or short that had been. Boken had no idea as he'd been deep asleep. For Shengli, she was already struggling to remember the conversation she'd just had. It was almost like it never happened except in a way it was like it had always been happening. Shengli smiled at herself. She was making less sense than Old Tam on one of his odder days.

"I must have dropped off as well. I didn't think I had but I guess I must have. I feel like I had some sort of wonderful dream but I can't remember now what it was. Just that it was lovely. I want to dance, Boken: I want to do the dance. I haven't done it for a couple of days now. I am so ready to do it again. Come on. Let's get back to the city. If Tongman is still looking for us well, I don't care! With you by my side, my little brave doggy companion, there could be twenty Tongmans and we'd still not have anything to fear! Come on!" And she skipped a few steps before breaking into a run and Boken bounded alongside, yapping and snapping as if they were charging through the forest as normal until they got back to the bridge and then, with secretive smiles, they went back into the old 'prowler' mode, bought some mushroom and chickpea fritters from a street stall, eating a couple there and then and shoving a few more in the pack for later, and worked their way through the early evening crowds, comrades on a mission.

Chapter Eight

The twins were already outside the Academy when Shengli and Boken arrived. She couldn't see them but Durfin whistled with one of the secret calls they used in their games in the forest and she found them straightaway in the shadows, between two buttresses.

"How are you?", she whispered. "Everything okay?"

"Yes. We got down to the old docks and we saw the ships bringing food and other things in. Durfin is feeling sick but it serves him right."

"I've told you, like, a million times, I didn't have any choice. I was a prisoner, remember?"

"All right, what's done is done." interrupted Shengli. "We've got to work out what to do now."

"So," Shonan spoke thoughtfully, "We're going to have to decide what we're going to do about tonight. It's too cold to stay out on the streets and it can't be safe and I think you're right about not heading straight to Zamai. But we don't have a lot of monies and we probably need to take care of every last coin and if we go to an inn, who's to say it isn't run by someone who's friends with Jiong or Tongman? Have you eaten? Durfin doesn't want anything but I found a place where I could get some soup."

"Yes, me and Boken are good. Look, this place is derelict. Or most of it seems to be anyway. Maybe we can sneak inside and find somewhere we can camp? Even maybe get a little fire going? I'm freezing. Then we should wake up super-early, get to Zamai, try and do the dance and then get out of Lungdou."

"Oh Dragons, yes!" said Durfin. "I hate this place. I never thought I'd miss the forest so much."

They edged around the wall to the main gate. The Academy was a group of buildings inside the boundary wall they were now against. Everything was built of pinkish bricks that had once had a coat of plaster with yellow paint, still evident in places, but that had mostly flaked off, revealing the dusty masonry beneath. The wall was topped with scalloped coping stones in the royal style but moss had mostly claimed the territory and where not, much of the decoration that must have been there in the golden days had faded or become overgrown with lichen. Ferns and thistles had sprouted at the base of the wall and in the corners by the buttresses. The main gate itself was intact. There was a large double door of heavy timber that was long overdue a paint job but still firmly closed and you didn't have to approach closely to see the great bolt that had been fastened across the two brass bosses that had been made to last and still served. The stone lyke-gate that framed the doors was topped with curling eaves and more stonework in the scalloped style.

There was no way in, through, or even over the gate. But the children were good climbers. All of them had spent hours in the forest pushing each other to new challenges and a crumbling brick wall with buttresses was like a stepladder to them. They turned back from the gate, walked around the wall for the first corner so as, hopefully, to be away from anyone who might be watching, and with Shonan going first to check the best holds,

Shengli came behind so she could lift Boken as far as she could and then pass him up to Shonan. With Durfin up last, nominated as bagman, they were up and over like cats.

Scuttling between the buildings and the outhouses they explored the old campus. The main buildings were more central and they chose to stay with the outhouses near the outer wall. It wasn't long before they found a small shed, built from the same pinkish brick with red roof tiles but less decoration than the wall or the main buildings nearer the gate. There was a broken window and they peered in.

Nothing. There was nothing there. A totally empty shed. Dusty and cobwebby but otherwise totally empty. The door was locked, unsurprisingly, but Shonan, being so agile and flexible, was able to reach through the broken window to the catch and open it from the inside and they all climbed in, stood in the middle of the room and catching each other's eyes, suddenly burst out laughing. "A palace!", Shonan joked, "We've got ourselves a little palace!"

They busied themselves with making a camp. This was no problem for forest kids who almost didn't need to speak to each other as they got on with practical tasks. It didn't after all seem smart to light a fire and draw attention to themselves and there was nothing really suitable for fuel anyway as the grasses and ferns growing between the cracks in the walls outside would be no better than tinder. But the hut gave shelter from the wind and relative to the outside it was cozy. They took it in turns to go and gather some of the bracken from base of the outer wall and that made good bedding as well as material they could use to block up the window and the gap under the door. Draft-free, snug and secret! They curled up and with a view to that super-early start that Shengli had proposed and they tried to go to sleep. But that wasn't easy and there was too much on their minds just yet.

"Durfin" asked Shengli, "How did you feel when you ate the flesh?"

"I told you, I had no choice!"

"I know, I'm not saying anything. I just wondered what it was like."

"To be honest, at first it was really nice. It's easy to see why city people eat it if they just don't think about what it is. It's like nothing in our world. But afterwards, you just feel weird. Like, something died, I don't know what, maybe a pig or something, I don't know what, it died just so you could have a sandwich. I wish I'd never had it but I told you, I didn't have any choice. And you don't have to say anything because Shonan has given me a really hard time all afternoon."

"I know. It's all right. We've all had to deal with some tough things. You have some knowledge now. You know something. Maybe the best thing you can do is use that to help other people understand?" As these words came out, Shengli heard herself and felt a bit awkward. This wasn't the silly chatter that they lived off. There was something there, she felt it. But then she wanted to get things back to their usual ways so she added: "And besides, you're too fat and stupid already so you shouldn't be eating anything for a while."

"Wha...!", spluttered Durfin.

Shonan laughed, Boken snuggled up to Shengli and Durfin turned his back on the others feeling a little wounded but deep down, grateful for the forgiveness and understanding that Shengli had given him. Sleep came.

It was still dark when something caused Boken to wake and he stirred and nudged Shengli. Shengli, Shengli, old girl: there's someone coming. A man and a dog. "Uh, wha'..." Shengli was struggling to come back from the deep sleep she had been enjoying. It was still dark and she couldn't see or hear anything.

Outside, Shengli. There's someone there. A man and a dog.

And then there was a rattle in the door, a rusty lock turned and the door creaked open. "Hello, hello? What have we got here then? Babes in the wood? Huh huh! More like babes in the hut, eh? Better than sniffing out a nest of rats, eh, Bolu?" The frame of the door was filled by a huge dog, shaggy-haired and taller at the shoulder than any of the children. Standing beside this enormous hound, feet splayed and wearing a fluffy hat that drooped behind him and in a coat that looked many sizes too big, was a little pointy-faced man. The two creatures, one huge for his kind and the other barely taller than a child, looked into the room, their eyes level like four little lights in a row. Shonan screamed. Durfin pulled his pack to his tummy and shuffled backwards to the wall. Shengli grabbed Boken and Boken, Boken barked at the giant dog and felt his fur rising on his back.

"Hey, hey, don't go fearing!" said the little man. "What's going on here then? Bolu told me he smelled something and led me here. No need for anyone to get upset. Easy does it. Easy. But let's have some stories, eh? Who are you, why are you here? 'cos something 'ain't right, no there 'ain't, not with kids sleeping in the sheds there 'ain't."

Bolu, the immense beast dropped his snout and loped gently towards Boken. Boken held his ground and, pulled back his chops and growled fiercely. Bolu sniffed gently and came close enough to nuzzle Boken softly. Boken gradually felt the fur on his back relax and settle. *This fellow doesn't seem so bad. Big, no question, and that can unsettle a chap y'know but it doesn't seem like he means harm.*

"So," said the little man, "If you aren't going to introduce yourselves, let me go first. I'm Pangti and this, as you've already heard, is Bolu and we are the night watch here at the Academy. Now, come on, who are you?"

Nobody spoke. "How about if you come with me back to my little hut, and you'll have to anyway because Bolu will insist, and if Bolu insists then you'll be inclined to agree with him, and we have ourselves a hot drink together and we get acquainted? I've got some rubyberry-broth just mulling nicely on the stove, I have, and it will do you a power of good, that will. I normally add a little dash of mulberry wine but I'm thinking that might not be right for you young 'uns but the both'll warm you anyway. What do you say?"

The twins looked at Shengli and she, hearing in Pangti something of the world of home and the village, nodded. Bolu nudged round them, bustling them like a sheepdog and they followed Pangti as he led the way, walking with feet at ten to two, bent forwards and his fluffy, floppy hat bouncing gently.

"Do you think we can trust him, Shengli?" asked Shonan, under her breath.

"I don't think we have any choice." Shengli replied. "We're all on our own and besides, he seems all right."

Pangti led them to his watchman's hut, near the main gate and they entered the homely, cozy little room. There were stools and wooden chairs with rough old blankets scattered over them; there was straw on the floor and the little stove in the corner had, as promised, an enamel jug of rubyberry-broth steaming gently and the rich, fruity smell filled the room. The stove, and the soft footing on the straw and the sight of the blankets filled them with warmth for the first time in days. Pangti signaled to them to sit on the chairs and they wrapped themselves up in the blankets and sat and watched him as he shuffled about, fetching little tin mugs and apologizing for the mess that didn't seem very messy to the children and gradually they were all settled, mugs of broth in their hands, blankets drawn around them, Boken and Bolu curled up by the stove. Pangti leaned forward,

"Right, now we might have a story, eh? What is this and why aren't you with your parents? From your beads, you're a ways away from home, although that's not so strange these days. Old Pangti 'ain't to be feared of but something 'ain't right and what I do know is that if something 'ain't right, it needs putting right tidily and before someone somewhere gets upset and makes things worse."

And Shengli, deciding that this was not a time for secrets, began the story, from Old Tam and his calculations to Renzi and the plan to get to Zamai and all the trials and troubles in-between. The only thing she didn't say anything about was the insoles which stayed in their bag around her neck. She felt that trusting Pangti would do more good than harm but there was a limit.

"Well, well, well...three holes in the ground, eh?" mused Pangti.

"What?" asked Shengli.

"Wells - they're holes in...oh, never mind. Just, well, well, well... What a tale."

While Shengli had been talking, Durfin and Shonan had fallen asleep. She too was drooping with the warmth and the feeling of security and the rubyberry-broth warming her from the inside.

"Why don't you let that sleep come, little 'un, and we'll sort it all out in the morning. Bolu and me, we've got to get out on our rounds again. Now you're safe, don't go thinking about running off, eh?"

"What will you do?"

"That's for the morning."

And he got up and with a low whistle, stirred Bolu who rose slowly up and the two left the room. Shengli thought she heard the key turn in the door behind them but then, she was half asleep so then again maybe she didn't and then the other half of that sleep came and she was as deeply gone as the others.

All four were awoken later by Pangti and Bolu coming back in. The open door showed that it was daylight, and he was bringing with him a jug of berry-broth while from Bolu's mouth hung a basket filled with steaming barley cakes.

"Breakfast, woodland babes! Barley cakes and berry-broth. There're some seaweed fritters here too -- I don't know if you've had them before. You maybe don't get them in the forest I expect but you might like them."

The children stirred, stretched and took a moment to realize where they were and how they'd come to be the guests of this pointy little man who seemed to be friendly but who, it was clear, was holding them captive if only in the nicest possible way.

"After breakfast, Shengli, you've got a little appointment with a lady who is keen to meet you."

"Who? Wha..." Shengli tried to say with a mouthful of barley-cake.

"The Dama herself. Yes, turns out she'd heard from somewhere that you are in Lungdou and she is most keen to meet you, most keen indeed. Me and Bolu sniffed out a prize little nest of creatures we did, last night, eh, Bolu? Better than our usual. We're usually lucky to sniff out a nest of rats, we are. It's a good night's work to find a nest of woodland babes and one of them turning out to be of special interest to the old lady, eh? Not a bad night's work at all, not a bad night's work."

Shengli began to wonder if she had made a mistake in being so honest with Pangti. And yet: here he was, handing out the barley cakes and the three of them were hungry enough for sure and the seaweed fritters, which were not so strange because dried seaweed was familiar to the villagers as the peddlers brought it, but this was fresh and so they approached a little cautious after Durfin's experience yesterday, but they turned out to be really tasty and not like anything they had ever had before but they were still plants after all so that was all right. They ate, took turns to go and visit the sluice room, accompanied by Bolu, where they had a welcome wash and clean up and then Pangti indicated to Shengli that it was time for her to come with him to see the Dama.

"I won't be locking the door on you two, er, three...sorry, little dog." He said behind him, as they left. "But Bolu will be here and sure he's a nice old thing but he can be a bit sensitive, like, and if he thinks you're not doing what he's there to see that you do be doing, then he can get upset. And if you don't mind me saying, I do suggest that you don't upset him. Really, I do." Bolu yawned sleepily and as his huge mouth stretched wide the opportunity to evaluate his resources in terms of teeth was enough to convince everybody present that it would be best not to hurt Bolu's feelings.

The gigantic hound curled up in the doorway, blocking it completely and settled his monumental snout on his paws and rolled his head sideways to get comfortable. They walked across the courtyard that opened up after the main gate, ignored the Great Hall of the Academy, which faced that gate and turned between two larger buildings before coming to a small bungalow with steps up to a painted door. The scalloping and decoration were more ornate than on any of the other buildings but the flaking paint and the gathering of dust and debris was everywhere.

Pangti indicated to Shengli to wait, knocked on the door, and entered. Waiting that moment, she thought about running -- but where to? This wasn't part of the plan but she was here now. This was the Dama. Dama Tiyun. The Dama who took over after the old Dama, who'd expelled her mother. This was the Dama who'd presided over the decay of the Academy and the end of the dance. Was she an enemy? Or a friend? She must have been a dancer herself once. She must know nüshu. She might even have known Shengli's mother. She must have done. Her thoughts were racing when Pangti came back out and told her to go in by herself.

"Quite a find, you were! In you go. Mind your Ps and Qs, there's a good girl. And if you get asked, try and put in a good word for old Pangti, eh? I treated you nice and just doing my job, you understand."

Shengli stepped cautiously through the doorway into the dark room. It took a moment for her eyes to adjust and at first she was only aware of the smell, a musty, dusty smell of damp old blankets and hearthrugs. Around the room were little tables and shelves cluttered with ornaments and pictures, curly legged sidetables and a long, low chaise longue with braided decoration and patterned cushions. Mirrors looked back at her mistily through the dust, their swirly frames with flaky gold paint enclosing her reflection. Across the room, a black fireplace with a mantel-shelf, vases, and little ceramic figurines of dancers, all coated with the same dust. Gauzy material hung across a bookcase and the backs of a couple of upright chairs. Light came from an oil lamp on one of the sidetables, washing the scene in an amber glow. Gradually Shengli's eyes came to settle on the lean, sharp-faced lady in the deep, leather, wing-back chair beside the fireplace. She was dressed in yellow muslins and lace that fell about her loosely. She wore little yellow dancing shoes and sat with her hands folded on her lap and her legs to one side, crossed at the ankles, one foot curled awkwardly behind the other. The light reflected golden off the rings she was wearing, big and bejeweled; she wore a necklace of some sparkly metal that glowed in the gloom. Her face was lean and her streaked hair was tied back in a tight bun. She waved gently to Shengli,

"Come closer, Dear. Bring over a chair and sit down."

Shengli did as she was asked and sat facing the old lady.

"Do you know who I am?"

"Y-yes. You're the Dama. Dama Tiyun."

"Yes, that's right. The Dama. The Dama. The Keeper of the Dance and one of the three Ecclesiarches of Zamai. Warden of the Academy, Regius Professor of Nüshu and Pattageyna of the Courts. Do you understand?"

Shengli nodded.

"And who are you, young lady? Who are you?"

"Er, no one, really..."

"Exactly. No one."

There was a silence before the Dama spoke again. "I knew your mother. We were friends."

Shengli's heart missed several beats at once. That mysterious hand that seemed to grip her chest whenever she thought of her mother took tight hold.

"We trained together. We learned the dance together." The Dama spoke slowly and her voice dropped and became quieter. "We were like sisters. She was the youngest but I was only a few years older so we were friendly together when all the other dancers were like grown women when we still felt like girls. And then she got herself expelled so she could be with your father. And then the new age came and no one believed in the dance anymore and gradually the other dancers died or retired and then the old Dama died and the King remembered his job for just long enough to appoint the first person he saw and that was me. And here I am."

"What, what happened to the Academy?"

"For some years there would be entertainments. We would do shows. There would be a recreation of the old ceremonies and we would do sequences from the dance but we got old, although that needn't have been a problem, and we could have trained new dancers, but there was no interest and no monies and in time it wasn't worth it any more. Now I sit here, sending messages to the court, waiting for invitations that never come and trying to find ways to get some monies together, selling off the old treasures, trying to slow down the decay of this place until someone, somewhere, wants it again."

"Can you still do the dance?", Shengli asked.

The Dama uncurled her feet from each other and Shengli saw how one of her ankles was twisted badly, distorted and lame.

"I fell. And there was no treatment. I can hardly walk, let alone dance. But do you know it? You know it?"

"Yes, I know it."

"Please, dance for me? For your mother's memory." Shengli stood, took a moment to gather herself and then gently, not with the same intensity as when she was calling the Mang dragon but with care and deliberation, she performed the first sequence. As she ended, she saw tears on the Dama's face, reflected in the dull orange light.

"Do you have the insoles? The nüshu? The spells?"

Shengli didn't answer.

"Shengli, it was I who sent Tongman to get them. I'm sorry now. It was foolish but we are near the end and that can make you do desperate things. Don't worry. He won't trouble you again. We have sold nearly all the treasures now but there is still interest among some of the merchants in buying and selling things from the old days. The spells could fetch a lot of monies, enough to do a lot of work here. And if you were here, we could maybe train new dancers? I don't have long left, I don't think. I can hardly walk, and I have little will left to go on. Shengli, you know, you could be Dama. Shengli, you could bring back the dance! Show me the spells, Shengli."

In the amber glow of the oil lamp, Shengli looked hard at the tight, lean figure with the yellow muslin drapery and the filigree lace. They looked at each other in silence for what seemed like a long time. Shengli's thoughts began to meander.

To be Dama? To bring back the dance? To honor her mother and to restore the traditions of the old ways? That would be worthy for Old Tam's memory, too. Perhaps this was her fate? Her destiny?

"You would be like a Queen, Shengli. You're young, you know the dance. The King would notice you like he has never noticed me. You could dance for the Court, there could be shows and riches and there'd be monies and there are a lot of merchants and traders who'd pay well to see dancers if you found some nice girls and got them trained up. Really, you could be very rich! We could both be very rich! I'd show you how to do it! It has been long enough now, people will want the dance again and if they want the dance, they'll want dancers."

Like a Queen? So, thought Shengli, she could bring her Ba to Lungdou, and he could be comfortable and not have to work anymore. A life at Court, advising the King; an Ecclesiarch, Warden of the Academy, a Pattageyna...little Shengli, bringing the Golden Days back to the Dance Academy? Shengli's mind started racing. She could perhaps use power to stop the eating of creatures? She could use these gifts to reduce pain and suffering like The One Who Sees Cries had said? Was that what was meant? She could be the one to bring the people of Tianya out of the misery she saw all around? The age of engines might give way to a new Golden Age? Everything made sense. Surely this was what Old Tam had in mind all along! This would be her: little Shengli! She was nodding.

"Yes, Shengli, we could get monies! Lots of monies! You and me!"

"First I have to do the dance at Zamai..."

"What? Don't be ridiculous! No one cares about that. But if we can sell the spells and use some monies to get some girls in again we could..."

"But...the Li Dragon..."

"Oh, for dragons' sake, Shengli! Please don't be such a bumpkin. You'll need to be smarter than this." The Dama's eyes glowed and she leaned forward. "I've been waiting for this day. Little Shengli, you're going to make me rich, make us rich, I mean..." Her face pushed towards Shengli and she reached out a bony hand to stroke Shengli's cheek. "There's monies to be made Shengli...monies to be made..."

Shengli felt the chill of the Dama's hand touch her face and she looked into the Dama's eyes and what she saw there was like a splash of cold water and she snapped back as if waking suddenly. She jumped up.

"But -- don't you believe in the lore? Don't you believe in the dance?"

The Dama curled her lip in an ugly and dismissive way. No spoken answer was needed. And Shengli turned and ran out and sprinted across the courtyard, tears stinging her eyes as she stumbled on the ice and the cracked paving. She stopped and pressed her back against a wall and breathed deeply as she felt her heart beating. She felt somehow ashamed although she couldn't work out quite why. She calmed herself down, breathed slowly and counted to a hundred before walking carefully back to Pangti's hut where she almost fell over Bolu as she stepped inside and there, as well as the friendly and familiar if puzzled faces of Boken, Shonan and Durfin she saw a bearded gentleman sitting in Pangti's chair nursing a mug of berry-broth.

"Hello," said a deep and gentle voice. "You must be Shengli. I'm glad I've found you at last. Are you all right?"

Chapter Nine

"Who...who are you? "It's all right, Shengli," burst in Durfin, "he's a friend of Old Tam's!"

"That's true. Tam and I were friends. My name is Kang, known as Lord Kang but you don't need to be formal with me. Tam and I were schoolboys together and students together, we were in the wars, but no need to talk of that now. He told me you would be coming."

"But Old Tam is..."Shengli started.

"I know. The twins here have told me about it but I'm not surprised. The time was about right. I shall miss him hugely but of course he is still here in all the ways that matter. When you love for real, there is no such thing as separation. Now, it sounds like you've had a bit of a journey?"

"Why should I trust you? We trusted Renzi and he turned on us. I trusted Pangti and he reported to the Dama. I nearly trusted the Dama..." Shengli's breath was quickening. The twins looked uncomfortable but could say nothing.

"It's all right." said Lord Kang. "I understand. You are right to be careful. These are difficult days. Here is the letter that Tam wrote to me. He must have sent it just as you left the village. You may recognize his writing, I think? And as you can see, when one knows what happened next, it's clear that he wasn't expecting to reach Lungdou. I didn't see that when I read it first but I see it now. He was cleverer than any of us. Dear old comrade."

He handed her the sheet of paper. She recognized Old Tam's script immediately and she read, *'Dear Kang, Greetings, Old Friend. How are things in the city? No, don't bother. I can guess. Well, it is all as always out here and that is some comfort but, of course, as you'll have realized yourself by now, there's an imbalance in the lower ennea and I'm convinced that the only thing that can save Tianya is for the dance to be performed again at Zamai. I know you'll agree and that you have probably come to the same conclusion. The good news is that little Shengli, who you'll remember from our conversations before, has grown such that she now has dancing shoes that fit the spells. She remembers the dance perfectly and can do it while activating the nüshu. We may be saved. I am writing this just as we are getting ready to leave the village and travel to join you in Lungdou but Kang, Old Man, I am beginning to think that you may have to look after this for me. Really no time to write any more just now and have to finish to get this to the forest courier who will pass any minute; otherwise, we'll probably get to Lungdou faster than this letter. Shengli will have three loyal friends with her, one of whom goes on four legs, and she is to be protected by the son of our old friend Han and they are good companions. If I could have any wish, it would be to sit with you in your garden again and talk of Halteres-lore and to sip a cup of mulberry wine one more time -- although nothing you have in the city matches what we have here! -- and -- no time. Must dash. Your old friend, T.*

"I trust you. That's Old Tam all right. What shall we do?"

"Thank you. Your trust is important. We will go to my home -- which is very near here -- and you will be safe. You can all stay, I've plenty of room, and you can rest and we will arrange to go to Zamai through the front door."

"Sorry, what do you mean by 'through the front door'?" Shengli asked.

"Durfin told me you were planning to sneak into Zamai early this morning and do the dance secretly. That is a delightful thought, and very brave, but you would never have succeeded. Zamai is well guarded. While the King has happily forgotten about the Dance Academy and pretty much everything else to do with the old ways, Zamai is still important to him. If you are to dance at Zamai, it will have to be with his approval."

"But surely, since the Age of Engines began, he has been against everything to do with the old ways?"

"And with good reason. He is too young to remember the wars but he grew up in their shadow. The Age of Engines has brought peace, or at least the end of wars such as we knew at one time. With engines, people can move goods around more easily, the merchants and traders have prospered, there is food in the markets, even now after a long winter, and there is entertainment for the people, steam fairs and organs and suchlike; the streets are safer with the light globes and the methods of the New Learning are starting to help us understand some of the causes of disease and illness. Many things make sense in the new learning. The engineers make a law, they test it and if it works, they use it, and if it doesn't, they drop it and try another law. In many, many ways, suffering is reduced. And that is what we all strive for. By through the front door, I mean we need to ensure the King wants you to do the dance. There is a path to that. I have some influence."

"But..."

"Yes, I know that this must sound shocking when you have sat at Tam's feet and heard his views and I am of his camp. But the essence of Halteres-lore is balance, as you know, and the new learning is powerful learning and we must understand it if we are to find the harmony that we currently lack. Let us talk more back at my house."

And they gathered their few belongings and made ready to leave. Lord Kang smiled at Bolu who stepped aside from the door and reaching into his gown he pulled out a little flask and left it beside the berry-broth jug.

"A little drop from my private collection! Pangti has done us a big favor. I would have struggled to find you otherwise. He's a good man at heart and he serves the Dama because that is his way of trying to hold the old ways together. He came to see me after he left you asleep and before he reported to her. He's earned a cup of this although I would have saved it for Tam if he were here."

They were taken to an elegant courtyard house in the classical style. A simple and proportionate gate opened to a small garden surrounded on three sides by single-story buildings. A raised, circular pond stood in the center of the yard, figuring the traditional model of the circle within a square. Even with the long winter the garden had a delicate beauty that was in contrast to the messiness of the street outside. Nor, on the other hand, was it like the natural loveliness of the forest. Instead, it expressed a calm refinement. Ornamental trees in pots, carefully sited chairs and tables under canopies with the bare winter lines of vines and climbing roses.

"This is so nice," said Shonan. "But it must be even lovelier in Spring!"

"Oh yes, I'm very lucky. And even in high summer, we enjoy the shade from those canopies as the foliage fills out. Come and meet my friends, the fish!"

They leaned over the side of the circular pool and watched the speckled and golden carp circle and weave among each other. Lord Kang held his fingers to the surface and two and then three of the fish came and nuzzled him.

"You know, some city people tried to make a theory that fish couldn't feel pain and had no intelligence. This, they said, made it all right to eat them."

"You don't eat creatures, either!"

"Dear Shengli, of course not! The objective of all our learning is to reduce suffering. How on earth could that be consistent with the torture and slaughter of creatures for the unnecessary eating pleasure of a species like ours, which is blessed with the intelligence and sensitivity to know better? These fish: if you try to catch them using one method, and they escape or, for some reason, the catcher returns them to the water, then they become harder to catch. They remember bad experiences and learn from them. And they remember good experiences and learn from them too which is why they have come to my hand like this because they're expecting to find some food so I'd better get some or they won't trust me anymore!"

He stepped away for a moment to a box at the edge of the courtyard to collect a pinch of something from a jar and brought it back and the reaction from the fish showed he had brought them something they enjoyed. "See: pleasure, pain, learning… you know, they can be tricky and deceitful too! But it is better not to feed them too much in the cold weather so that's enough now." He showed them round the rest of the house. There was his study with books, an astrolabe and, of course, a lute, very like Old Tam's den. There was also a formal room for guests with smart chairs arranged around the edge and a simple ceramic set for serving wine or berry-broth. They were told to leave their packs in two guest bedrooms, one for the twins and one for Shengli and Boken. Neat little bedrooms, plain but clean. There was also a busy little kitchen where Lord Kang introduced them to the kindly looking lady who wiped her hands on a cloth before greeting them.

"This is Old Sun. She has been with me for many years and she looks after things. Cook, housekeeper, whatever you like to call it, but she manages this place and I would be lost without her."

"Hello, Guests! How are you? Have you seen your rooms? Are they all right? If you're cold I can always put some more blankets on the bed. There's hot water in the mornings and evenings when I get the stove going and you just let me know if there's anything you want. Anything at all! Kang tells me you are friends of that other old fool, Villager Tam and…"

"Sun," said Lord Kang, "the children told me that Tam has left us. He picked his time and place in the forest and closed his eyes. His time has finished. I'm sorry to tell you so suddenly."

The old lady's eyes filled with tears, and she bit her lip.

"Oh no, not another one. Soon there'll be none of us left. Oh my, but I know he'll have been ready but…oh dear, he might have been ready but, dear me, I'm not ready to think I'll never see him again…"

"The last night we saw him" said Shengli, "when we were camping in the forest, he was so happy. He was telling stories of the old days and full of life and then the next morning he just went off into the forest, sat himself still and…"

"A good end for a good man," said Lord Kang. "Camping in the forest at his age! May we all have the good fortune to go out in a place we love with people who make us feel young and are working for something that we believe to be good. Let us not grieve too much, dear Sun, you know how he'd react if he were here!"

"Yes, Kang, you're right. Come on." and she wiped the corner of her eye with the cloth, pulled a smile and said, "You must be hungry -- come on -- how about some breakfast? I've got a pot of porridge on and it's lovely with a big dollop of my homemade syrup. And as for you, little dog, I keep something just for visitors like you. Don't tell the others but if you come this way, there's a couple of bones that were mislaid by the flesh-merchants and that are just nice when I have a visitor like yourself for whom it's only natural."

Ah, thought Boken. What a fine woman! It is all well and good, all this talk about the rights and wrongs of eating creatures, but that's a people thing. The Yu dragon made him a flesh-eater after all and for sure he could get by on barley cakes and whatever but...

The children weren't at all hungry after Pangti's hospitality earlier but she pressed them hard and the first to give in was Durfin, of course, but then that made it all right for the others and soon they were seated around the stove with huge bowls of porridge which they sweetened with the syrup. Lord Kang was watching them eat when the peace was disturbed by the sound of a steam hooter, three notes rising, repeated three times, right outside, it seemed, the gate to the courtyard and shaking them all and causing Shengli at least to cough and choke on a spoonful of porridge.

"Well, I never!" said Lord Kang, "a herald!"

They all walked out to the street outside the gate where a herald in the dress uniform of the Palace Guard stood to attention in front of the shiniest, fanciest, most ornate looking steam-wagon any of them had seen yet. The herald raised a sparkling brass megaphone to his mouth and took a deep breath and in a huge voice that had them all pressing their hands to their ears, launched the proclamation, "HEAR ALL, HEAR ALL, BE IT HEARD AND UNDERSTOOD…"

"Dear chap, no need, no need!" Lord Kang smiled and waved for the herald to stop. "There's only us here. If you have the missive I'll read it out and you can spare your tonsils for the next job. Now, what is all this about, eh?"

The herald drew a small scroll from a pouch attached to his belt and handed it over to Lord Kang with a sheepish smile, "Thank you, Sir. Busy day today. Fair bit of proclaiming ahead…"

"I understand. The King has been very active recently. Now, what do we have here?" And Kang unfurled the scroll and in a soft and slightly amused voice he read out to the children, Boken and Old Sun,

A Proclamation Sent by His Magnificence, the Most Royal Personage, Exalted and Resplendent, Defender of the Lore, (at which point Kang sniffed in a significant sort of way), *Conduct of the Ecclesiarchs, Margrave of the Pattageynii, Warden of the Seas, Lord of the Isles, Friend to the Dragons, Protector of the People, Benefactor to the Creatures, Guardian of the Forests, Rivers, Mountains and Plains of Tianya, his most High…*

Lord Kang smiled and said, "Actually not that 'high'. He's no taller than you are, Durfin!" *…most High Loftiness the King of Tianya. To his dear old tutor, the learned and altogether just really excellent 'Yes-He' Kang!*

"That would be me, by the way…not strictly my official title."

"You were the King's tutor?" Shonan asked.

"Still am, actually." Kang replied, with a smile. "It's a lifetime appointment, which is, I confess, why I get to live in this rather nice home and enjoy this lifestyle of leisure and relative comfort. I assumed you knew, sorry. Arrogant of me. It hasn't been an onerous position in recent years but the King is a sweet boy really, at heart, and he enjoys teasing me and I have to admit, he looks after me nicely. Now what's this all about?"

"Dear Kang," the King's missive continued, *"take a look at this and then tell me that you don't love engines! This is the latest model from the workshops at Dalongkou and if this doesn't win you over, then*

I don't know what will! Take a ride! The driver and the car are yours for today!

"Go out to the countryside or something! There are new technologies that make it cleaner, smoother, faster than any engine before now. The upholstery is lined with septicium and if you look at the passenger seats you'll see an amazing little gadget for you to put a cup and keep it just handy when you're rolling along and isn't that just skills? -- so pour yourself a nice glass of mulberry wine (there's a bottle on the backseat!) and sit back and let the open road unroll before you. Then come and see me and tell me that you just love engines because you must, really! I will await your presence at the change of the afternoon watch today. - (signed) Binbin

"Well, that settles any plans we may have had for this afternoon. But timely." Lord Kang slipped back into the house to find a brush and drafted a quick reply onto the scroll and returned it to the herald. With a smile he bowed and the officer returned the compliments, turned and jogged off smartly, carrying his megaphone.

"Now, what to do with this thing?" asked the old teacher who had already noted the change of expression on the faces of the twins since they had seen the wagon. "I really can't be gadding off around today." he mused, "and I need to spend some time with Shengli planning strategy for our meeting with the King this afternoon and I'd like to show her some of the old texts pertaining to the dance and Durfin, perhaps you have an interest in some of the manuscripts?"

"...er, y-yes, of course..." mumbled the boy who had hitherto never shown any interest whatsoever in anything that could even be mistaken for a manuscript.

"Or perhaps, I wonder, Shonan, could I ask you and Durfin to cover for me and take this wagon out while Shengli and I work here? If the wagon returns and there is no sign that it has been out it will appear that I have defied the King's wishes and that would most seriously upset the little plan that I have developing in my old head. Do you think you could deputise for me? And help Shengli and me out with this?"

Shengli was fighting to keep a straight face as she completely understood what the cunning old fellow was doing, and it was soon settled. Lord Kang spoke quietly with the driver, seated high on the forward platform of the wagon in his coat, helmet, and goggles.

Old Sun hurried to put together a picnic basket and gathered some blankets and even hot water bottles. Kang made it clear to the twins that they were doing an important job that freed him up to plan for the operation at Zamai and so they climbed into the passenger seat, the two of them fitting neatly into the single, armchair-like, heavily upholstered throne, admired the nifty little bracket for holding a cup, and after some further discussion between Kang and the driver, the wagon steamed up and started to ease away, only for Kang to cry out in a chilling voice of panic,

"Noooo....Wait, wait...stop...just a moment..."

All of them, the twins, the driver, and back in the gateway, Shengli, Boken, and Old Sun shared a moment of horrible anxiety, wondering what in the name of the dragons it could be that caused him to shout out so dramatically, while Kang trotted the few steps over to the wagon and reached inside, "Where, uh, what the...ah, there we go!" And he pulled out the bottle of mulberry wine that the King had left him.

"Hm...Sanjianhua...not a bad drop. Not a totally wasted education after all. Off you all go."

And with smiles and laughter the wagon pulled away and Lord Kang turned back to face Shengli. "Now, young lady, we've got work to do."

They returned into the quiet old courtyard, and it felt like passing into another world after the steam, the noise and the novelty of the King's intervention in Lord Kang's day.

"I'm sorry not to offer you the chance of the ride out, Shengli, but I do need a chance to speak with you and this has been most opportune."

"I hate engines." she said, "Really, I do. They make me feel sick and even if they are beautiful wagons and all the rest, it is still everything I hate."

"Well, hating is never good but I have some sympathy with your feelings. Come, it is a little cold, let us settle in my study and I'll warm up some berry-broth."

In a brief moment they were settled in deep and enveloping chairs, nestling into soft cushions, and enjoying the tranquility of the little oasis of learning and scholarship. Scrolls gathered on shelves and in corners of the room. Lord Kang's lute was propped up in the corner, brushes hung from racks and on the desk and in cabinets around the room there was a collection of curios and oddities. Between them there was a broth-set with a small charcoal burner heating the rustic looking pot. Lord Kang poured them each a bowl and they sat, warming their hands on the rough ceramic and after a period of quiet, during which Shengli began to wonder if the old teacher had forgotten she was there, when finally he spoke,

"Shengli, what do you know of Halteres-lore?"

"Old Tam would say all sorts of things and he obviously taught me to read but he was funny about things like that. Often, often when I asked him a question about something he would say," and she slipped into her 'Old Tam' voice, 'plenty of time for that later'."

Lord Kang smiled. "Tam had a view that you could only understand Halteres-lore after you'd experienced it. Which is to say, you had to, if you like, live it before you could then start to study it. This is why he would never make the move to the city. He believed, and I agree with him to a very large degree, that Halteres-lore needs to be kept alive in reality, not just in scrolls. And in his view, it could best be preserved in an environment such as your village. He would argue with me here that as soon as someone like me tried to explain what it was, that meant it stopped being the true Halteres. In a way, as he would put it, the Halteres that can be analyzed and explained, isn't the true Halteres."

"Then this may seem like a stupid thing to say, but can you explain it to me?"

"I intend to try. I have thought hard about this. When we go to Zamai, your dance will be part of the practice of Halteres-lore and I think it will be more likely to be successful if you have some understanding. But Tam's words are with me and he would challenge me that you already have an instinctive understanding that might be destroyed by what I want to do."

"I want to understand."

"Let us start with the engine we saw just now. That is really quite an amazing thing, isn't it?"

"I suppose so."

"Yes, we must acknowledge that it is. It is remarkable and a piece of cleverness that certainly improves the world in a way in that one can now move from one place to another much more quickly, and carry things that you could never carry before and so on. But it works through an engine that means you have to take coal from the Jiao dragon's back; you have to scrape away at the surface and dig deep holes into the mountains. Scars that no one knows how to heal or if they will ever heal. We have a success over a brief time period at the cost of what may be tragedy in the long run.

"How can people be so stupid?"

"It is based on an illusion. The illusion of separateness. A kind of feeling that one is not part of nature but outside it, like the engineers themselves are, after all, outside their engines, acting on them, rather than part of the system itself. It isn't being stupid. The engineers are very clever. That is almost the problem, if you like. And their intelligence has some success and they get the idea that you can straighten out a world that is, well, all wiggly and crinkly. Only the universe is smarter than people can ever be and it works quite well by itself."

"You sound like Gan!"

"Who?"

"Someone we see in the forest sometimes. Old Tam and us, we met him…", and she felt herself getting upset when she wanted to concentrate and she coughed.

"This is exactly what Tam would say to me." And he took his turn to mimic Old Tam's voice, 'The lore lives, it isn't studied'." he smiled reassuringly at Shengli. "You are sitting where he would always sit. He would be very happy to know that.

"How does this all work with the dragons?"

"The dragons are the four poles of Halteres. The Yu dragon is order and regularity; the Mang dragons are disorder and randomness. They channel vibrations along their veins and ensure there is the order and stability we need, balanced with the energy of spontaneity and creativity. The Jiao dragon and the Li dragons are the things of the earth and the things of the sky but, of course, you know that. And when the earthly elements and the atmospheric elements are in balance then we have all the good things of nature and they in turn are sustained by vibrations along their veins. And the veins intersect at Zamai. Two axes, order and disorder; earth and sky. That is the universe. Simultaneously simple and unimaginably complex. Think about the seed of one of the bamboos in your forest. How tiny is it?"

"Very tiny!"

"And yet an entire forest is potentially in the seed of a single bamboo. So simple and yet so complicated."

"I never thought of it like that."

"When you look at nature, Shengli, you look at yourself. And when you dance at Zamai, you will be connecting with the vibrations that restore rhythm to the dragon veins. I'd like to show you some of the scrolls, I think it will help you to understand in more depth…"

And signaling her to rise, he took her to the table and after some rummaging in the muddle of papers and parchments, he found the one he was looking for and unrolled it and started to point out graphs and illustrations. Shengli stood beside him and nodded and asked more questions and the morning fell away from them in the quiet, cozy study.

Chapter Ten

The two studied together for the rest of the morning until Old Sun came and interrupted them and insisted that they have some soup and no sooner had Shengli finished her bowl of the warming mixture of vegetables, mushrooms, barley, and beans flavored with herbs and spices than she yawned an enormous yawn and felt her eyes closing and sleep coming to claim her.

"Poor little thing -- after the night that she had and everything else and you going on all morning with your scrolls and stories. It's time she had a nap."

"You are right as always, Madam Sun. I have a brief errand to run also before the twins get back. Perhaps a bowl of soup and a nap for them too? They'll need to be rested and ready if we are to see the King at the change of the afternoon watch and I rather hope and plan for them to have a very important job to do this evening."

"What are you plotting, you old devil?"

"All good, Sun, all good. And hopefully in a short while we can have some fresh spring greens to make a change from these stews."

"Why, you…"

And with a laugh he shimmied out of the kitchen and made ready to disappear on whatever the task was that he had in mind. Shengli and Boken took themselves off to their guest room and a moment after climbing between the crisp, clean sheets Shengli was deep asleep with Boken snoring gently in his usual place, curled up on the bed by her feet. She didn't even wake up when the twins returned, speaking with voices that had grown used to making themselves heard over the sound of the wagon's engine, faces bright red from the wind and the cold on the road, and gabbling excitedly about their experience but it wasn't long before, with bellies full of soup, they too were in their room, letting the events of the past couple of days fall away and exhaustion take over. While they slept, snow began to fall again for the first time in several days.

Back in the forest, Ba looked up from his vegetable patch and sighed deeply. As it had been over a week since the last fall, he had had half a thought that that might be it, and he could turn over the bare earth, ready for the first sowing. But it seemed not and it didn't look as though Old Tam and Shengli had succeeded yet in raising the Li dragon. So be it. He shouldered his hoe and went back to the cottage. It looked like it was going to be another long evening alone by the fire.

In the second row, Durfin and Shonan's parents looked out at the new snowfall and sighed. The two little ones were keeping them busy but it was quiet without the twins. Without the spring there weren't the chores to keep their minds occupied in the same way either and time was starting to hang heavy and that allowed plenty of space for imaginations to work and to conjure up thoughts and ideas of what might have happened to their elder children.

"But they've got Old Tam and Renzi, they'll be fine..." they would say to each other before going back to whatever they were doing but the mind would work away and their hearts would be troubled.

In the Dance Academy, Dama Tiyun grabbed her walking stick and hauled herself up from her chair. She limped over to the door of her bungalow and looked out at the freshly falling snow, white when it landed but quickly merging with the grimy cobbles and becoming discolored. Perhaps if she could just talk to Shengli again? Help her understand the value of what she had and how with some monies they could start to bring this place back to life?

In the streets of Lungdou the city people looked up at the skies and felt their hearts sink. Snow had long ceased to be a novelty and this winter had already lasted too long. What a shame that in this age of engines there still wasn't a way to control the weather! No doubt the engineers would fix that soon enough but for now it was time again to pull collars up over the ears and push on through the slush and mess and to keep on with the business of daily life in the Royal seat of Kings, Lungdou, the capital city of Tianya.

And in the mountains, the snow followed the arrival of news of the death of the wolf prince and how that came to pass. Han, King of the wolves, howled to the skies as the first soft flakes fell and settled on his fur. First Old Tam, his dear friend, and now his son, and in circumstances that brought pain and confusion. Han raged with anger, upset and frustration as he withdrew to the crevasse in the Mutian Mountain where he and the pack were sheltering for the winter. Warden of the mountains? He could not even protect and guide his own son in a mission vital to his dearest friend, the truest ally the wolves ever had. These were dark days indeed.

Meanwhile, Lord Kang hurried himself through the little, windy streets around the College of Learning. He found Basha and Geng and after speaking with them, made one extra call to the dusty old store in the alley between the College and the Dance Academy. He felt the fresh snow falling on his head and shoulders but paid it no mind. It would only be a matter of a short time now.

Shengli stirred. Refreshed from her sleep and comforted by the warmth and steady breathing of Boken at the foot of the bed. Out of the little window she saw the snow and how pretty it looked on the dark branches of the little cherry tree outside. She wriggled her toes under the blankets and found herself thinking of the dance. It was all going to be all right.

Everyone gathered in the homely kitchen. Basha and Geng were musicianers. Not, as they pointed out more than once, that they got do much musicianing at all these days since the steam organs were now so popular and all the old gigs at weddings and festivals and so on had dried up.

"Not a lot of work these days, kids. Don't bother learning to be musicianers. No one cares. Just get some tupenny'ha'penny engineer to put a card into a steam organ and off it all tootles." explained Basha, his curmudgeonly old face still kindly as he tenderly tuned his zither.

"He's a miserable old sod, he is and no mistake," said Geng, cheerier and he winked at Durfin as he tweaked and tinkered with his bagpipes. "Don't listen to him. I'd be gloomy if I played the zither. Now, if you get yourself a set of small pipes like these you'll never have any friends nor money but you'll always have something to cuddle, see...", and he gave the bag a squeeze, causing a comical moaning sound to squirl out of the odd-looking bundle. The children laughed and Lord Kang set about explaining his plan.

"These two rapscallions are, in fact, honorable maestri of the King's Consort of Players and they performed many times for ceremonies at Zamai in the old days as well. The Consort has disbanded given the lack of interest in the modern world in hearing music played by real people on real instruments and most of the old players, those that are left anyway, have moved on to find work elsewhere, especially if they had families to support. But these two are still around."

"Nowhere to go, old man," mumbled Basha

"Which is very handy from our point of view." smiled Lord Kang. "I've been thinking about your description of how you configured the dance at the way-block in the forest and in particular, the importance of the music. You've lost Tam and Renzi since then, although I hope I can play a part, but it seems sensible to enlist a couple of pros. What do you think, Shengli?"

"Oh, yes!" she almost shouted. "But do they know the music?"

"Yes and no." replied Geng. "We were never required to play for this dance. There hasn't been a dragon-calling in my time or Basha's and it has been a long while since we played any of the ritual music for real, as it were, but from what his lordship tells us, you have a clear idea of what you need and we reckon that with a bit of working it out together, we'll be tidy."

Shonan's face had dropped a bit, listening to this conversation, but Lord Kang, sensitive as ever responded immediately.

"And twins, I have these for you. I picked them up for you especially from the old store."

He stepped outside for a moment and returned with two percussion instruments: one a kind of inverted metal pan with beveled surfaces and the other an hourglass shaped drum. "Durfin, I think you can do your thing on this. It happens to be called a zurdom," and he handed Durfin the drum.

"And Shonan, this is for you, it comes with these little sticks. Try it out." Basha and Geng stepped over and showed the children how to strike the two instruments. For Durfin it was a case of slapping in the middle or striking at the edge with his thumb. As long as he kept it simple, he thought, it would be all right. For Shonan there seemed much greater scope for invention: the convex metal disc, called a quan by the two musicians, made a sweet ringing noise to a different pitch on each of the surfaces. By marking out the rhythms in different patterns, Shonan was able to make melodies in time with the rhythms that Shengli had taught her.

"The quan is one of the most ancient and sacred instruments, Shonan," said Geng. "In some ways simple in that you can't really make a bad noise – whatever you play is going to sound nice given the tone quality and the tuning, but in other ways tough, as you will be playing lead. We'll be accompanying you, thickening out the texture and sculpting different shaped vibrations through the fluence."

They set to work. Shonan could remember every detail of the three patterns and taught the two old musicians who not only grasped them immediately they also found ways of adding drones and harmonies to enrich the sound. Durfin pounded away on the head of the hourglass shaped drum, slapping and tapping the solid, single pattern that he had memorized and decided to stick with and Shonan found that by varying not only the three patterns as she had done before, but by mixing up the sequence of notes on the quan she could develop more complex variations.

"Who will play the part of the King?" asked Shengli.

"The King," said Lord Kang.

They all looked at him, stunned for a moment, and then Basha stood up slowly and reached for his zither case.

"Well, that was all fun and it was nice to meet you kids, but as you've seen, things ain't exactly easy around here these days and I need to get some supper on the stove and I'd like to get back before dark as when you're carrying this thing it is easy for an old bugger like me to slip and take a tumble and one of these days…"

"Stay with me, Basha. Trust me, please. I think I can make it happen. And in all the ancient records there was always a zither and you have to be there."

"Why on earth would the King agree to be part of a performance like this? He'd send for a steam organ and have it huffing and puffing away all mechanical and he'd do it just to prove a point."

"Trust me, please. And whatever happens, you'll be my guest here for dinner and the best of my cellar, such as it is these days, afterwards."

"Now there's talking," said Geng, and he leaned over and winked at Durfin before adding, "Lord Kang is showing a bit more sensitivity to the needs of us performing artistes there, than we've seen in a good while in these parts."

"All right," said Basha, "for you, you old devil. But if the King wants nothing to do with it, don't say I didn't warn you. Let's try and get this thing together then. You'll just have to play the King's part for now." And there were more sounds of tuning up, tinkering and experimenting and Basha and Geng then insisted on a 'proper rehearsal' and the band started to come together.

Shengli, feeling a little bit surplus at that point, stepped out into the courtyard. It had made her feel a bit weird, hearing the music come together, and she didn't want to get drawn into performing the dance at this stage. Like all dancers, she knew that every performance, every rehearsal, carried a risk and while she would stretch and warm up gently, if Lord Kang had a plan that included her doing the dance for real any time soon, then she could not contemplate anything that might lead to a slip or a sprain or whatever kind of injury. She was feeling the weight of the responsibility on her. There were four poles, the four dragons, Kang had said, along the two axes that formed the structure of the universe. One of them was asleep and it was her task to reawaken it by stimulating the vibrations through the fluence in the proven and proper manner through the dance that only she could do. She was ready, no question. And that meant taking no risks. She wandered through to the kitchen and found Old Sun there, kneading some dough.

"Hello, little Shengli! What's going on out there and how come you're in here?"

"They've got a band together but, of course, I'm not in it as I will be dancing and I didn't really want to sit around hearing it in case I felt like doing the dance and then slipped or something."

"Now that sounds very sensible. Why don't you sit yourself down there and keep warm by the stove."

"Can I help you?"

"Well, why not? I'm setting about making some dumplings as it looks like we might have a bit of a party together tonight but no one can tell me what time to eat so I can have these ready on the side for whenever they'll be needed. I've got a filling here made out of mushrooms and pickles and a few other bits and pieces and with a bit more work on it, this dough will be ready… have you made dumplings before?"

"What? Have I? Thousands of times! You watch!"

And Old Sun gave the dough a bit more of a stretch and a tug and then pulled off a portion, rolled it into a sausage shape, and using her giant cleaver with feather-like delicacy, chopped off walnut-sized sections. Shengli took a few and with the heel of her hand flattened them into discs. Old Sun took them back and using a little rolling pin, gave them a quick spin and rendered them as thin as paper and in moments they had a pile of little wrappers and they switched to stuffing: taking a small spoonful of the mushroom and pickle mixture, placing it in the middle of one of the discs and then with a pinch and a twist, sealing the mixture inside a perfect little package.

"You're good at this. Who taught you?"

"My mother. We …we would make dumplings together sometimes. Especially in the winter when there wasn't much variety in food and we could make a whole load and leave some in the snow to freeze and have them later."

"Aye, that's good housekeeping. She was a lovely little thing, was your mother."

"You knew her!"

"Oh yes, I was in the kitchens of the Academy before the King, that is, Prince Binbin as he was then, was assigned Lord Kang as his tutor and I moved over here."

"Tell me about her. Please."

"She was pretty, of course, just like you are, dear, and she was a lively one, she was! She was the youngest of the dancers by quite some way so we used to adopt her a bit and spoil her and she'd often hang around the kitchen, teasing us and making mischief. Just a child, really. But we all liked her because she was like most of us, country-folk at heart and her ways made us feel homelike even though we'd moved up to the city."

"You're from the village?"

"Not your village, dear, there's more than one village you know! But I guess they're not so different from each other. My old home is to the north, the other side of the mountains there and in a little valley. Pretty place but poor and if you came from a big family, it made sense, see, for one or two of you to move to the city to find work. Takes a bit of pressure off the land. So that's my story."

"I bet there's a lot more than just that…"

"Well, perhaps, but there's time enough."

"You sound like Old Tam!" And they smiled at each other

and settled into the steady rhythm of rolling, patting, folding and crimping the dumplings. Noiselessly and gently, comforted by the soft glow from the stove. Boken had stolen in quietly and curled up on one of the chairs and the snow continued to fall gently outside.

From across the courtyard they could hear the band coming together: the soft humming of the small-pipes; the harmonies of the zither; the steady rhythm of the zurdom, and the bell-like tinkling of the quan. Unconsciously, they adapted their actions over the kitchen table to the tempo of the music, folding and crimping; rolling and filling to the patterns of sound that drifted on the air until eventually it came to rest.

"Now, that was lovely, that was." remarked Old Sun.

"Life can be quite simple, can't it?" said Shengli.

"That's been my way." said Sun, "But people have a habit of making it more complicated."

They heard steps come crunching through the fresh snow and the musicians all burst into the kitchen.

"How's about a nice mug of berry-broth, Old Sun?" called out Geng.

"Why should I do that, now, when you've not called round and seen us all these ages? As if we're all too busy these days to share a cup of broth from time to time."

"You know, that's a totally fair comment, you old darlin', and right from today I tell you now, I'll be calling round so often for a cuppa that you'll get sick of the sight of me!" and he came round the kitchen table and gave her a cheeky hug.

"Why you...!"

Everyone was laughing and Lord Kang leaned over to Shengli.

"Shengli, I'd just like a bit more of a chat if you have a moment?"

The two of them stepped out into the courtyard. Lord Kang

first strolled over to the fishpond and looked into the water.

"What happens to them when it freezes?" asked Shengli.

"Oh, they're all right as long as it doesn't freeze right to the bottom and this pond is much deeper than it looks: it goes below the ground level there. They'll drift down to the bottom and just wait it out like the fish in your village pond. And even in our most wintry days, this courtyard still gets the best of the sun so we've never had more than a thin surface of ice. Shengli, what do you know about the King?"

"Nothing, really. Just that he became King very young because his father and mother and elder sisters were killed during the wars and that he survived because he escaped to the islands."

"Those were terrible times, Shengli. I was with the King, or Prince Binbin, as I'll always think of him. We don't talk of those days now and maybe we should but when he became King he was determined that Tianya would never know such unhappiness again. After the years of disorder, the idea that there was some kind of balance between regularity and randomness just seemed impossible. He had only known chaos."

"Did no one try to call the Yu dragon?"

"Of course! The old Dama had kept the Academy strong and the dance was performed many times. The ceremony of the three foxes was held and the old King fired the golden arrow from Qiangkun's bow just as outlined in the scrolls."

"And didn't any of it work?"

"No."

"Why not?"

"I don't suppose we'll ever know. But in the end, Binbin, myself, Old Sun and a small group from the household, we ended up escaping from Lungdou on an old ox cart. We were able to get a boat to the islands before the invaders entered the city but, of course, that was when the rest of the royal family met their ends. When the tide of fortune turned and Lungdou was at peace again and the Prince returned, so long had passed that no one recognized him. He had to prove his identity with fingerprints and toe prints. Even his old friends wouldn't believe it was him until he had done that. Can you imagine what that must have felt like on top of everything? Come, it's too cold out here. Let's step inside for a moment."

And they went into Lord Kang's study where he bent to blow on the charcoal that still glowed faintly under the broth-pot. "We'll get this going again. It's probably brewed a bit too strong but I could use a cup just as much as Geng."

"What happened to you and Old Tam during the wars?"

"These are long stories, and I am making it my work in these last days to write them down. I am not surprised that Tam did not tell you. They are difficult memories to share. He was captured in the campaigns in the mountains...his close comradeship with the wolves comes from those days. He also spent a long time in captivity. When you return to the village, someone will need to gather Tam's works. Perhaps that will be you? But that is for the future. However, he and I had both vowed to write the histories and he would not have let things end if he did not feel he had done his work."

"So what of the King?"

"That's really why we need to talk about this now. When the Royal house was restored in Tianya, after the experience of humiliation at the hands of the invaders, armed with all the power of their engines, the King launched the New Age. He rejected the old learning that appeared to have failed, sent the scholars from the College of Learning to other places, beyond Tianya, so they could learn the ways of engines and gradually, as you know, the old learning was rejected and then forgotten."

"That's so sad."

"But not from the point of view of the King. That's what you have to understand. The New Age has in many ways been an age of peace and prosperity. You can't assume others will see things as you or I, or Old Tam, or others do. They remember the wars and the disorder and for them, that was the old age. Now they see foods brought from far places, entertainments and conveniences and the power of the engines. It works. In the short run."

"But at what cost?"

"Yes. And that is our task: to find some kind of balance between the old and the new ages. The old age collapsed through some imbalance, the cause of which we may never understand. Maybe one day someone will discover why it was that the Yu dragon slept for so long and could not be roused. But order did return."

"How?"

"We can't really know but there is a theory that is consistent with the learning that, on a day in the occupation, a group of the Princes and Dukes from the invaders went hunting for pleasure only, not for any purpose that could be defended as necessary. They shot arrows at a hawk and killed it for no reason other than some sort of amusement and the Yu dragon was roused by this crime against the order of nature…"

"…they killed a creature for the fun of it?"

"Yes. There is much to learn, Shengli. You would find it hard to believe some of the ways of the world. But you will carry the learning forward, I know it. The key thing now is for you to understand why the King is hostile to the old learning. He is not bad or foolish. Do you see?"

"Yes. Yes, I do. So what chance do we have?"

"Well, the years and our shared history have given me a little freedom. He rejected the learning that I represent but he has never rejected me. And with the years of peace, there has come a mood of playfulness and a search for amusement and I think with a little theater-acting, we will have some fun with His Royal Highness King Tiebin the 23rd and in the process, accomplish our serious business. The change of the afternoon watch approaches, let us get everyone together and make our way to the Palace."

Chapter Eleven

The walk round to the Palace was a short one and as they were expected, there wasn't any delay and they were shown through the elegant main gate. The palace was, as Shengli had noted on her walk only the day before, smaller than one might have imagined from the stories of the court that they had grown up with. However, the modest size was offset by the elegance and decoration and the widespread use of gold leaf that glittered even in the smoky gloom of a Lungdou dusk. The familiar scalloping trimmed the curling eaves which spread from the wall, held up by highly decorated corbels that were so delicately structured they seemed too light and slender to support the extended roofs giving the impression that the upturned tiles were floating away from the building. Roof-top decorations along the ridge were made up of figures drawn from the old legends of Tianya.

Passing through the gate, one entered the courtyard, which was laid out following the classical principle of the circle within the square. Buildings ran down the four sides, their walls shining with gold and inlaid with shiny gemstones of all types, mosaic tiles, and carvings. Passageways in the four corners suggested that the palace complex continued beyond this open square, presumably to more private gardens and residences. The courtyard itself was made of multicolored cobbles. Stones of all types: chrysoprase, jasper, onyx, moonstone, and turquoise; hematite, sunstone, golden obsidian, and agates of various sorts were laid out in a fan pattern that radiated inwards from the walls towards the circular building at the center. They faced the throne hall directly as they entered through the main gate. A perfect circle inside the perfect square and with a shallow, ogee roof that drew the eye upwards to a center-point, which was in turn topped off with an inverted sea purslane flower, the symbol of the royal family since they first arrived on the mainland of Tianya from their ancestral home on the outer islands back in ancient times. As the children knew, as everyone in Tianya knew, the ornamental sea purslane flower above the throne hall was decorated with rare pink sapphires and had stood atop the throne hall since the building of the palace in the reign of the remarkable Queen Fafan. A herald led them the short distance from the gatehouse to the throne hall and rapped smartly with his ceremonial mace on the gilt-patterned door, which was immediately opened by two guards.

Stepping grandly into the little hall, stamping smartly to attention, he lifted his chin and cried out in a clear and well-trained voice, "Your Royal Highness, members of the Court, here, calling at the hour of the change of the afternoon watch, presenting to the throne His Erudition the Royal Tutor, the Lord Kang accompanied by", and he checked a card in his hand, "the Advanced Engineering Rationalist Enchantment Demonstration Party." The children looked at each other but Lord Kang signaled gently to them to be still.

"Yes-He Kang!", called an excited and youthful voice.

The floor rose in the form of three concentric discs and at the center of the room, beneath the point of the roof, under the sea purslane flower itself, sitting cross-legged on a mushroom shaped stool, its stem rising from the very mid-point of the disc, was the King. Around him on the disc, scattered variously, were other men and women sitting similarly cross-legged on large cushions and they too looked and smiled at the entrance of Kang and his party.

"So good to see you, old professor! What did you think of the Pankongxu 3.1? Skills, eh? What about the cup-holder? Jokes, or what? Come on, now, you love it? Right?"

"Your most Royal and Excellent Highness…"

"Oh, away with that! Come on over, pull up a cushion and bring your new friends. I'm rather intrigued to learn more about this…what did you call it?" and he looked over at the herald, "The Advanced Engineering Rationalist Ench…" …yes, yes, yes…got it. Jolly good. So…come on, the PKX, eh? She just purrs, right?"

"Most remarkable. A very splendid wagon."

"See, I knew it…didn't I say, Tamzi?" and he turned to one of the young men sitting near him, a chubby fellow with shiny hair who made a sort of grunting noise.

"I knew you'd come round sooner or later. Now, what's this all about, eh?"

"Your Highness, I have a little wager I'd like to try with you.

"That's not like you. What's up?"

"Oh, I'm not averse to a bet if I know that I'm going to win."

"Ho, ho, ho! Come on then, spill it. Your note this morning was enough to get me interested."

"I have indeed become fully converted to the ideals of the New Age and as you have not had much call on my services of late…"

"Now…er…well, one's been a bit busy what with reigning and being King and whatnot, you know how it is."

"Indeed, and I have still wanted to do work of value and so it is with enormous pleasure and pride that I wish to present to you the fruits of my studies and labors."

"Now," the King made a pretend warning voice, "you're not going to waste my time with any more superstitious guff, are you?"

"Not at all, Sir." Kang made as if to look shocked at the very idea. "I intend to demonstrate to you engineering advances beyond anything you have seen so far that will have you convinced that what you are seeing is magic. Even though, of course, it will be engineering."

"Explain…"

"I have assembled a team of these young engineers," and he indicated the children, "and with this pair of musicianers would like to stage for you a special effects display of theater, using the latest engineering technology that I predict will cause you to say that I have used magic. My bet is simply that we will perform for you and you will say that what you saw was, indeed, magic. If you do not, then the forfeit on me is yours to decide. If I win, however, then you will come to my home for berry-broth and you will have to listen to me talk about Halteres-lore for a full hour."

"Please no! But I'm intrigued All I have to do is to not believe that what you are going to show me is magic, and then I win, and I could, say, insist that you go to mechanical engineering classes for a full term?"

"If that were your chosen forfeit. Although I would be happy to let you take time to think of something else."

"Well, I have to concede that it has been getting a bit dull around here. Let's do it. What do you have in mind?"

"To give us a chance, we need a good setting. I would like you to grant permission for us to stage the performance at Zamai."

"At Zamai?" The King paused. "But is that appropriate?"

Kang smiled, and said, "Surely, in our New Age, we none of us have any scruples about that?"

"Of course not." replied the King, although perhaps a little uncertainly. "When?"

"Tonight? We have no reason to delay."

"Very well. Let me make arrangements. Meanwhile take your little team away and do what you need to do. We will meet at Zamai in...two hours. Is that acceptable?"

"Most certainly!"

"Advanced Engineering Rationally what?" asked Durfin as they walked away.

"Advanced Engineering Rationalist Enchantment Demonstration Party. Yes, I was quite pleased with that. It seems to have worked. Now let us get ourselves over to Zamai and prepare. We'll get home first and collect the instruments. Shengli, you have your dancing shoes and the insoles, of course?" Shengli tapped the shoes, which she had tucked in her belt ready before they set out and then felt for the cotton bag around her neck. It was there as it had been throughout. Her heart was racing and she had a range of emotions running through her. She had just seen the King, she was going to Zamai, she was to perform the dance; she was to summon the Li dragon.

She felt Shonan lean towards her as they walked, and that thoughtful girl asked, "How are you feeling?"

"I'm good, Shonan. Bit nervous but I'll be glad when this is over, to be honest. What did you think of the King?"

"He just seemed like any other person. I'm not sure I see the point of Kings and Queens."

"Me neither. Or palaces, or any of it. It just seems to say that one person is more special than all the other people and I just know that that's not true. Whoever came up with this idea must have been pretty stupid, if you ask me. Probably an ancestor of that tubby man, Tamzi!"

And they giggled and then Durfin had to ask, "What's funny?" and for some reason that set them both off even more and Durfin looked confused and the watching Geng leaned over and said, "That's girls, Durfin old man. They're all mysteries, all of 'em. You just stick to drumming, that's my advice, and worry about girls later!" and that brought a snort from Basha, and Durfin fell in alongside the two old musicianers. With the musical instruments collected from Lord Kang's house, they continued the walk round to Zamai and a herald was waiting for them.

"His Royal Highness has asked me to open up and let you prepare as you need. He will attend himself shortly. I am to offer you whatever assistance you require."

"That will be fine, thank you." said Kang. "Just let us in and we will soon be ready."

Zamai comprised four, crescent-shaped halls that surrounded the main dome. A simple structure consisting of a low, square wall, about knee height surrounding a plain, upturned-dish like building. The roof was perfectly smooth apart from the cross-shaped pattern cut into it. If one extended the four arms of the cross it took you through the spaces between the four crescent shaped halls. These were the dragon veins, of course. One entered Zamai by going down a flight of steps that took you under the square wall and brought you up again actually inside the dome. There was one of these subway-type entrances at each of the points marked by dragon veins. All the building work was totally plain and the contrast with the rich ornamentation of the palace could not have been greater. Inside, there was a square platform the four corners of which touched the dome at midpoints between the dragon veins. One stepped from the floor, through the stairs up, under one of the arms of the cross in the roof and at the middle of one of the sides of the square.

A step up from that, there was a circle platform within the square and the pattern continued for three more pairs so that in total, including the first square, there were four, square platforms and four circle platforms. The central, circle platform was directly under the center of the cross cut into the roof of the dome. Everything was constructed of plain, white, polished granite stone that sparked with quartz crystals but there was no other decoration at all of any kind. Light came from candles in glass bowls set into the walls at even spaces around the inside of the dome.

"It's beautiful." Shengli was first to speak.

"This is Zamai." Kang began, "The meeting point of the two primary dragon veins. The central point as far as we in Tianya know it of the network of channels that distribute vibrations through the dragon plane. That means that it provides the main point of contact between <u>this world of dust</u> in the domain of Tianya <u>and their world.</u> In the domains beyond, where these veins exhaust and other dragon-spirits lie, they have other designs but for Tianya, this has always been the most direct point for correspondence with dragons. I don't suppose I will now ever see how they manage these things in the far outer islands, where the sea dragons circle, let alone in the domains outside Tianya but the network extends, must extend, in ways and to places beyond our imagination and these things must be so, even if they are beyond our full understanding at present. But that is no matter to us here and now. For we of this domain, and for our ancestors, this has been the focal point."

"Nice that they keep it clean." noted Bahsa. "I've not been here for how many years but it's nice and clean, I'll say that. I was expecting it to look a bit dusty, you know."

"Thanks, Basha." replied kang. "Actually, I feel that privately, the King has a deep sense of the sacred nature of this place. He comes here alone sometimes. That isn't common knowledge so don't repeat it. Come on, let us set up. Shengli, how would you like to prepare?"

"Please, all just start playing and practising in your own way. I'm going to just warm up gently and then walk through the sequence in slow motion. I daren't do it for real for so many reasons but mainly because this polished surface is enough to make me nervous about a slip and an injury. Especially where some of the snow has come in through the crossed lines in the roof."

"In the old days, they used to put chalk dust on the floor for the dancer," said Geng.

"Really? Why didn't you say before?" asked Kang.

"I assumed you knew."

"No fear. I have no role now. I will return home. I have some chalk in my office that I use for sketching and there is a mortar and pestle in the kitchen. Leave that to me. I'll bring a broom as well to clear that bit of snow." And Lord Kang turned and disappeared down the steps through the subterranean exit. The four musicianers began to set up their instruments, to tune and twiddle and experiment with the acoustics in the shiny, closed, domed space. Shonan in particular was enchanted by the sound of her quan as the notes rang against the polished granite.

"Boken…" Shengli turned to the faithful little dog. What is it, old girl? All looking good! "Boken, I'm scared."

Well isn't it time that we had a cuddle and you tickled my tummy? I'm not saying anything, but it's been a while, you know. And with laughs and smiles, Shengli grabbed Boken and gave him a vigorous cuddle, a thoroughgoing tummy-tickle and the two of them rolled around on the floor of sacred Zamai until Shengli forgot why they were there and after a serious face-licking from Boken she shook herself, stood up and thought about what a very intelligent and sensitive friend she had. He was such a smart little dog. She wasn't at all scared anymore.

Kang returned with a little bowl of chalk dust that he sprinkled on the central disc. Shengli went through the dance in slow motion, stopping at the end of each sequence, the boys and the girl in the band played together a bit and then took a break and Boken thumped his tail in time to whatever rhythm they created. They had Zamai to themselves until they heard crisp footsteps coming up the steps of one of the entrances.

They stopped what they were doing, and saw emerging from the tunnel the King, alone and unaccompanied.

"Well, Kang my man, here I am." he said. "I don't see a lot of evidence of engines but I'm looking forward to whatever it is you've come up with. Just one thing. I would prefer no one to know that I was here this evening. I told the gang from the palace that I was scrapping this plan and having an early night. If word gets out that I'm attending Zamai with you, my Lord Kang, after dark, and with some total strangers, it could have very unfortunate consequences. Do you all understand?"

The King's tone was serious but soon gave way to a playful amusement when he was instructed in his role as conductor. Lord Kang made it all out to be part of the 'illusion' that he was organizing and although the King kept asking questions about the engines, Kang's reply was always "all in good time, all in good time!"

In the closed space, cut off completely from the outside world apart from the cross cut into the roof looking out onto the dark gray sky, they all forgot that this was the King in front of them, not just a playful but curious former student of Lord Kang, and that they were engaged in a deadly serious ceremonial ritual with no lesser purpose than saving Tianya from an eternal winter.

There was no reason to delay further. The chatter subsided. Lord Kang swept the central disc for one last time and rubbed it dry with a cloth he had brought back with the broom and he spread the chalk, removing any traces of the recent snowfall. The musicianers placed themselves on three of the sides of the disc, under the lines of the cross, and the King and Boken stood at the fourth. The King had a mild, indulgent smile on his face but the others were deep in focus. Shengli then stood to one side, her face turned away from the others for a moment as she gathered her thoughts. In her mind, she ran through images and memories of practising the dance with her mother. Playing around in the cottage; on walks in the forest; by the edge of the village pond. She then thought back to the day at the way-stone with Old Tam and the sight of the Mang dragon and she thought hard to bring back that feeling.

Some deep breaths and she took the little bag from round her neck and looked at the insoles for the first time since they had arrived in Lungdou. She gasped with anxiety at what she saw but took care not to reveal her feelings to the others. The nüshu embroidery was starting to unpick in a couple of places. Clearly, the dance at the way-stone had done some damage and all the bouncing around in the bag, rubbing against each other, had caused wearing at some of the fragile threads. Shengli was fighting to suppress a feeling of panic. She couldn't tell anyone and she cursed herself for not checking them earlier but after the experience with Renzi and Tongman, she had not wanted to take them out at any time and keeping them close to her chest had felt safe. What if they wouldn't work now? It felt for a moment like her heart was scoured by a blast of cold air even though at the same time she felt almost like she couldn't breathe. She could feel the eyes of the others on her back, waiting for her. Oh, how stupid she had been! How careless! But there was nothing for it now.

She slipped the insoles into her dancing shoes and squeezed them on. Already they were feeling tighter. She had grown again. No time to think of that now. She turned and walked slowly over to the central disc, stepped up and took her place directly on the intersection of the dragon lines, marked symbolically in the roof above. She nodded at the King who smiled, looked in a kindly if amused way at the others and, mouthing Old Tam's 'Mulberry, mulberry, mulberry wine', rhythm, he started to beat time using the handle of a writing brush that Lord Kang had brought for the purpose. Boken joined in with his tail thumping on the hard floor and in turn, on a nod from Geng, Durfin began, with his simple but solid rhythm, followed by Geng who picked it up himself, first with a drone from the bag and then the sweet notes of his small-pipes.

Basha picked up with the zither, strumming in rhythms with his left hand and articulating points with improvised melodies plucked with his right. And finally, Shonan entered taking the lead as the instrument with the brightest sound that rang again like silver bells over the top of the rich, layered texture of the rest of the band. The notes from her quan ricocheted off the shiny granite walls of the dome like glass marbles, as if the the village beads she was wearing were pinging against the smooth surfaces in patterns. This was magical music. Music that hadn't been heard for a generation or more. The candles in the glass bowls flickered a little more, caught in some way by the patterns in the air or perhaps it was an illusion, but surely it was real?

Shengli took a deep breath, pushed her hands down to her sides and then as high up as she could reach, paused, and the dance began. The dance like never before. Shengli was no more simply a dancer performing a dance. She was the dance. There was no dance that was not Shengli and no Shengli that was not the dance. The dance was her. There was no dancer, just a dance; the dance was alive in Shengli, and she was alive in the dance. There was no Shengli. There was the dance. Only the dance. The music flowed through her like water rushing through a stream, as if it was cascading through river rapids and she wasn't even there. She felt the air, the fluence, as if she could see it swirling from the ends of her fingers, the points of her shoes, little runnels of colored energy forming patterns in the space around her and then shooting away. Her feet tapped and slid on the smooth but chalk-dusted surface with no thinking, no control, alive and being, it seemed, owned by the dance. From the first sequence, the arcing of the hair, the lines of colour drawn by her beads, the stretching upwards, the hands gesturing and directing to the sky towards, as it was always meant to be, the intersection of the two crossed lines in the roof of the dome of Zamai. The hair flicks along the dragon veins, directly under the incised lines on the roof; the dance in place, in context.

The second sequence then, the feet: driving vibrations out along the horizontal plane, the spins, rising through the levels and then, the third sequence, the moves to activate the nüshu spells, the words of the ancients, encoded in script and preserved in the most fragile of forms in the insubstantial needlework on fine-spun cloth. Dainty, delicate, and endangered. Shengli kicked down on the soles, arched her feet and slid; en pointe and then tapping; first, second, third, fourth, fifth positions; pivot and releve; flicks and jettes; a toe-spin, and taps in triplets.

Deep in concentration, no more the smile of indulgent amusement on the face of the King. Now, he had fallen into a full sense of loss, of a loss of self, of himself as one, and instead a total absorption into the ensemble, into the music, into the dance. The King felt, perhaps for the first time in his life, what it was to give over completely to something greater than himself. And that thing was the dance and to be in service to the dance.

And so it started to happen. In the glimmering light of the candles, with the dizzying turns and shapes of the dance, the pulsing drum; the hypnotic drone and the sweet notes of the small-pipes, the relentless urging of the strummed chords, and the light runs and counterpoints from the zither, the crystal clear, jewel-like rings of the quan, and the thump-thump-thump of Boken's tail; in the middle of this sound and movement, the air started to thicken as it had in the forest. And as before, the thickening air became misty, and then twisted into a spiral of incense-like smoke. And the color came and it was green: a hint of green in the colorless mist then a clearer green, light and delicate like the first leaves of spring; translucent then and jade-like, then more solid but still that light, spring-leaf shade but firmer, seemingly marbled with veins of gold that formed, clearly, into a pattern of scales. Spinning itself, the long, thin form, entwined and spiraling with Shengli in the dance as if, for a moment, they were embraced and in the dance together. The little legs, too small surely for a creature of that size? Claws, horns, the face, the long, coiling form of the Li dragon, green and gold, the focus of the energy of the skies and the seasons, of all things aerial and ethereal.

Shengli and the dragon spun together on the central disc, on the intersection of the primary dragon lines beneath the skies of Tianya that were revealed through the crossed incisions in the roof of the dome, placed there by ancient scholars, and the focus of power for dancers and dragons through ages and eras, yes, even before Queens and Kings; to bring peace or harvests; creativity or security; the point of focus for hopes and passion, for the love of the people for their land and for their neighbors, and their vesting of those hopes in the laws of the universe as revealed by the learning and channeled through the dragons.

Shengli threw her arms upwards, flicking her wrists outwards in a move that made sense as in that gesture, she seemed to throw the Li dragon upwards, or perhaps instead he took it as a cue, because at that point the coiled spiral straightened and in an instant had shot vertically through the center of the cross in the roof and was out of sight. Nothing changed with the dance. Shengli completed the moves, finishing in the ball as before and the musicianers, concentrating to the last, brought the music to a natural cadence, and the final notes echoed around Zamai until there was silence. Shengli, curled up in the ball on the center point of Zamai, sucked in the cold air in deep breaths and did not move.

Finally, the King spoke, his voice at first hushed before recovering to his previous detached self-confidence. "Magic. That was magic. I don't care what anyone says, that was magic. How did you do it? Kang, Kang?"

They all looked around but they could not see Lord Kang. Then Boken ran off, down the steps of one of the entrances and a moment later he returned with the teacher and guide who had brought them all together.

"Hey, Kang, where were you? Behind the scenes? Operating something? Where did you go?" the King asked.

"Something like that," the old tutor replied.

"That was fantastic. Superb engineering."

"Not magic, then?" asked Lord Kang, carefully.

"Lord Kang, the first word he said afterwards was 'Magic'," Durfin spoke. "You won the bet!"

"Ah yes, the young feller has me there. You won. But you must tell me how it's done! Amazing trick. Amazing. Made me feel different, I'll admit that. Little Shengli, that was sensational."

Shengli straightened herself and cleared her throat. "Th-

thank you, Your Highness."

Suddenly the King seemed rather irrelevant. Shengli wanted him to go so she could just hug the twins and perhaps he picked up that feeling too.

"I-I'd best get back to the Palace. Look, this never happened, all right? I'm not sure it would be understood. I don't understand it. But I'd like to meet with you all tomorrow. I'll send word."

And he walked slowly off and down and out through the one of the exits and as soon as he was gone there was an explosion of noise as the children, Boken, the two old musicians and Lord Kang embraced and cried and laughed and threw themselves at each other with elation, relief and joy. Joy at music and dance and service to the land and all that lived on it.

As the mood calmed, Shengli turned to Lord Kang and asked him, "Where did you go?"

"I stayed outside. I had no role in the ceremony, and I feared that would disrupt the events."

"So, you didn't see the Li dragon?" Shengli asked.

"No, I did not. And maybe I never will see a dragon. I am convinced that you can only see the dragon if you are in the performance. I think your experience in the forest confirmed that and I had to be outside. But, there are more important matters now. There are dumplings back at my house that I know, Shengli, you were part of preparing earlier today and there is mulberry wine for Basha and Geng, and berry-broth with syrup and I think it is time for some sort of party. We won't know until tomorrow if the dawn brings the spring or not but let us have faith. You have done your work and it is time to relax. Any objections?" There were none.

PART 3

A DANCE TO WAKE A DRAGON

Chapter Twelve

They all slept late and Shengli was woken by the bright sunlight that washed into her room. She blinked and rubbed her eyes, emerging from the deep sleep that had overwhelmed her and then she got out of bed and walked across to the window where the slender branches of the cherry tree twisted upwards.

She looked closely, blinking in the unfamiliar sunlight.

There were buds on the branches. There were actual little green buds. As tiny as they could be, just little shiny jade colored pimples, but there was no mistaking: winter was over. She had succeeded. The Li dragon was now spinning and dancing in the skies above and the seasons had turned at last. Her heart felt like it would burst out of her chest as it swelled with happiness and relief and she closed her eyes for a moment to feel the joy flood through her.

Pulling on her clothes quickly she stepped out into the courtyard and she felt the warm, spring sun on her face. The sky above Lungdou was blue with a few fluffy white clouds drifting across. The snow of just yesterday was already melting and only remained in little patches in corners that the sun hadn't yet reached or in those places where it had drifted into deeper piles.

On the branches of the trees and on plants around the courtyard, in their containers or planted directly into beds marked out by neat little paths, more spots of green broke up the dark fingers of the winter patterns they had grown used to. It seemed as though nature was in a hurry to make up for lost time and all the pent-up energy of spring was being released in a rush to recover the missing days.

Suddenly, Shengli was startled by the arrival of a swallow that swooped into the courtyard and then found its neat space under the eaves of the house. It was all happening so suddenly: no easing in of the spring as sometimes seemed to happen: gently, tentatively, uncertain at first with new grass taking a cautious look above ground before feeling confident enough to push upwards. By contrast, this was a spring that seemed to be exploding into life with impatience and confidence.

"Good morning, my dear! You're finally up! Isn't it a lovely day?"

"Hello, Old Sun and yes, it is lovely. What about the others?"

"I haven't seen the twins, so I guess they're still asleep but, of course, Lord Kang has been up for hours like always. He's been in his den." Shengli smiled and went over to the study.

She pushed the door gently open and saw the old man, standing behind his table, studying some charts carefully with the astrolabe in his hands. His hearing as acute as ever, Shengli's attempts to creep in were no use and he spoke without looking up.

"Good morning, Shengli, and I must say, 'Congratulations'!"

"The spring has come!" she replied. "It is just like Old Tam said! The old learning is true and it works and we have saved Tianya with the dance! Isn't that amazing?"

"Yes, yes, it is. And in an interesting way, the process of spring seems to have been accelerated. I'm curious about that and I've been trying to find some explanation so I can better understand what has been happening but that can wait. Let us go and have a look outside."

He lay down his astrolabe and they stepped out to the courtyard and Lord Kang bent down over one of the beds and pointed. "Here they come! The crocuses." And sure enough, and Shengli was convinced she hadn't seen them even only a few minutes ago, the shiny green spears of the little crocus flowers could be seen pushing through the last of the snow. Smiling and shaking his head in surprise and happiness, Lord Kang collected a handful of fish food from the jar in the box at the edge of the courtyard and went to look in at the fish in the deep, circular pond in the middle of the yard. Sure enough, the fish were livelier than they had been before and they took food greedily from Lord Kang's hand. "Better not to give them too much yet. They'll be better able to digest it when they warm up a bit. But a little won't hurt!"

"Lord Kang…"

"Yes, Shengli"

"What happens now?"

"How do you mean? Spring comes, people get busy with planting and so on. As a village girl, I'm sure you have a better idea than I do!"

"But the King saw the Li dragon. We have proved that the old learning was true and that we have to live in harmony with the dragons and that the new ways are putting us out of balance. People need to know and understand that while there may be good things to come from the engines and so on, that has to work with the old learning. And we can show them. I could do the dance again for some of the engineers to see. We could go to one of the places for the secondary lines and call a Mang dragon and people would witness it and then they would believe again and maybe they'd stop eating creatures and digging the black stones out of the mountains to burn them and cutting down the forest and just destroying Tianya even though I know they're not bad they just lost the learning but we have it and we can show them and then they'll have it again and...and..."

"Steady on, there! Perhaps we take one thing at a time and we start with breakfast? As you heard yesterday, the King will send us a message today so we can see how things are then. Have you lost Boken? It isn't often I see you without him by your side."

"He was still sleeping when I came out. Yes, yes, of course. One thing at a time. But we should think ahead! We could talk to the King about the Dance Academy: Dama Tiyun isn't bad, I'm sure, but she doesn't believe in the power of the dance, so she thinks it is just for show and making money. The King will understand now and we could start again, training dancers and you could get some young students into the College of Learning and pass on the lore that you and Old Tam protected and we could...oh, we could do all sorts of things!"

"After breakfast." and Lord Kang smiled at Shengli whose eyes were shining with enthusiasm and impatience. Shonan and Durfin appeared and rubbing their eyes and blinking crossed the courtyard to join Shengli at the kitchen.

"Shengli, I'm so proud of you!" said Shonan.

"Yes, me too! Big proud, really!" said Durfin.

"But it wasn't just me, you two were really important. Shonan, you made such lovely music, and it was like magic just in sounds and Durfin, so strong and certain. It made it easy for me. Thank you, thank you my loyal and wonderful friends! Has anyone seen Boken?"

No sooner had she spoken than the little dog bounced into the kitchen and jumped up at her, licking her face and as excited as anyone, Great stuff, old girl! Look what you did! Spring, by the Dragons! Really, a most impressive feat and a dog is, you know, awfully proud to be your friend.

There was porridge with syrup and some leftover dumplings and more of the fresh seaweed fritters for which they had acquired something of a taste.

"We'll be getting a bit of variety soon, now, thanks to Shengli. I need to get that lazy old man out of his den this afternoon to help me sow a few seeds in the tubs so we can have some fresh herbs and salad leaves in a short while. Not like you'll be getting in the village but it still makes a difference, having a few fresh leaves…"

"We'll help!" they chorused and then there was the to and fro of politely offering to help, being politely declined, politely re-offering and so on. They were interrupted by the sound of a herald outside the gate, this time the refrain of rising notes being less of a surprise than the previous day. There was no shiny wagon this time, just the wiry, athletic young herald who warmed himself up and unfurled the scroll but before he could begin was interrupted by Durfin, "We can all read, you know! Just hand it over!"

"Oh, ah, all right. Just doin' me job, y'know. But thanks all the same. Any reply?" Lord Kang had taken the scroll and reading it, he nodded and said, "Yes, just tell the King that we will be there as he requires." And the herald saluted smartly, spun on the spot and trotted off in an official type of jog-march.

"What is it, sir?" asked Shonan.

"We are to have lunch with His Majesty in one of his private rooms. In the grounds behind the main throne hall square. Rather an unusual honor for people who are not closely connected to the King. Indeed, I haven't been past the throne hall myself for, oh, a number of years now. Ever since we stopped formal classes and my current idleness was forced upon me."

"Perhaps we'd better tidy ourselves up a bit?" suggested Shengli, and the rest of the morning passed quickly with a mixture of routine maintenance to their clothes, a good scrub, and just lazing around before it was time to report to the palace. They were shown across the square that seemed ablaze with the spring sunshine sending the light bouncing in kaleidoscopic fashion from the gemstones and the gold leaf and they passed through one of the small archways in a corner that took them into a gentler, less decorative place with fish-ponds, clumps of ornamental bamboo and some small pavilions. These were intricately decorated in the royal style with the scalloped eaves and for sure, a certain amount of gilding, but the whole effect was more of delicacy and subdued elegance after passing through the rainbow-like throne hall square. They were shown up some steps to a little bungalow where the King greeted them, alone, apart from two serving folk bringing dishes through to the table. He caught sight of the children looking anxiously at what was on offer,

"Don't worry! All the food is from plants. None from creatures. Kang sent word during the morning. Please, come on through and take a seat."

Cautiously, aware that they were being invited into a private dining room of the King himself but, all the same, still not that impressed when all was said and done, the children, and Boken, took their places at the table.

"Now, before we begin, I have a few things for you just to reflect my appreciation of your show yesterday evening. For you, Durfin and Shonan, the Order of the Lyre, an ancient honor given to musicianers but, oddly, I note that it hasn't been awarded for a very long time indeed. Rather nice to bring it to life again," and he beckoned them over and, from a little box in front of him on the dining table, took out two medals and pinned them in turn to the chests of the twins.

"Your majesty," said Durfin.

"Yes, little feller, what is it?"

"Basha and Geng were in the band, too. And they taught us really. They should get the medals."

"They already have done." replied the King, I saw them earlier. Indeed, it was they who reminded me of the old things in the first place. Now, for you, Boken, a medal is a little less appropriate since nothing to pin it to, eh?"

Well spotted, said Boken although of course only Shengli knew and she fought to control her smile. Boken, to be frank, wasn't altogether enamored of the King. "So, er, here's the ribbon anyway and maybe you can tie it up, you know, around your ears or something?" Boken's already low opinion of monarchy in general and this King in particular slid a little further down the scale.

"And now the star of the show!"

"It wasn't a show," said Shengli, under her breath.

"Yes, for the star, well, a star, of course!" and he picked out another medal from the box that was, indeed, in the shape of a twelve-pointed star studded with shiny gemstones.

"The Star of Honor, first presented by my illustrious ancestor, Queen Fafan. Pretty cool, huh? Look, it's the same on both sides which isn't always the case, you know, with medals."

"It wasn't a show." she mumbled again.

"Jolly good, jolly good. Now, some lunch, eh? And then perhaps, Mr Yes-He Kang, you might share some of your trade secrets, eh? Dam' impressive illusion. How was it done?"

"It wasn't a…" and then Shengli felt a gentle tug on her arm from Lord Kang and he smiled, indicated with his eyes and she understood, took her place back at the table and they settled in for lunch. Lord Kang did a good job of stalling and bluffing the King, giving the impression that he was reluctant to reveal too much about the engineering technology that had created the 'illusion' while also leaving the King with a sense that that was, indeed, exactly what he had seen, that the dragon was the product of some particularly sophisticated machinery that he would very shortly be sharing with the engineers at the College and at the workshops at Dalongkou and then he started to pretend to explain but he used such comically technical sounding language that the King, unwilling to appear stupid, pretended to understand for a while before changing the subject.

They chatted of other things but the King started to seem bored and he yawned quite ostentatiously at one point and it was clear that it was time to go. Lord Kang stood, the children followed his lead and they made the requisite bows and curtseys and walked backwards to the door.

"Ah well, if you must go," said the King in his Kingly voice and then, very much more softly "Funny, though, for a period yesterday evening I really believed it was magic and that we were calling a dragon. And I have to admit, I haven't felt like that since I don't know when."

And then, he started being a King again, "Now, off you trot and work hard at school and whatnot, jolly good, eh? Take care of the medals. You're supposed to wear them on my birthday and on state occasions."

Shengli was almost exploding as they walked away but Lord Kang's hand on her shoulder kept her quiet until they were out of the palace and some way down the street and then she could hold herself no more.

"But it wasn't a show! It wasn't an illusion! It was real. How can he be so stupid?"

"He isn't stupid," Shengli, "but he is convinced that anything that might lead to a return to the old learning will take Tianya back to the days of wars and, as he sees it, superstition."

"But he saw! With his own eyes! He was there and he was conducting."

"Yes, but he needs to believe that what he saw was an illusion that depended on some very sophisticated application of engines. Just as you needed to believe that what happened was that you summoned a dragon with the dance."

Shengli stopped walking and looked hard at Lord Kang. "That is what happened. Why did you say that?"

"Truth is a funny thing, Shengli. After all, much of reality is what we make of it in our heads. When I see a flower is red, and you see it is red, how do I know that the red that you see is the same as the red that I see? Maybe the red that you see would be what you would call blue in my eyes? But every time I see the flower that would look blue to you, I call it red, because that is what I have always done, and you see it as red. I can't see through your eyes and you can't see through mine. And thereby I suspect is much of the mystery of the world."

Shengli started walking again but she was biting her lip so hard it hurt. She was fighting her own feelings that were mixed between anger and betrayal on the one hand and confusion and self-doubt on the other.

"I know what I saw. And we all know that the spring came. Old Tam was right, the Li dragon lay beneath, and the dance was what brought it above."

They walked back to the house in silence and Shengli went straight to her room, with Boken, and shut herself in for the rest of the afternoon.

She could hear the twins as they played around with the quan and the zurdom. Now, she thought, that was really real and she could hear the music and she found herself thinking about how the instruments actually sounded like her friends. Not, of course, sounded like their voices or any other actual way but sort of representative. The silvery-bell sounds of the quan were like Shonan: clear, sweet, perhaps a bit fragile but cutting through everything else as if with a crystal light while the zurdom was warm sounding, and admittedly, one had to say it, perhaps not that bright, but grounded and secure. She smiled at the memory of how Durfin had stood up for Basha and Geng when receiving his medal from the King. That was typical.

But Lord Kang had hurt her. It seemed he doubted her. That somehow, they had imagined everything and the spring had come by coincidence. Well, she would show him. That evening they gathered for dinner back in the kitchen and the twins started to talk about the journey home. They told Lord Kang and Old Sun about the village and their little brother and sister and how they missed them although as soon as they saw them again they'd remember all the ways little brothers and sisters were really annoying but not really and then there were the antics that they would get up to in the forest with Shengli and Boken and what it would be like to get back now that spring had come and there would be work to do with the vegetable plots and for sure there would be that lean time between the end of winter and the first early vegetables when you had to make the most of what was left of the winter stores but then there would be all sorts of foods to enjoy that tasted like nothing you could get in the city and they'd be busying themselves in the forest, collecting mushrooms and wild herbs and, thank all the dragons, there'd be no more steam-wagons hey! Did you see what happened there? A rhyme! and isn't that funny given how they'd so wanted to see engines but now they were sick of them and that was fine, thank you, and no one ate flesh in the village, which was just so much happier and Durfin would never get rid of the feeling but he would really in time and just wait 'til they told everyone about seeing the Li dragon and how Shengli was so amazing and well they hadn't been too bad themselves and then they could play the zurdom and the quan for everyone in the village and they'd worked out a way they could play as a duet and maybe Shengli could work out more dances and…and…

"I'm not going." Shengli snapped.

"What…not going? What do you mean?" asked Shonan. "Not coming home?"

"No."

"Why not?" asked Durfin who was more than a bit muddled. For all his words, he was still a bit fascinated by engines and to be honest, to be really, really honest, that bit of flesh he'd eaten, he was never going to admit it to anyone but it had been, well, really, really good. And he'd had fun with Geng and Basha and was really going to miss them even though he'd only known them for a day, really. So he wasn't, actually, feeling too down on the city in truth but his instinctive loyalty to his sister and to Shengli was overriding those feelings so he was all up for the journey home.

Except, now Shengli was changing things. Again. He'd do anything for her, really he would, but she could be a bit confusing. Really.

"I'm staying here and I'm going to do the dance again and I'm going to show people so that they have to believe, they have to know, that the dragons are real and then they will respect the old learning. Even if that means that just some people stop eating creatures, it will be a start."

Lord Kang spoke next, "I don't think that will be a good idea."

She marched out into the courtyard and went to lean over the edge of the pond and she looked in at the fishes as they circled and nibbled at the algae on the brickwork.

Lord Kang came up beside her. "Are you going to explain to

the fish about Halteres-lore? About the dragons?"

"Stop making fun of me."

"I'm not, Shengli, I promise. I promise, I do believe you. I have believed in the dragons all my life even without ever seeing one. Without the dragons, the universe doesn't make sense. Even if you never saw one, you can see the effects of their activity. That is evidence enough for me and even without that I would still believe in the dragons because of the love I have for the people who taught me the lore and because of my faith in them."

"Then why did you say the things you did?"

"I want you to understand the people who don't believe in the dragons. They are right too, in a way."

"How can they be, when they're wrong?"

"Look at the fish, Shengli. Imagine they were invited to come and join us for lunch, to leave their wet and slimy world and join us in the spring sunshine knowing that Old Sun has fried the last lot of the dumplings in peanut oil and there's a fruit pie for afters? And Durfin has filled himself up too much on the seaweed fritters before lunch so there'll be plenty more for everyone? Would that spotted fellow there, would he hop out of the pool with a cheery 'Hello', trick Boken into getting out of the rocking chair and take his place and then chat amiably about recipes for mulberry wine until the food was served? And would he prefer to sit in the dry, away from the wet and slimy world that would be such a misery to you or I?"

He said this in such a way that of course it made Shengli laugh although at the same time she felt he wasn't taking her seriously.

"Of course not. But I'm not talking about fish. I'm talking about people. People who are living in a way that causes suffering whether through damaging the mountains and forests or eating creatures or just caring too much about having things they don't need and, you know, all that…"

"And how will that change?"

"I can talk to people about our experiences. I can show them. They'll see!"

"Like the King did? I'm asking again, can you talk to the fishes about Halteres-lore?"

"No, of course not. But they don't need me to! They already know it, I guess."

"Does talking about food fill your stomach? Does talking about a coat keep you warm?"

"Again, of course not. So what?"

"Because this what I have learned from Old Tam. And if I was unsure before then I am certain now. If Halteres-lore is to survive these days, it needs to be lived, not preached. Then there will be an alternative for people to see when they are ready for it. And maybe that will be the King one day."

"So there is nothing we can do?"

"That isn't what I've been saying. Shengli, can you read the nüshu on the spells in your dancing shoes?"

"I can make out the sounds from the writing and I can say the words, but I don't know what they mean."

"Would you like Old Sun to tell you?"

"Wha…"

"Yes, she knows nüshu, She is, in truth, a great scholar with wisdom and knowledge way beyond anything that I or Tam have ever possessed but in the old society, the learning of women was not respected so silly fools like us were enrolled in the College and got to spend our days playing around. Meanwhile, the women of the valleys and mountains, the forests and the islands, recorded and remembered wisdom far more sophisticated than anything we can ever understand with our clumsy scripts. In some of those far places, out of the way of the world, I understand, there are still priories where some women keep the lore. But the old days, and perhaps these days too, were days when stupid men would feel threatened by women who knew wisdom and they would call them witches or other bad things and so the women learned to keep their secrets. And although it has mostly been lost, unless more survives in the outlying regions than I know, there are just a few left now who carry the knowledge. Actually, the interesting thing is that..."

But Shengli had already raced to her room where she had left the dancing shoes the previous evening with the embroidered insoles still in them. It was then that she saw the damage that had been done. She sat on the edge of the bed and looked at the delicate little pieces of fabric and saw how threads had run and entire symbols had been torn out of the cloth. Some of the symbols had completely unraveled and the thread lay loose in the bottom of her shoe. Of course, she knew the words that came in the spaces but these soles, the spells that she had guarded since her mother had died and which had been exactly the right size for her feet only through this past adventure, these spells were gone.

Oddly, she felt a sense of relief. She had lost the dance. She could still do it of course but there could be no expectation of these spells ever working again. At least not for her. But she knew what she had to do. She walked across the courtyard and smiled as she passed Lord Kang. She called for Shonan who came out and joined her, she spoke swiftly to her childhood friend and the two of them went into the kitchen. A little while later, Durfin came out looking a little hurt and Lord Kang waved him over, "No cause for unhappy feelings, Durfin, old man. That is a world that isn't for you or I, and all that we need to know is that we should respect it, protect it, and look to it for the best hope we all have. In the meantime, this is the first day of spring and we still don't have any seeds in the ground. How are you with a trowel?"

RICHARD PRATT

The two men, one young and one old, exchanged smiles and Lord Kang led the way to a tool cupboard, dug out little packets of seeds and twine and marker sticks and the pair of them got busy on the bare containers and tubs that surrounded the courtyard.

Chapter Thirteen

The following morning the sky was gray and for a moment Shengli feared that the previous day had been an illusion but no, it was no more than Lungdou's grimy smoke and dust gathering again and the temperature was still warm and what was more, some of the little buds on the cherry tree outside her window were showing the first pink blossom. She thought of how beautiful it was going to look in a couple of days but she would not see it as talking late into the previous night, they had agreed that they wanted to get back to the village and there would be an engine this day. The contrast with their arrival in Lungdou struck them all. They walked with confidence through the crowded streets, weaving in and out of the crowds, sidestepping the garbage and alert to the passing wagons.

"You are all real city kids now!" laughed Old Sun who was sorry to see them go and she and Lord Kang were both accompanying them to see them off.

"No," said Durfin, "I'm a villager and proud of it. The city is too confused and city people are too confusing for me!" Lord Kang put his arm round Durfin's shoulders and said something softly in his ear that the others couldn't hear but whatever it was it set the two of them laughing and they strode out ahead, the others coming behind.

At the mounting bays, the mass of people was as before, but less alarming given the familiarity. Shengli saw the man who had asked her for some monies the first day when Renzi had stopped her. This time she leaned down to him and put a coin in his hand and said a kind word. Lord Kang looked after the business of organizing tickets and they saw the railway engine waiting. It was similar to the previous engine but seemed newer and larger. Like the earlier one, it was a kind of barrel on the side but at the end with the engineers there was a great copper dome that shone even in the muggy light of smoky Lungdou. Most striking though were the wheels. With two small wheels in front, there were a pair of giant ones in the middle, taller than the tallest man, and then two smaller ones under the engineers' platform. It gave off an air of arrogance and a look of greater power than the engine on which they had arrived.

"Ah, the new Stormdart!" said Lord Kang, "I've heard about this. A friend of mine was involved in the design. Well, this will get you home faster than you can imagine."

They boarded and after promises to visit again, and hugs and a few tears, and a last-minute gift of a huge bag of barley cakes and apples for the journey, there were whistles, fresh bursts of shouting, guffets of steam and the big driving wheel turned, and they drew away from Lungdou and settled back to watch as the buildings of the dirty city gradually gave way to the fields and hedgerows of the land to the south of the river. The open wagon was crowded and that put them off talking and so dreamily they rocked gently, feeling the rhythms of the engine and the rattle over the sections of track and the twins were soon fast-deep asleep and failed to wake even when with a jolt, the train stopped, not suddenly but even so, with a rattling and bumping as the wagons knocked against each other.

"What's happening?" asked Shengli, to no-one in particular.

"We're taking on water, Dear," said a kindly seeming lady. "This new engine is faster, they say, but it does seem to stop sooner than the old one. I can't help wondering if it isn't just change for change's sake, you know what I mean?"

Suddenly Boken perked up his ears and sniffed the air. He looked over at Shengli, Wonder if we might pop out for a minute or two, old girl? Quick call, if you understand my meaning? With a smile, Shengli nodded and opened the wagon door and the two of them climbed down to the side of the track. She smiled at the kindly lady who made said, "Ah, so this is where you get off! Well, all the best, mind how you go."

Shutting the door behind her she stretched and watched as Boken sniffed the ground and then with a start, sprinted into a clump of foxgloves and brambles. Oh no, thought Shengli, the naughty creature! He's after a rabbit. And indeed, the return to the sounds and smells of the countryside had overwhelmed Boken after the misery of the city and he'd quite lost his head. Shengli chased after him, "Boken! Boken!" And she scrambled down the side of a banking after the little dog. It was just like so many times in the forest but really, what a pest. He'd get a talking to when she caught him but you couldn't really blame him but then, with horror, she heard the sound of the Stormdart as it got up steam and the giant driving wheels turned and she shouted as loud as she could but of course with the noise of the engine no one heard her and faster than any engine in Tianya before, Stormdart accelerated away and Shengli watched it disappear getting smaller and smaller and her heart sank with misery and her face grew hot with anger. She screamed for Boken who trotted back a little sheepishly. Sorry, old girl. Really I am. I don't know what came over me. It's just been so long, you know. Old instincts kicking in and well, you know, I am a dog and that was a rabbit and that's what happens, really. I'm awfully sorry. Please don't be too mad. And his eyes grew big, and his shoulders fell inwards and his ears flopped forward and Shengli couldn't be angry anymore.

"It's all right. I know. We've had some funny days and we've all had moments when we've been a bit mixed up. And I'll never ever be angry with you or if ever I am I'll remember how you stood up to Renzi and were so smart and brave and oh, Boken, you have put us in a bit of a pickle, though. There isn't another engine for two days or something and even if the twins wake up, they won't be able to do anything until the engine gets to Quiczu. I guess we're going to have to walk. Well, we know well enough how to do that. I expect they'll wait for us at the mounting bay there." Shengli didn't have a detailed knowledge of the geography of Tianya but she knew that the railway line took a big bend to follow the flat land towards the coast and she had the idea that they could make the walk a lot shorter by following paths through the peaks that rose up ahead and to her right. She didn't really know what that would mean and although completely at home in the forest, she had never spent any time in the mountains but the ancients would pass through that way, to and from Lungdou before the railway line, on trails that must still be there and, well, how hard could it be? You just put one foot in front of the other and cutting off the big curve of the railway line should mean a lot less walking. Maybe they'd get there before dark? That would still be six or seven hours and you could walk, oh, a really long way in that time.

The peaks certainly made a fantastic sight in the spring sunshine. Gentler foothills first appeared as one's eyes followed the flat land away from the sea which lay across the plain and out of sight to her left but the mountains really began with the steep ridge that rose ahead of her now and which marked the northern flank of the salient that jutted out from the great ranges behind. Shengli knew that if she just kept heading south, and she had no difficulty calculating that from the sun, she would hit the river on the other side, hopefully not too far from Quiczu.

It seemed the smart thing to do compared with following the railway tracks on their long bend avoiding the very barrier she now planned to cross. They set off in good spirits. It felt like old times again with Shengli chattering away to Boken and Boken running ahead then turning to watch as Shengli caught up. For the little dog, after the long winter when it had been so hard to run with the deep forest snow and then the claustrophobic city where one was always either indoors or negotiating crowded alleys and the legs and feet of clumsy city folk, it was a glorious relief. He ran ahead, turned, saw Shengli following, raced back to her, turned and ran ahead, as always covering three times as much distance as he needed to but feeling his heart pumping and his spirits soaring. The old tracks were still clear even if they looked neglected. The ancients had laid level stones across the paths on the slopes to assist the peddlers and the packhorse drivers of the age before the engines. The way across the mountains had never been popular: the sea route down river from Quiczu and round the coast to Lungdou had always been the main route for traders and travelers and the mountains had a reputation for bandits and, of course, wolves. But there were the mountain people themselves, scratching out what lives they could in the steep valleys and there would always be adventurers willing to take the risks involved in searching for the precious metals and gemstones that the mountain guarded tightly but for which there had always been a demand in the city, not least during the building of the Royal Palace, as Shengli herself had seen only so recently.

RICHARD PRATT

The going was hard and loose stones and sharp edges meant keeping a secure footing was a challenge. The snow had melted from the paths but there would still be slushy spots and the sun reflected harshly off the snow that still clung to the higher ground. The path would take a steep slope, which would leave one out of breath but then there would be a sharp descent and the challenge on ankles and knees. Shengli was a fit young girl, tough and healthy, but she was still small after all, and more used to the athleticism of dance or chasing through the forest than the stamina sapping strain of mountain trekking. No matter, push on. She had the idea at each slope that as soon they reached the crest, she would look down and see Quiczu in the distance as they had when approaching from the forest side. But every crest showed only a slope down and then a climb up to another, even higher point. The sun passed overhead and Shengli was aware that while it was a blessing not to have to carry her pack, left on the train, she would have been glad of Old Sun's bag of barley cakes and apples. There were mountain streams to drink from, rushing with the snow melt and that was fine water, crisp and cold, refreshing and bright but the mountains didn't offer the same easy wayside food that Shengli would have found so simple to gather in the forest. There were strange plants that she didn't recognize and she was smart enough to know what she didn't know. But she was hungry. Dark clouds came over and the drop in temperature after the bright sunshine was welcome but the first big drops of rain were not. A mist fell, and then a new problem. The path split in a fork, both tracks equally neglected. What if one of them bent away from the route? And with the sun hidden behind the dark clouds it was getting harder to be confident about the route south.

Boken raced ahead first up one path and then the other and came back, Not at all sure, old girl. They both start off about the same and then drop down a steep slope either side of this peak here. They tried the left fork until before long, that path forked so Shengli then chose right, hoping that this would keep the general direction straight but that path grew windier and twistier such that she could not feel sure that they were headed in the right direction. The mist meant she had completely lost her bearings in relation to the sun; the rain grew heavier and the path narrowed between steep cliffs. She was fighting to keep optimistic and talking to herself, "Come on then, up this next peak, I bet we'll see Quiczu down there and then we'll just skip down and be in the town and then we can try and ambush the twins…"

But the conversation kept shifting to something more angry and irritable, "Oh, you stupid girl, Shengli, you stupid girl. You're lost. Why didn't you just sit down and wait by the railway line. Someone would have come. Oh, you think you're so smart. Just a quick walk, eh? Short cut through the mountains, bring us out right by Quiczu? So clever…" But mostly it was just, "Oh please, please, make this the last climb before we see something…please."

The rain fell more heavily, the skies darkened further and there was the first flash of lightning followed by a grumble of thunder. "Boken, we need to find shelter, a cave or something. We'll just have to sit this out." Got it, I'll scout ahead. Don't worry, we'll be fine! And he scampered off, sniffing and stopping to look up and around. Something seemed to catch his nose and he darted left and right and then out of sight. As always, he was investigating every corner, every curiosity. Shengli had her head down as she tried to watch her footing on the now very slippy rocks and in some sort of shield to the rain. With Boken out of sight she felt so alone. It was a great relief when he skittered back into view every few moments and yapped cheerfully to encourage her to keep going before disappearing up ahead again. But then he didn't appear again for what was probably only a minute or two but it felt like an age. Shengli couldn't tell if the heavy feeling that came on her was just her fatigue and the thickening air but she felt like lead weights were pulling her insides down. She picked up the pace but slipped and struck her knee on a sharp rock and the sudden pain both made her feel sick for a moment and then even more cross with herself. Her heart was pumping and she was fighting to keep control of her feelings. She needed to be strong and sensible.

Don't rush, stay calm, Boken will be waiting up ahead where he has found a cave or at least some sort of outcrop something we can hide under to see out this storm. Come on, Shengli. She pulled herself up and turned one more bend and through the rain and the mist she thought she saw something like an animal, moving oddly and unnaturally. She couldn't see yet what it was and it was odd that Boken wasn't around. She walked closer and started to feel a deep fear come up on her. She started to run, slipped again and scrambled to her feet and as she gained ground the truth of what she was looking at seemed to choke her off at the throat. "Boken! Boken!"

The little dog had his head caught in some kind of a trap. He was kicking with his back legs but his head was caught in a pair of metal bars that were crushing him by the throat. His eyes were clear and still but his jaws were stretching desperately as the arms of the trap closed over his throat. Shengli grabbed at the steel bars of the trap and tried to pull them apart. They were sprung tightly around the neck of her dearest friend and she struggled to get a strong grip, wrapping her fingers around the cold steel and she strained and pulled. She tried to get her legs braced against the earth and slipped and pulled both dog and trap in a sharp jerk. She was crying and screaming into the wind as she strained at the powerfully sprung arms of the trap and she felt the life slipping out of Boken as the unbearable sound of his breath, his life, slipping away from him came as a horrible watery gurgling.

It was moments. Only moments. Maybe he was already close when she found him but that fight with the arms of the steel trap was the hardest fight she had ever fought and yet she lost. She was too weak. It was like trying to pull apart the iron bars of a prison window and she was just not strong enough. With a final jolt, Boken's body went limp and his still clear and bright eyes froze as they stared out ahead at the world he had now left. His jaws were still extended as they had gasped for the last fragile touch of life but the tension had gone. Shengli stared and then hugged at Boken and her first feeling was simply refusal to believe what had happened. "Boken, Boken, no, please, Boken…"

For a moment she just refused to accept what she could see in front of her. A man-made steel trap had closed over the neck of her dear friend. A man-made trap. A trap made by her own kind. Had killed Boken. Boken, the little foxlike dog who was smarter and funnier, braver and more loyal than any person she had ever met. It can't have happened.

But it had. And the grief welled up within her and she just howled out in misery and rage. She cried out to the storm, to the rain and the thunder. She had never been so angry. How can this happen? How? Why? She clenched her fists and beat them against the rocks in frustration. And the tears mixed with the rainwater rushing down her face and the end of the world was about her as the storm battered against the rocks, the winds circled and lifted the earth and she hugged and pressed her face against the amber fur of the dear, dear little dog.

Time passed, how long? Shengli didn't know or care but she needed to get out of the storm. She couldn't take the trap of Boken's neck but the trap itself was only held in the ground by a slender spike, which she pulled out easily. She lifted Boken, trap and all, and stood up. She had no plan but she was going to find shelter and wait out the storm and then Boken would have the same, simple but dignified funeral that they had given Old Tam so very recently. And whatever happened after that, she could not think that far ahead now. She struggled on. Boken was no weight, even if she still had to carry the awful trap as well.

And then, through the mist, a little up the side of the slope to one side she thought she saw, she did see, the small entrance to a cave and she clutched Boken with one arm and using the free arm for balance, she scrambled up the slope and into the welcome shelter. She lay Boken on the dusty ground in the most dignified way she could and curled up herself in a hollow, closed her eyes and cried and cried until she was overwhelmed with exhaustion and she just collapsed asleep where she was on the bare rock, cold and wet as she was. She no longer cared about anything and if she too died in the night, well then that would be just fine.

In her sleep, Shengli felt without being conscious the familiar warmth of a furry body and the reassuring sound of steady breathing. She nuzzled up against the side of the comforting presence beside her and slept deeply until she turned slightly and felt a sharp stone dig into her and she shook herself half-awake. In the dark of the cave she could see nothing at all and yet she could feel the comfort and protection of...she reached and stroked the side of the creature she had snuggled up against. Soft and soothing. But...it couldn't be Boken: Boken was dead. She stifled a choke. She moved as slowly as she could and tried to make out in the darkness some sense of who had joined her while she was sleeping. She could hear breathing of more than one creature and reaching out gently, she could feel that she had the serene, soft bodies on either side of her and she could hear them deeper in the cave. Dog-like but larger. In the mountains, in a cave. A group. A pack? It could only be wolves!

Paralyzed with anxiety she fought to control her breathing and feelings of fear and frustration. One nightmare after another. She did everything she could to keep as silent as possible but every breath she made seemed to sound to her like a roar. The wolves must know she was there. With their sense of smell, their sophisticated awareness and sharp intelligence they would know. And it felt almost as if they had surrounded her, whether to trap her or to warm her and care for her she didn't know. She mustn't move; she tried to empty her head to stay calm, to slow down her mind and to create some space. The thoughts and fears that were galloping through her had to come under control. She counted her breaths slowly. They seemed so loud and she put all her attention onto slowing down the rhythm of in and out, making it softer, calmer. The concentration was making her eyes water but she couldn't move to wipe them so she blinked to try and clear them.

The effect was to create that rainbow like fuzziness of refraction and for all that it was dark, she could see the flower-formed spectrum of colored light. She couldn't blink, or rub but she didn't want to after all. The rose-shape, the sunburst of lights formed gradually into the willowy, delicate and comforting, clear and defined form of The One Who Sees Cries. In the small cave, she yet still appeared larger than life, filling Shengli's vision as if there were no walls, no boundaries, to the space in which she swayed gently. She reached out with the small flask and allowed a drop to fall onto Shengli's face and Shengli felt calmed and comforted, blessed and reassured. The One Who Sees Cries spoke but her voice didn't disturb the wolves who slept on, warming each other as a pack, protecting each other and, it was clear now, Shengli also.

"Shengli, do not fear. The wolves have come in here to protect you. They will care for you and keep you safe."

Shengli found, as before, that she could speak with The One from inside her head and so make no noise. "In my village we have always cared for and respected the wolves. Old Tam would speak of them with love. But that was before Renzi. Now I don't know. And I am in their space."

"Renzi had man-spirit and wolf-spirit combined.", said The One. "Although he was the true-born Prince of the wolves, he had acquired man-spirit so that he could enter the world of men. The new age has seen more and more damage to the lands where the wolves had dominion and the war of men on wolves, killing them for their skin, and even for their amusement, using the crossbows or the traps, like the one that took Boken, this all convinced him he had to enter the world of men to try and save his pack. Since men became flesh eaters, they have seen the wolves as enemies. They take the animals from the mountains so the wolves struggle to find food in their own realm and they are hungry and then, as the men imprison animals and prepare them for killing, they in turn fear the wolves who, unlike men, must eat flesh and who are hungry and who would take some of the prison animals if they could. These are sad days and the suffering is great. Do not blame Renzi for what happened. His mind had been corrupted by acquiring man-spirit and that mixed with his powerful wolf-spirit desire to save his pack. When he was loyal and true, that was his wolf-spirit. When he turned on you, after he had heard of the monies that could be won from your treasure that was his man-spirit. The wolves feel shamed by what happened and although they grieve for the loss of their Prince, the Great Han, the King of the wolves, has vowed to protect and care for you. You are safe, Shengli. You are safe."

"How did he mix man-spirit and wolf spirit?"

"The ways of Tianya are many and the learning is long. There will be time, there will be time. You are safe. Rest and trust the wolves. And weep no longer for Boken. Take strength from his memory and love him by being strong. You are safe...you are safe..."

And the elegant, beautiful figure swayed gently and the colors faded and she was gone with only the words, "You are safe...you are safe..." echoing softer and softer. Shengli sensed a deep calm and her heart seemed to fall into rhythm with the breathing of the wolves around her. She felt the warmth and comfort of their bodies and although she could not sleep again, she lay peacefully and in the dark and she played through in her mind all that she had seen and learned of the past few days. She understood so much more. The dance for the Li dragon had been a momentary thing: an urgent task for a particular crisis. But the loss of balance in Tianya turned out to be a much greater and more complex matter. There was so much to know and understand and so much to do. For now she chose simply to play through in her mind her memories of Boken and to bring him back to life in her heart, chasing through the forest, being playful and brave, loyal and understanding but also pompous and funny at times. She wouldn't grieve for him now. She would just be thankful that she ever knew him at all.

Chapter Fourteen

The wolves awoke in turn and seemed to ignore Shengli at first. The morning light reached into the cave and it was easier to see now. They nuzzled and licked each other's faces and some of them started to play and roll around in the entrance to the cave. Shengli stayed as still as she could while also taking the occasional glance over at the body of Boken which still lay where she left it, the horrible steel trap still clamped over his throat and face. But it is hard to stay completely still for very long and eventually she could not help but shuffle slightly and the noise caught the attention of the wolf beside her who turned his silver gray face to her and with a cock of the head, a twitch of the brow and a turn of an ear spoke as clearly as ever Boken had. Shengli was astonished to find that all the years of 'speaking' with Boken meant she could understand Lupine, the language of the wolves. It was like being with Boken although slightly different, like a different accent or something, but understandable and clear.

"Good morning, young lady. Please be at peace. You will come to no harm with us. We have followed your story and your journey. We know of you from our dear old friend, Tam-ha, and are committed to your protection and safety."

It was like Boken, although the wolf used his tail a bit more. For Boken, the tail was more about emphasis and color in speech; when the wolf spoke, the tail had a more direct purpose. But Shengli found it was easy to follow. Her only concern was would they understand her? She could only speak the people language of Tianya with the accent of the southern forest folk. It hadn't mattered before. Boken had grown up around her so presumably he knew it as well as she did.

"Er...hello. I'm Shengli. Can you understand me?"

The wolf smiled with his eyes. "Yes indeed. All wolves know the language of people. Sometimes it is what saves us and how we know of danger. You are rare in that you understand us. Only Tam-ha apart from you has ever understood us that we know of."

"Why do you call him 'Tam-ha'?"

"Ah, I forget. You do not have that in your ways. For us, Tam-ha was a great friend and so we honor him by calling him 'ha'. It is our way of showing respect. I am Han. My role is to be King of the Wolves, but here that only means I have a different job. All members of the pack have their jobs. Mine is what it is."

"I have heard of you."

"Renzi was my son. He was sent to help you but through his man-spirit he lost his way. His wolf-spirit desire to save his pack, ourselves, here in the mountain, mixed with his man-spirit belief that he could control and influence events and he became infected by the idea that if he could obtain monies he would have power. He wanted power to serve his pack. To serve the pack is a wolf-thing; but the pursuit of power is a man-thing. I am very sorry and ashamed of how he turned."

"Please don't be. I was scared then but I understand now. I'm just very, very, sad it all happened like it did. I really liked him until that day but then I was very scared."

"Nonetheless, it is my duty to protect you now. This is our atonement. You have the service of the pack. Now, your little dog-friend…"

"Boken. The best and truest friend anyone could ever have."

"It is our intention to honor him as a member of our pack. He cannot lay here as we use this cave in rain and storm but if you will come with us, we will show you a place where he can lie."

"What is that thing that killed him?"

"It is a trap for us. People place them. They have two types that we know: one type is like a metal mouth that closes suddenly on your leg. Then you cannot move and the people come and kill you with a crossbow or some other thing. This is the second type where usually there is some food or something that brings your attention and then the mouth closes over your head. We older wolves are more aware and we try to teach the cubs but still, every year, we have some of the younger members of the pack who get caught. At least you die quickly with this type."

"But why?"

"We did not know and that is one reason Renzi took on man-spirit so he could learn and understand and maybe protect us. It made no sense to us. We know about killing and hunting. We are wolves. But we only kill when we must. Why would people kill us? They do not need to eat flesh, and even if they choose to, they do not eat wolf. Then Renzi came back and told us, people take our skins and decorate themselves with them. Mountain people can get monies from city people for our skins. But they are our skins! And then, and I am sorry to say this to you as it must cause you shame, but some people kill animals for amusement. They call it sport."

"I have heard of this, but I didn't believe it."

"It is true. I am sorry. Now let us take this poor martyr to a high place where the wind and sun and the birds will ensure that his body decays cleanly and from where his spirit can take its next journey."

Shengli picked herself up with difficulty from the cage floor. She was stiff and sore from the previous day and the effort to keep still since she had awoken had been almost more work than being busy.

She was aching more than she could ever remember aching but she gathered Boken's little, furry body in her arms, felt her heart twist again at the sight of the steel trap still clamped over his head and which she knew she could do nothing about and she followed Han out of the cave. Han led her up a slope, following a narrow trail that he explained was usually used by the mountain goats but with the wolf-pack in that part of the mountains, the goats had mysteriously chosen to forage elsewhere. He smiled again in that way with his eyes. The other wolves came behind and after a short while they came out to a more level piece of rock and Han showed Shengli where to lay Boken. She tried one last time to pull the steel trap off his face and head but it was impossible.

"It is no matter." said Han. "A body is just a vehicle. This one is broken now. Death is part of life just as life is part of death. It is all one."

And he began to walk around Boken's body in a figure eight pattern. The other wolves followed and soon the pack were walking slowly and mournfully around Boken and looping back. Han changed direction and the wolves all followed him as they kicked some dust and fallen leaves over Boken, but no more than that, and then they formed a circle and at a signal from Han, they howled. All as one, at first, and then breaking into howls that were personal and spontaneous. And in each howl was a cry of incomprehension and despair at a world in which there was a species who killed without necessity, that caused suffering, and who never seemed to have enough. Han lowered his head and that was the signal for the howling to cease and there followed silence. It was an odd silence in that the wind in the mountains blows and sings and one forgets it is there until there is supposed silence and then the noise of the wind is deafening. The sound of birdcalls carried on that wind although the greatest of them all, the Tianya Mountain Eagle, circled over a distant peak in silence and watched everything, saying nothing. Tears rolled down Shengli's cheeks but the dignity and elegance of the wolves and of their simple but powerful ritual had given her strength and she was comforted. The wolves dispersed and settled to grooming and licking each other.

Han walked over to Shengli. "The pack is hungry and we will need to hunt soon. But first we must help you to return to a people-place. We can take you to a ridge from where you can look down and see the plain and the river. From there, you cannot get lost. I'm sorry that we have no food for you. The winter has been long and we have been hungry often. The people in the plains have some animals in prisons that we will take if we have to but we will not risk it today. The snow is melting and soon we will be able to hunt in the true way."

"Thank you. I can feed myself on the walk. I must try and find my friends again. I guess they'll be in Quiczu. If I can see the river, I'll know to follow it down stream and I can find the town."

Han was ready to leave at that moment but Shengli took a few minutes to kneel beside Boken's body and to say good-bye for the last time. Then she stood up, brushed herself down and biting her lower lip slightly nodded at Han and as he turned to walk she fell in beside him, feeling his smooth, almost weightless loping contrast with her own, clumsy seeming, stepping and scrambling. "Sir, King Han, Sir, thank you for respecting Boken like that."

"It is our way. One day, perhaps, I will have the chance to say goodbye to my son in the same way but as yet I have no news as to what has happened to his body."

Shengli felt a sense of guilt that she had been the cause of Renzi's being in Lungdou and the tragedy that had followed. "I'm...I'm so sorry."

"There is no cause for sorrow. It was a risk to merge the two spirits. We are wolves. We live with risk and danger and we accept that in the service of the pack."

"Can you tell me about your time with Old Tam, I mean 'Tam-ha' "

"That was in the time of your people-wars when terrible things happened. Tam-ha had been captured by the enemies but escaped into the mountains. He lived with us through three winters and served alongside us, caring for the little ones, playing and protecting and he had a skill with the traps that he could make them into pieces. He told us stories and we shared our wisdom and together we walked the dragon lines as he searched for the place of disturbance on the Yu dragon's vein. He did not find it with us but then later, but you must know about that?"

"N-no..."

"Then you must find answers in his world, not ours. We hunt in order with the Yu dragon's wisdom; we do no harm to the Jiao dragon but rather we feed the earth in line with nature; we play among ourselves with the spirit of the Mang dragons and we live in harmony with the seasons of the Li dragon. For wolves, there is simplicity. The lines, the dragon veins, they are of no anxiety to us. We walk them without knowing we walk them. But your species..."

There was nothing Shengli could say. She felt more at peace with King Han of the wolves than she had with, say, King Tiebin of the people, but yet she was of people. She thought back to the evening with Old Sun when the elderly lady had shared with herself and Shonan some of the secrets to nüshu and the learning of the women of Tianya. Somewhere, in the middle between Old Tam's and Lord Kang's philosophical speculations and the understanding and wisdom of the women who wrote nüshu there was an answer that would help people find the way to the kind of oneness with nature that she could see in the wolves. She would find it.

They reached the top of a ridge and suddenly, below them, the mountains fell away to the river valley below and in the clear, bright light of a spring day after the storm of the night before, the panorama stretched seemingly endlessly. She could see how the winding river, silvery in the sunlight, weaved through the valley and how the flat lands either side had made homes for the farming people of these fertile reaches. To her right, the west, she understood, the river twisted away and the mountains curved round such that in the distance, all was the range of the great heights. Across the river, she saw how the land rose and then the forest began and how the sight of that green sea lifted her heart, the bamboos like a fluffy carpet that stretched, rolling over the gentler hills of the south, as far as far. But she could see no sign of Quiczu.

"The town is to the east. As the river bends round these mountains here. You will have to make for the river and then follow that. It is maybe two- or three-days' walking," said Han.

How could she have got so lost? She must have turned completely to the west and off her so-smart route to cut off the mountain salient. She would never walk in the mountains again, unless she had a wolf by her side! But she would be all right from here. There was a goat track leading down the slope and from there, the river and the forested hills across would always be in view. She turned to King Han, "Your Highness, thank you."

"There is no place for you to address me like that. Being leader of the pack is a job like any other. Simply address me as Han. If you were willing, you could simply call me 'friend'. I would be pleased if you felt that despite the events with my son, you could consider myself, the pack and all wolves to be your friends."

"Oh yes! I would be so proud! Han, my friend, I hope we will meet again. I would like to spend time here with you and learn more about the way of the wolves."

"I have a feeling that is very likely. There is imbalance in Tianya and when that occurs, there is need of one who can interpret the dragon lines and cross between their world and ours and there will be need then of one who can go between the different creatures, not only the people and the wolves but all the feeling-creatures of Tianya. I have an idea that may be you."

"Wha..."

"Shengli, communication with the dragons is through dance and music setting vibrations along the lines, the veins. Only a dancer can do that."

"But I have lost the spells to put in my shoes."

"One who has studied the learning of the old philosophers and who has been given the gift of nüshu will write new spells."

"How do you know all this?"

"Tam-ha and I remained in contact until the end. My joy was that Renzi could be the go-between. I had hoped, as had Tam-ha, that he would bring wolf-wisdom to the learning of men but man-spirit was too conflicted in him. And as Tam-ha helped me understand, only a woman would ever have the gift of nüshu and so be able to write spells. Return to your village, study Tam-ha's learning and dance every day. Find people who can master the music and work with them..."

"Shonan and Durfin!" Shengli blurted out,

"...and there will be hope for all creatures that until people learn ways of living without causing unnecessary suffering. Then there will be a dancer with the art to bring succor and comfort, repair and healing to the dragons whenever they are threatened. I had hoped to give my son to this cause. Now I cannot and, tragically, he threatened you, but know this: whenever you are in the mountains, there will be wolves who will know you and watch you, even if you cannot see or hear them, and in these domains you will be safe. That is my promise."

"Th-thank you. Thank you. I am honored."

"It is we who honor you as you embrace this destiny. Go safely, Shengli. All creatures, including the poor people who have lost the way, all creatures need you and your dance. One day, maybe, Tianya won't need you but there will be very great need before then. Let us part now but I am sure we will meet again before long."

Shengli paused a moment as she looked at the great wolf. His amber-yellow eyes were kindly and smiled gently in a warm if worldly and weary way; the silver of his winter fur was lighter beneath and darkened to a line of near-black that ran down his spine; his alert ears, triangular and pointed, stood symmetrically atop his head and from between them, a band of darker fur extended forwards along his muzzle. He was the handsomest creature she had ever seen and in wisdom and dignity, compassion and loyalty, he was, from his jet-black nose to the last hair of his bushy tail a King as a King should be. Later he would lead the hunt and he would kill and that would be ruthless and bloody and it would be necessary. In their lives, the wolves would play their part in the ever moving, ever pulsing patterns and cycles of Tianya just as they always had, in accordance with the laws of the Yu dragon. There was nothing for it. She knelt on one knee and threw her arms around Han and embraced him, pressing her face into his beautiful soft fur.

"Thank you, thank you. I will always be your friend. Always. Always."

"Now, Shengli, go back to people. And be cautious what you tell them of our meeting. There is fear and hatred of wolves among people."

"I will, I will. Oh, goodbye, great King. I will see you again. Goodbye." And she had to turn because the little track was steep and irregular and she had to watch her feet but after a few steps she turned to wave again but Han was gone and Shengli was on her own for the first time.

Shonan and Durfin had slept soundly all the way to Quiczu but when the engine pulled into the mounting bay there and they were woken by a worker from the railway, their first thought was that Shengli had already jumped off and would be waiting for them beside the wagons. But they couldn't find her and went through all the possible explanations as they tried to talk each other into reassurance. She'd gone to find food? She and Boken were exploring? She'd be back soon. She'd gone into the town and got lost but sooner or later she'd ask someone or something and then she'd look for them and of course she'd come to the mounting bay. She was by the river talking and had lost track of the time; she was, she was...

And as the hours passed it became harder to explain why she wasn't there. Something had happened and the evening grew darker and they were at a loss as to what to do. The only thing they were certain of was that they must stay where Shengli would come to find them, at the mounting bay in Quiczu where they had set out with Renzi so recently and yet how that seemed like another lifetime ago.

As evening drew on, the crowds of people that gathered around the fancy building with its scalloped roofs and clock tower gradually dispersed. An official looking railway employee came and drove them out of the waiting building and into the square outside and he then locked the doors. Unless Shengli came soon, they might be facing a night in the open. No matter in itself, they were old hands at sleeping in the open and it was a clear spring night but this wasn't the forest, this was Quiczu, and none of the stories about Quiczu that they had grown up with suggested it was all right for children to sleep in the streets. As the open square in front of the ornate railway building cleared of passengers, and as darkness came, different people came and started to set up stalls. They unloaded boxes and packets of foodstuffs and flasks of drink and set up little tables with low stools. Some put up canvas shelters but some were heard saying that for once they wouldn't bother, it was such a nice night, and there were braziers and stoves lit and as the daylight slipped away finally, the red and orange glow of charcoal and wood stoves lit up the space.

On some of the stalls, people burnt lumps of flesh over hot coals, threading them onto little sticks and the smell was simultaneously gross and appalling while also alluring and tempting. Others were baking cakes in charcoal ovens; there were bread-buns and barley fritters and then men who dipped ladles in wooden barrels of mulberry wine and served it out in beakers; a great kettle of berry-broth had only a few takers but it steamed comfortingly by itself. Slowly, a crowd of people gathered and, swapping monies for the foodstuffs and drinks, settled around the area on the little stools and ate and drank and in some cases smoked little pipes, something the children had not seen since their last visit to their grandfather's and the smell made them homesick.

"Shonan, I'm hungry. I could really go for some of those fritters at least."

"Me too, but we've hardly any monies and until Shengli

comes back I don't suppose we should spend any. We've still got some of Old Sun's snacks: if we eat those, she can't really mind as they were for the journey although she didn't have her share."

"Perhaps it would be wrong to take her share now?"

"Yes, I suppose you're right. Why don't we get out the zurdom and the quan and play around a bit to pass the time?"

And the twins, bored and tired, lonely and hungry, but determined to stay put for as long as it took for Shengli to come back and find them, set up their instruments and started to play around a little, Durfin setting that solid, reliable pulse that he found came so easily to him while Shonan experimented with the metallic ringing sounds that rang out prettily from her quan. They became so absorbed in their music that they forgot about the food market and the people. They had found a system for themselves whereby Durfin began with a rhythm that had a fixed number of pulses, which he would repeat, creating a kind of cycle. Shonan would listen to it for a while and then set up a rising pattern of notes from the quan, a simple ascending sequence. Durfin found that he could keep the pattern while occasionally playing around the pulses, on them and off them while still keeping the feel of them. Shonan then began, over the recurring pattern that Durfin supported, to mix up the notes: simple sequences at first, sometimes just a few notes at a time and then, gradually, getting more complex but sticking throughout just to the notes of the first sequence so that it held some sort of sense in her mind. The mixtures of notes would get more complex and rapid, but still fitting over Durfin's pattern, until she felt it time to, kind of, unravel the knot that she had created so then she would feel her choices of notes resolving in simpler sequences until at the end the only thing that felt right was to play, again, the rising sequence that she had started with.

It was something they had worked out playing around in

Lord Kang's courtyard but it was very satisfying. As she came to the end, Durfin heard it and knew and he brought things to a close at exactly the moment that the last note of the quan faded away. They looked at each other and smiled but then were broken out of their private moment by the sound of clapping and the stamping of feet. There were cheers and people slapping the little wooden tables and a kindly lady brought over a couple of barley cakes and some berry-broth.

"That was lovely, kiddos, how about something we can dance to? We haven't had anything like this since I can't remember when. It seems no one can do music anymore, not now we've got the steam-organs, but that was lovely. Better, I dare say, than the organs, although who'd have thought that, but I don't know why. Lovely, it was. Can you do another?"

"Go on! Another tune!" roared a portly gentleman with a big, greasy, but smiling face. And then there were other cries of "more" and "a dance!" and so on.

Chapter Fifteen

Shonan looked at Durfin. "Can you make a rhythm that is like a dance? Maybe", she looked at the group of people, none of them looking noticeably athletic or lithe, "maybe not so fast?"

"Can I? Easy. Listen." And he started a rhythm over six beats, strong on the first and fairly strong on the fourth but weak on the others, switching between slaps to the middle of the drumhead and sharp clicks on the rim, and Shonan got it immediately and set up a simple, recurring tune, taking care to accent the pulses in Durfin's rhythm and building in repetition of phrases, rather than constantly coming up with new patterns. The greasy-faced man pulled himself to his feet and like a huge bear, started to shuffle his feet backwards and forwards in time, while comically holding up his trousers by the loose cloth over his knees. Others cheered him on and broke out into applause, clapping and stamping their feet.

Some of the older men and women with pipes took them out of their mouths and started conducting with them in time, with similar looks about them as Old Tam had had when he first tried to conduct the dance back in the forest by the way-stone when they first tried to make music. A big, cheery woman with some kind of paint on her face grabbed at one of the men and took hold of both his wrists and started to spin him round in time to the music and that was the signal to others to get up in pairs. Before long there was a group of maybe a dozen people jigging and bouncing around in carefree manner and while it wasn't dancing like they had seen Shengli doing, it was funny and happy all the same and then finally, when it felt about right, Shonan nodded to Durfin, they brought their made-up little tune to an end. There was huge laughter and applause and they were called over to join the people at the tables and were given food and drink and when they were asked where they were from and they told as much of their story as they felt appropriate, they were offered places to stay the night but they said 'no' as they were waiting for their friend so they were given more food to keep for her and told not to worry, if she hadn't turned up the next day they'd look out for them and not to worry and they'd always have a friend in Gentong or Bang or Liangkou or Shoumen or whoever it was had been the last to speak.

And then there were calls for more music and so they played twice more for dancing but then that seemed to be enough for everybody so they finished with another go at the kind of more complicated, kind of 'looking-for-something' tune that they had worked out for themselves only they deliberately set it to a slower rhythm so it felt like evening and Shonan made it sound thoughtful and not quite so busy as before, and Durfin found that sometimes he could hint at the pulse by missing beats and there was a way that the music happened, if you like, between the notes and then when it felt right, they brought this different piece of playing to its end, although they didn't really know how they knew it was time to stop but they did.

They put the zurdom and the quan away and they were offered more food and more drink and were made more promises about how they didn't need to worry about anything and how they'd check in on them the next day and see if they needed anything and don't you worry, Qiangfeng or Awen or Xiangxiang would see they'd be all right, never fear. And gradually the crowd slipped away with farewells and promises, a cheerful belch and a tummy pat and the occasional slip when standing up and taking a step on the uneven cobbles and then a wave and another farewell and so on.

With the last of the eaters and drinkers away, the cooks and peddlers began to extinguish their fires and stoves and disassemble their fragile stalls until before long, apart from the detritus of little sticks and dropped, uneaten, foodstuffs, the last farewell to the twins and promise of help if they needed it any time, just ask for Langzurdom or Langxiang or whoever and they'd see them right and the twins were alone in the square. They gathered up their own and Shengli's, packs, the instruments, and their generous supply of foodstuffs, thanks to all the party people, and found a sheltered corner under the canopy at the front of the station.

"People are funny, aren't they?" said Shonan.

"Yes, sister, they are. Sometimes you think they're just horrid because of all the awful things and then they're all so kind and really it felt like the village in a way, although different, of course."

"Maybe not so different."

"You know what I think? I think it was music and dance. That's the trick. But in Lungdou, did you see any music or dancing, apart from the steam organs? And that's not really music, is it, because it doesn't have musicianers there so it can't be music, can it, like, not music that is there, if you know what I mean. It seems to me that if the music is right there, like being made by music-people right there, then it is really there and then that has some sort of trick, I don't know what. I wish I could ask Old Tam about it only I probably wouldn't understand his answer anyway. I can't help thinking there's something to this, though. You and Shengli work it out since I'm the stupid one, obviously. But I think there's some sort of thing in all this. I really do. And you know what else..."

"Go on..." his sister said, with a smile.

"It all starts with a drum!" and Durfin gave his a cheerful thump and then dodged the slap from his sister that he knew was coming even before she thought of it and they got on with the business of making themselves comfortable and getting what sleep they could, assuming that Shengli was doing the same somewhere else and she'd come and find them the next day and no doubt she'd have a story to tell but whether it compared with theirs, well, that they'd have to see about.

Shengli's knees were screaming by the time she reached the bottom of the slope. It had been hard going and however hard she tried to be mindful, she couldn't help landing her feet on loose bits of scree that ran away when she stepped on them. She'd tried silly running as a way of getting down quickly with a view to one of her famous crash landings but the snow had largely gone and the rocks and occasional gorse bushes didn't make that too attractive. So mostly it was a sort of shuffle sideways, step a bit, slip, scramble and slide but after what seemed like forever the slope started to level and before long, she was at the edge of the river valley and walking across farmland.

Growing up in the forest, Shengli hadn't had much experience of farmland. They grew their own food in the plots around the village and foraged in the greenwood but big, open fields with hedges around them were strange and alien. Snow still lingered on these but some of them had already been ploughed and she guessed that spring sowing must be due to start soon. She stuck to the edges of the fields where the plough hadn't quite reached but still, the furrows and ridges and the earth thrown up by the hedgerows meant it was once again hard going even if of a different type. She was pleased to find some chickweed and henbit in the hedgerows and she ate greedily as she hadn't had a proper meal since breakfast the previous day but what she'd give now for a barley cake and mug of berry-broth! She knew there must be people nearby somewhere but she didn't see any and she was keen not run into anyone who might ask difficult questions. Her objective was the river and hopefully a better path that ran alongside it and that would take her to Quiczu. It was impossible, surely, that Shonan and Durfin were still there and she tried to guess what they would do. Perhaps they would have spoken to someone? Or started the journey back to the village? Although the more she thought about it, the more she came to reckon that they'd be waiting for her. How did she know? Well, that was just what they were like.

Finding her way through the hedges that divided the fields was tricky, and she was scratched and stung in places, but eventually, she entered a field that didn't have a boundary down the southern side ahead of her and she could see that that was because it bordered the river. Thank the dragons for that: compared with the mountains, this was easy walking on soggy but level ground and she couldn't get lost. As long as she followed the river downstream, she would see Quiczu sooner or later.

The river here, above Quiczu, was clean and fresh and full of eagerness as the first of the snowmelt chased down from the mountains. Shengli knelt beside the water and washed her face and that felt so good she did the same with her feet and dangling them in the running water was so soothing that she lay back on the bank and let them soak in the cool, fresh, rushing river and she felt the late morning spring sun on her face and let her eyes close for a moment and there was nothing for it, there was no fighting it, in a moment she sank into a deep sleep.

"'ello, Miss! This is a funny looking fish to have been landed by somebody, ain't it, Bofan?"

Shengli jolted awake but with the sun direct in her eyes she was befuddled and blurred for a moment before she began to make out just about the hugest man she had ever seen in her life. He towered over her, wearing a great cape with a hood that covered his head leaving a face that would have been visible if it weren't for the thick, bush-like beard that made Shengli think oddly that it looked like a swarm of bees had attached themselves to his face. Beside him was a sleek, skinny kind of dog, its tongue lolling out and dull, its silly-looking eyes protruding almost like a frog's.

"Er...hello, I'll just be on my way then. Nice to have met you." Shengli climbed to her feet dopily.

"Now then, are you all right? You look like you've been sleeping rough and while that's no crime, and for sure I'm no constable, don't the dragons know I ain't, but are you all right?"

"Yes, yes. Thank you. Must go. Well, lovely day, eh?"

"Very well. Not my place to intrude. We'll just get back to our boat then. Come on Bofan, with the river this fast we'll be in Quiczu in no time." And the great big man turned, his oily cape swinging with him and he stepped down off the bank to where a simple boat lay pulled up onto the shallows, flat-bottomed and flat-ended with a canvas, arched cover towards the stern and an empty space with baskets and other equipment towards the bow.

Shengli paused for a moment. Maybe she needed to be a bit smarter here? "Ah-hum", she coughed, "You are, er, going to Quiczu?"

"That's right. I'd like to shift some of these fish here before the day's ruined. We were late starting out for reasons I don't need to go into here and we'll have missed the best of the market but there'll still be something for these, especially that fat old sea trout there. I'm hoping that someone will be late shopping for their bit of supper just as I was late catching it!"

"Erm...I wonder, would you mind, sir, if I may ask, most kindly, if you would..."

"Out with it, girl, out with it!" smiled the huge man.

"Could you take me to Quiczu? I have to get there too." She quickly told what seemed the most acceptable parts of her story about stepping out of the railway wagon when it stopped and then trying to walk to Quiczu through the mountains and getting lost and so on but deciding on balance not to mention the wolves nor, in the circumstances, share her feelings about men who killed animals such as trappers who laid head-traps for wolves or anything more than just that she had fallen off the train and got lost. That seemed to be enough for now.

The fisherman paused and tugged at his beard. Shengli smiled at the dog to see if she could communicate with him as she had Boken and the wolves but he seemed a silly thing and although she could make out what he was saying, it was pretty uninteresting. Maybe that was what you got if you lived your life with a man who never troubled to learn how to speak with you himself? And how could he, after all, when killing creatures was what he did so of course he couldn't know that you can't have any kind of relationship with a creature as long as you see creatures other than your own type as just being there for you to use in any way you like. Silly old man. Shengli actually felt sorry for him all of a sudden.

"Well, I don't see why not, although I can't help wondering if I shouldn't know something about your parents or something. Little girls shouldn't take rides on boats with strange men, you know. But if you're in trouble, then the right thing is for me to help you. I don't want any trouble of my own though, you understand? We'll drop you outside Quiczu and you can walk the last bit. If I turn up with you in one of my baskets some of those fellers down there won't half have something to say."

"I understand," said Shengli, although she didn't really.

The fisherman showed her how to climb in the boat and asked her to sit at the very front while he took up his place at the back, the stern, where with a quick shove with a boathook, they were afloat and he took hold of the handle of a long tiller that doubled as a kind of oar that he could sway with a twisting motion to create an effect ironically just like the tail of one of the poor fishes that lay in the baskets in the boat. The quick current carried them rapidly and the fisherman's main task as helmsman was to hold the line and weave the boat safely through the tight meanders. Shengli looked in at the basket where the fish were held. The basket was itself inside a watertight, bamboo bucket and the fish were still alive but they were pressed against each other and could not move. The largest of all, the one the fisherman had called a sea trout, lay across the middle of the basket and Shengli marveled at the beauty of the fine creature. Silver and muscular with a pattern of black spots, his eyes were shiny and alert towards the top of his head and he seemed to look up at Shengli with an accusing expression, his mouth turned down no doubt in nature but Shengli, for all that she knew she was being fanciful, she felt he was angry with her and defiant. She suppressed the urge to tip the basket over the side of the boat and release the fishes and instead turned away and enjoyed the unfamiliar experience of watching the landscape rush by from the point of view of a boat gliding down a briskly flowing river. The ploughed fields gave way to brown and busier lands where the last of the winter barley had been harvested and the straw lay gathered in clumps, awaiting collection and then in alternate strips of land, fresh earth where the first shoots of spring barley would soon be nudging through, alerted by warming of the soil in the spring sunshine.

As they approached the town of Quiczu, barley fields gave way to market gardening: plots of winter greens and onions and bean plants that had been planted hopeful for an early spring and that had been waiting for a day just such as this before letting their first flowers pop open.

To her left, the north, she could see the mountains she had so recently been among and how they gave way to the plain before the sea beyond; to her right, the south, she felt a surge of love for the gentler, rolling hills, covered in the light fronds of the bamboo forest and all that was familiar and secure about home. In her mind she played with a map of Tianya. She had never given it much thought before but from Lungdou, the mountains wrapped around to south and north but the great ranges were to the west. To the north, the mountains then fell away as the valleys, one of which had held Old Sun's home village, opened out like dry rivers down to the grasslands and then, beyond, the desert. One day, she thought, she would like to see the desert. They were lands from which had come the invaders in the days of the wars but from where, she imagined, they must have looked on Tianya with longing. And to the east, the islands. The ancestral home of the royal family; the strange people who lived surrounded by the sea and who farmed the kelp and sea algae and marine plants that they shipped into Tianya and which, by the time she knew them, were dried and served in seaweed fritters and other snacks but the royal symbol of the sea purslane was a reminder of what they owed to that rich source of food and how they had returned to it in times of trouble.

And among those islands, Lord Kang had suggested, were

priories where wise women still worked with nüshu and where the sea dragons spiraled beneath, and the dragon veins of the land were faint. And then south, the forested hills: forests of bamboo from the Quiczu river down to far beyond her own village but she knew, because she had heard others tell, of how the bamboo gave way to trees of different types and then to richer, thicker, mysterious forests that no one dared travel through. A land bounded by endless deserts to the north, by the sea to the east, by the great mountains to the west and endless forests to the south. At some point, she remembered Old Tam explaining, there was an end and one reached the sea again but she hadn't been paying attention properly. Tianya seemed so small and vulnerable when you thought about it like that. The people settled in the valleys and where the rivers met the sea; villages dotted the landscape whatever the terrain but the two main towns, Quiczu and Lungdou, had grown by waterways and where, she knew, the dragon lines were thickest. Only at Zamai did the primary lines intersect but the secondary and tertiary lines crisscrossed Tianya in a pattern that still hadn't been fully mapped by the scholars and no one was doing that work anymore. Looking over to the south, seeing the familiar forest undulating and rolling over the soft southern hills Shengli tried to see the terrain as Old Tam or Lord Kang or Old Sun might have done, in their different ways: veins and arteries of vibrations running in straight lines, intersecting and patterning and carrying the fluence that animated the dragons and kept Tianya in harmony.

And now there was all the muddle: the mess in the air from the engines that kept the Li dragon beneath; the scars in the earth in the excavation for coal and other stones that scraped at the Jiao dragon; the chaos among creatures when people set themselves as separate from nature and took for themselves the right to kill and exploit others outside the order of the Yu dragon and the defiant imposition of the laws of the engines on a nature that was made wonderful by the random playfulness of the Mang dragons. Maybe it was the crystal, sparkling water of the burbling river as it bounced between the bends formed by the two banks but Shengli felt like she could see Tianya clearly for the first time and she understood, thanks to Old Sun's teachings and the remarks of King Han, how it was that Old Tam had worked to plot the dragon lines and then to try and care for them, to look for damage and to sustain the dragons but he never had the dance or the right to use nüshu. She knew now what her work would be and she lay back in the boat and watched the clouds playing in the sky as she let her mind wander through thoughts of dragon lines, nüshu, wolves, Boken and around and around and she forgot where she was until with a gentle bump, the boat nudged the bank.

Neither wanted to be the first to say it but both Shonan and Durfin were wondering, as the second evening came, that maybe they should think again about waiting by the railway mounting bay another day? They had spent the day taking it in turns to wander round the town in case Shengli was waiting for them somewhere else, one of them always staying at the railway. It had been no good although they had at least become very familiar with the streets of Quiczu for what that might be worth. Perhaps Shengli had assumed they would head for the village? Whatever had happened to her, maybe she was already pushing on through the forest by now and who knows, bumping into Gan and asking him if he had seen them and she thought they were in front of her? But as neither would say the thought out loud, they stayed where they were and as evening fell and the crowd of travelers thinned out and the evening food sellers and the party people gathered again, at least they knew they had a way of making sure of a good meal. As the evening crowd gathered, a little larger than the previous night, and they recognized a couple of faces from before they set themselves to play and Durfin, closing his eyes as he now found this helped, started off with the rhythm cycle that suited his mood. And that mood was somber. It was a slow beat, not draggy but thoughtful and a bit sad. Somehow, he had found exactly the tempo and character of Shonan's own feelings and she too closed her eyes, felt around the surface of her quan for a moment with the palm of her hand and then, taking the little sticks, she picked out a rising sequence of notes that seemed to be just right. You wouldn't call it sad, but sort of thinking. They took the music on that kind of 'looking-for-something' journey that they had worked out and that now felt as natural as talking, or in fact, more natural in a way, in that you could say things that it would be hard to say in words. Somehow, Shonan seemed to be asking more questions this time. The sequences of notes didn't so much get more complex as more unsettled and then when it seemed to reach a point where it felt like the whole thing would strain and break down, she pulled it back with gentler choices and calmer patterns until eventually the answer, such as it was, was given by finding again the initial, rising pattern. There was a moment's silence from the people who had turned to listen and then they broke into applause, at first cautiously as if wondering whether this was something you should clap to as it had left them feeling a little unsure although not in a way that they didn't appreciate, and then, confident that others were feeling the same as themselves, they clapped more vigorously.

The twins opened their eyes and the first person they saw, seated cross-legged on the ground in front of them, clapping hard enough to hurt and with tears rolling down her face was Shengli. "You two...you two...how did you? That was...I don't know...." She was gabbling and couldn't find the words and they just stared at her before Shonan screamed and putting aside her quan threw herself at Shengli and hugged her for all her life and then Durfin stood by them, kind of awkward but with a massive grin on his face, forgetting to put down his drum and then Shengli reached to give him a hug but he was still holding his drum so she hugged him over the top of it which was funny and set them all laughing. Shonan let go of Shengli and looked around but she couldn't see what she expected, the little foxlike dog bouncing around them whenever there were these times. "Where's Boken?" she asked

"I've got a lot to tell you." said Shengli. "I'm so glad I found you. Can we sit down and have something to eat?"

And meanwhile, the kindly lady from the evening before had brought them over some barley cakes and seaweed fritters and mugs of berry-broth and she asked if this was the friend they'd been waiting for and it was all happy and joyful and then Shengli told the twins her story and they were silent and both of them wept for Boken but were proud and jealous at the same time of the experience with the wolves and they didn't really feel like telling their story afterwards as it didn't sound that amazing but Shengli made them anyway and they sat and wept a bit more for Boken but laughed to be together again and Shengli ate like she had never eaten she was so hungry and what with it all they didn't notice the constable come up in front of them or the lean woman with the twisted foot and hair in a tight bun just behind him.

"There she is, constable. Arrest her!" came the sharp voice.

All three children looked up and saw first the broad-chested constable, his crossbow across his back, his tall hat pulled over his eyes and his leather belts shining in the light from the cooking fires. Behind him, bending round him, was the pinched face and sparrow-like frame of the woman that Shengli recognized as the Dama and the twins only knew as someone who meant them no good at all.

"Arrest her! That one!"

"Steady on, Madam, Now, Miss," flustered the constable, "the lady here, and she's a most estimable lady, tells me you might have something that rightfully belongs to her. What do you have to say?"

"Who me, sir?" asked Shonan, innocently, with a smile.

"No," snapped the Dama, "the other one"

"Me, sir?" asked Durfin, cheekily.

"Is you a miss, young man? Was I addressin' you? Now, what about you, you, miss?" and he pointed at Shengli.

"I don't have anything that belongs to that lady and I don't know what you are talking about." Shengli spoke, jutting out her chin a bit.

"The spells, you thieving magpie. They belong to the academy. Hand them over!" screamed the Dama.

Shengli stood up and spoke calmly but firmly straight to the Dama, ignoring the constable.

"They were my mother's and now they're mine and they're ruined anyway."

Chapter Sixteen

As always when a constable is involved, a crowd had gathered round. Shengli and the Dama stared hard at each other and the constable shuffled awkwardly.

"Now, perhaps we'd be better all going back to the castle and talking about it there, nice and sensible, like?" he said.

"Arrest her! She's a thief!" squawked the Dama.

"I am not," said Shengli, slowly and clearly. And she turned to pick up her pack from where Durfin had laid it. "And now we'll be on our way, thank you."

"Now just you wait a minute, Miss." said the constable, and he reached out to put his hand on her shoulder but Shengli swayed and darted for a gap in the crowd. The constable lurched after her but the portly gentleman, who had started the dancing the night before, took a slight step to one side and the constable fell over him, crashing to the floor with a thud and a wheeze.

"Now then kiddos," said the kindly lady who'd encouraged their music, leaning towards the twins, "you'd better get after your friend there. Don't you worry about anything here."

And the twins gathered up the quan and the zurdom and their two packs and the bag of food and the crowd parted to let them through, and they scuttled across the square in the direction that Shengli had taken. Behind them, they could hear the Dama shrieking, "Stop, Thief! Oh, for dragons' sake! What's the matter with you people! Stop, Thief! Get up, you stupid plod. Chase them. I will be speaking to the Captain later. He's a very good friend of mine. Get up. Stop, Thief!"

And the constable pulled himself to his feet and gave the greasy-faced gentleman a hard stare and muttered something about how he wouldn't be forgetting and then he galumphed across the square, but with no idea which way the children had gone, he stopped and looked around feeling a little foolish. The twins had hidden in a doorway on one side and were trying to make out Shengli in the shadows but they had lost her again. Durfin stamped the ground in frustration.

"We can't stay here," said Shonan, "the constable may be slow but he'll get round to us if we stay still.

"But where shall we go? Shengli must have run farther. I don't know. Oh, I just want to go home!"

"That's it!" said Shonan, "We have to cross the river by the bridge. We'd have to do that to get over to the south side for the journey back to the forest. We'll have to do it; she'll have to do it. Let's go and wait, the two of us, one at each end. She'll think the same, I know she will."

Carefully keeping to the shadows, moving from doorway to doorway like city rats, they darted across the roads and down alleys that had become familiar during their wanderings in the daytime. At one point they had a near-miss, dodging a steam-wagon, and then they were slipping through the crowds on a busy street as they approached the bridge and when they arrived, they separated, Shonan taking the north side and Durfin making himself as anonymous as he could carrying two packs and a drum as he crossed over and hid in a corner near the arch where he could see anyone coming or going.

Shengli was kicking herself for losing the twins again. She couldn't go back to the square in front of the railway mounting bays and she didn't think the twins would be there either. She tried hard to think but her head was too full and busy and she couldn't concentrate, which made her think straightaway of the The One Who Sees Cries so she pulled back into a shadowy place, behind some rubbish bins where she was sure she couldn't be seen and she started, bit by bit, to empty her head of everything that was racing through it. She forced herself to stop feeling guilty for bringing trouble to the twins; she stopped feeling bitter and angry towards the Dama; she stopped feeling sad for Boken; she stopped feeling homesick for Ba and the village; she stopped trying to think what Lord Kang or Old Tam would want her to do; she stopped her busy thoughts about Old Sun and the nüshu; she stopped thinking about the pain in her feet from the walking over the past two days; she stopped her thoughts about the twins and their music and her dance and how she could maybe... Stop thinking, Shengli! She stopped thinking about the smell from the bins and the hatefulness of the towns and she stopped thinking about the friendly fisherman and the tragic fish and she stopped.

She suddenly found that all she was thinking about was her mother and she forced herself to stop thinking about her as well. She completely stopped thinking and for a second, maybe, it seemed she had succeeded in stopping thinking about everything and as soon as she did it came to her: they've gone to the bridge to wait for me there!

And she relaxed and her head filled up again but it didn't matter as she knew what to do, so she let all those thoughts rush back in like water being released through a dam that has burst and she felt strangely tired and elated at the same time. Not thinking about anything was more exhausting than anything else she had tried but it had worked: a clear head created space for her to see the thing she needed to see. The only problem now was finding out where the bridge was.

She had no idea about the layout of the town. The walk from where she had been dropped by the fisherman to the railway had been easy as it was daylight and the clock tower was visible from a long way away. She crawled out from behind the bins only to see the clumsy constable lumbering down the street. He hadn't seen her though so she hid back behind the bins and thought hard what to do, looking out at the people coming and going and she saw not her fisherman, but another one with the same sort of cape and hat and a basket that he was carrying upside down, empty. He was whistling and Shengli reasoned that, well, if his basket is empty, and he's in a good mood, then he's sold his fish and he's going back to his boat, and that will be moored at the riverside, so that's how to find the way to the river, so she slipped out and fell into step behind him and just caught herself before she started whistling along with him and right enough, he led her all the way down to the waterside where the fishing boats were tied up and from where she could see the bridge, only a short way away.

She approached the bridge from the riverbank and then saw a new problem. A constable had stopped by the head of the bridge, took out a pipe and leaned over the railing for a quiet smoke. It wasn't the same constable as the one they had run from but who was to know that he wasn't there to watch for them? And she was confused in her mind which end of the bridge the twins would be waiting. She had cleared her thoughts well enough to get a clear picture that they were waiting at the bridge but when she pushed that thought hard to see whether the north or south side, it wouldn't make sense. It was like they were at both ends at the same time. She thought for a moment about swimming the river but that was a ridiculous idea. It wasn't too far for her but the current was very strong and in the dark she could easily get disoriented. She was brave but not foolish. She slipped back into 'prowler' mode only because that seemed what you ought to do when trying to dodge a constable and she kept close to the walls and the boxes and packing crates around the wharves where the boats moored and as she approached the bridge she tried one of the forest whistle calls that she knew the twins would recognize.

To her surprise, she got an answer from the far side of the river, as clear across the water as if she were standing right next by. She knew it was Durfin; he'd always had a stronger whistle call than Shonan. They must be both over there. Then there was the lighter, less muscular response from Shonan but she was on this side of the river. That was it! No wonder she couldn't work out which side they'd be on, they were on both sides. Who'd be friends with twins? Things could get confusing.

Gradually, she neared the bridge, whistling and hearing their responses. She soon found Shonan and they whistled in unison to Durfin so he would know they were together. Shonan and Shengli pressed together under the arch of the bridge and waited. They could see the glow from the constable's pipe above them, and watched him through the gaps between the planks that made up the bridge, but they felt safe in the dark recess and they shared a barley cake and when the constable managed to belch and then let go with a ginormous fart they were crying as they bit their fingers and tried not to laugh and give themselves away. Eventually, his duties on the bridge apparently over, the constable stretched, indulged in a bit of a scratch which set the girls to chewing their knuckles and suppressing the kind of giggling fit that is only possible with a friend and off he patrolled back into the city and away from the bridge.

Moments later the three friends were reunited and there was

only one thing on their minds. "Let's get deep into the forest and find a place for the night and we'll be home tomorrow," said Shengli. "And far away from any trumpeting constables!" And she and Shonan exploded into a fit of unrestrained laughter and Durfin looked confused, and he shrugged his shoulders: situation normal.

For all that they were together again and excited to be returning to the forest it was hard going up the hill to the ridge where they had first looked down over Quiczu that day so recently. The time passed as Shengli told them about the story of Renzi and they were all silent for a good while after that and then the pain in Shengli's feet from her time in the mountains started to make walking harder and harder and eventually they reached the edge of the forest and they found the first place that felt safe and suitable and set up camp. But they couldn't sleep. They tried to restrain themselves from eating too much of the food they had carried but it was hard and they ended up nibbling until there seemed so little left they decided just to finish it anyway. They could forage in the forest tomorrow; that was no hardship.

"So, what do we do now, Shengli?" asked Shonan.

"Go home, of course."

"But what about the muddling in the heads of the city people? And Old Tam's work on the dragon lines? And what Old Sun told us?"

"Huh?" interjected Durfin.

"Shush, potato head."

"Hey," he argued back, "we're identical twins. If I'm a potato head then..."

"Do you mind? I'm trying to talk with Shengli here." Shonan shot back with a slightly superior attitude.

"Potato head, yourself." Durfin mumbled.

"Stop it, both of you. After so much you're still going on!"

A DANCE TO WAKE A DRAGON

Shengli said with exasperation.

"Of course!" they replied in unison and burst out laughing while Shengli looked at them and shook her head. "Twins, eh?"

She spoke seriously, "I don't know the answer to your question, anyway, Shonan. But I keep thinking about Boken and how maybe the trap thing is only a small part of it but it stands for a whole lot of something else. The dragon lines; what Lord Kang said about how engines could have benefits; the King and his pretending he didn't believe in the dance, because I know he was pretending; the wolves and even the fisherman earlier today. He was kind and good as he helped me and yet he was catching and killing those beautiful fish and, I don't know. But I think it is all connected somehow. When we get back, I'm going to see if it is all right for me to spend some time in Old Tam's hut looking through his studies and see if I can work out what he was at. And I'll have the advantage of the nüshu now, thanks to Old Sun. And somehow the answer is in the dance."

"And you can't have a dance without music!" said Shonan.

"And you can't have music without a drum!" said Durfin and braced himself to duck but the slap never came.

"Yes, you know, I think you're right." said Shengli, thoughtfully, and in full seriousness. "I've been thinking that whatever it is, it probably does begin with a drum."

There seemed to be no more to say after that and they drifted off asleep eventually under the shuffling of the bamboo leaves in the pleasant spring night. It was good to be walking through the forest again and the soft surface of the path, springy with the fallen leaves from the previous autumn and now clear of snow, meant that walking was easy. Shafts of sunlight slanted through the bamboos and the contrast with the snowy scene when last they had passed this way reminded them what they had done and why.

They were chatting about nothing in particular when they came upon a scene that caused them to stop and then take cover off the line of the path. A group of men and women were tying yellow rope around the bamboos and writing marks on the trunks. One of the men had a kind of board with papers on it and he was directing the others, "And then we'll take the access road through here. Kanting, mark the trees from that point through another twenty measures. They'll come down tomorrow. Henfang, where are you – Henfang, you lazy slob…oh, there you are…" A small figure, presumably Henfang, had been right behind the officious man.

"Here I am, boss. What is it?"

"Get me something to eat. Wretched forest. Miles from anything to buy. Sooner we get this developed and get some proper facilities around here the better."

"Right-oh boss. I've got some pig-flesh rolled in pastry. Will that do? And a nice mug of berry-broth although it's cold now, sorry."

Shengli nudged the twins, and they sat down out of sight to watch. The men and women were marking and measuring and there was a quarrel about something and the man who seemed to be in charge got cross about something and there was a lot of lining things up with sticks that were marked in bands of red and white and then shouting numbers at each other. There was a gentle rustle and someone sat down beside them. It was Gan.

"Hello, children." he said, "How are you? I seem to be running into you all the time these days."

"Oh, Gan!" Shonan cried first and threw her arms around him, but the others were only moments behind.

The old woodsman laughed. "Now steady on! But that's all nice, that is. What have you done with Old Tam, and your little dog?" And they told Gan the story of their adventures and he listened quietly and at the news of Old Tam's and Boken's deaths he nodded gently but said nothing and they all sat watching the men and women with their measuring rods and tapes as they marked up the forest and as they came to the end of their story they sat in silence for a while.

Durfin asked, "What are they doing, there?"

"Developing the forest. That's what they told me, anyway."

"What does that mean?" asked Shonan.

"I don't know. I don't know what it means to develop anything really. Everything that develops and flourishes just goes back to where it came from. Think about it, like a tree, it grows, it develops and flourishes, and then it dies back and one day it falls in the forest and then it rots into the earth and it is just the soil again, like it all started from. But I guess I don't really understand."

"I know that if Old Tam were here," said Shengli, "he'd say you understood better than any of us!"

"Ah, now, he was a good man. Although I didn't always know what he was talking about!" and they laughed together.

And then they heard coming up the path the unmistakable sound of a steam-wagon; familiar to them from their adventures in the cities but Gan tensed up and clutched his staff. "It's all right, Gan, it's just a steam-wagon." said Shonan.

"A what?" he spoke warily, "In the forest?" and he edged back defensively. And huffing and thumping the rattling pistons and rods knocked and hissed as the wagon, dirtier and heavier made than any they had seen on the roads of Quiczu and Lungdou, ground its way forward up a path that had never before known such a thing. Blackened by coal dirt, grimy with oil and soot but magnificent in a way in how it ate the earth before it and how it seemed unstoppable in progress and how it represented ingenuity and all the cleverness anyone could need to manage a world for good. The wagon pulled up and stopped by the group of measuring men and women and with a series of pops and hisses, gurgles and a long last exhale of steam like a sigh from an exhausted beast the wagon was still and settled to a gentle, even, burbling sound as, seemingly, it rested.

The engineers pulled their goggles back off their heads and looked down at the boss man who shouted up at them. "Ah, there you are, at last. What took you so long?"

"Not really designed for forests, ain't an engine, sir." said one of the engineers, "Going was a bit soft in places. Had to take it steady. But we're right enough we are. Where do you want us?"

And the boss man and some of the other measurers gathered round the boss man's board and papers and the engineers listened and shook their heads at something and the boss man got angry, and he shouted at the little man called Henfang, and Gan got up slowly and made to leave.

"Time for me to get on. I don't know what's going on here and I don't suppose I'll ever understand. For me, I tend to think like the world wasn't made to be mucked about with. From what I see, the more people want, the more they lose. Mess it up and you lose it, that's how it seems to me but anyway, I'll be seeing you kids some time. Give my best to your families now. I'll be by the village someday soon, I expect."

"Come and see us, Gan!" they said in turn and with promises of the next time, Gan took off into the forest away from the path for whatever bit of business he was on that day and the children set to the rest of their day's walking. The scene of the measurers and the steam-wagon and the idea of developing the forest had made them thoughtful and more eager to get home.

And what a homecoming it was! There was shock and upset among the villagers as they learned the news about Old Tam and it was hard for anyone to imagine the village without his wise presence but they all knew he would have chosen to go the way he did and that was consolation for them all. And although they hadn't known the little dog for as long, there was perhaps greater upset at the fate of Boken, and the realization that Shengli wouldn't have him skipping around her feet was hard for them to take, and especially so for Shengli's Ba, who hadn't realized how much he had relied on Boken to be family to Shengli after her mother had died. But the joy at the return of the children overrode these unhappinesses, and their tales and the wonders of what they had done and seen filled the villagers with pride and envy as well as anxiety as they thought of the complexity and yet nearness of the world beyond the forest.

A feast was prepared. of course, and there was all the best food imaginable to the children made up of all the different ways of preparing the good things of the forest and the vegetable plots, and the specialties that they traded with the peddlers, and the adults argued over whose mulberry wine was best for the occasion and then settled on the compromise that it should be Ba's and the twins' parents both and tables were set up outside the front row of cottages and all the village were invited and food was brought out from every cottage and smaller children like Shonan and Durfin's little brother and sister ran from table to table and the older adults settled back into chairs and the conversation gradually drifted towards mulch and recipes for mulberry wine.

Shengli's Ba squeezed her hand. "I missed you, you know."

"I missed you, too. But it turned out all right in the end." she answered. "

Do you think that is the end?" Ba asked. "I won't be surprised if you hear again from the Dama and from what you tell me, we will have more disturbances here in the forest than we care for."

They sat in silence for a while, Shengli fingering her beads in thought, and then she said quietly, "Ba, I'm going to walk up to Old Tam's hut. I won't be long."

"I'll wait here. There'll be a bit of clearing up to do and I'll do my share."

"Of course." And Shengli edged away quietly.

Durfin and Shonan were setting up to play some music and the villagers were excited at the sight of the zurdom and the quan and as Shengli stepped around the edge of the pond she heard the drum start up and then Shonan's quan start to ring and it was a melody that said everything that she was feeling and she wondered how it was that her clever friend did that, every time? Evening was falling in the forest and there was a slight chill in the air as the sun fell away to the west. Shengli let herself into Old Tam's hut and everything was just as he had left it. There were the scrolls lined up on shelves and in jars; the astrolabe lay propped up on its stand and the brushes and inkstones were just as they always were, lying about randomly. She picked the lute up in the corner and plucked a couple of notes. Old Tam had been convinced that playing the lute helped keep the Yu dragon from falling asleep and she too was coming to see too that finding the way forward for the people and other creatures of Tianya was going to involve music and it was going to involve dance. But how and what that meant she still needed to work out.

She blew some dust from off a scroll and unrolled it across the desk. The signs made sense, of course, she was a good reader, but she must have picked a scroll out of order, as it seemed to start up from something else. She rolled it up again. It would all have to be worked out in time but now was not the moment. The sound of the twins' music floated up from the village down the slope and mixed with the bubbling stream that ran down beside Old Tam's hut and the songs of them both seemed to combine and to say to her that 'yes, the answers are in here somewhere but not tonight'.

Stepping out of the hut, looking down to the village and protected by the darkness, she danced a couple of steps from the first sequence of the dragon dance and then she stopped and thought a moment, listened to the music that the twins were playing, and an idea came to her. She concentrated her mind on the rhythm that Durfin was laying down and she experimented with a couple of improvised steps and then she found that a sway worked, and then she tried a little rond de jambe, and then a thunder clap and a spin, and then she fell to the ground and started laughing. It was so easy! Lightly skipping she started to make her way back to the village.

She would keep her secret for a little while yet, but Durfin had been right to say it all started with a drum. That was how it began, it did, and it gained meaning with a melody and then it came to life and became magical with a dance. And she could make the dance. As long as she had the twins, she could make the dance and she had the nüshu and she would study the learning and there would be new spells and new dances and somehow the muddle that the people had got into and the confusion with the dragons and the funny ways of seeing things that people had got into, not because they were bad because they weren't, just think of the fisherman, and the King was all right really, Lord Kang said so, and she had seen so, but they were lost somehow and that was because they were looking in the wrong places but she, she and the twins, they had found it and it had been there all along.

And just then, a flash of amber fur caught her eyes, and her heart froze but then she saw that it was in fact a young fox, with a white throat and little black points on his ears, who turned and stared back at her. Then suddenly, as if he'd never been there, he leaped away over the stream but it turned out to be just a bit too far to leap clearly for such a little fox, almost still only a cub, and as he landed on the other bank he slipped back a bit, just catching the tip of his tail in the water before recovering and disappearing into the forest. And Shengli watched him, and she knew then that like the fox, her journey was just beginning and the slips and false steps that she had experienced as she went to dance at Zamai were in a way no more than the little fox's dipping of his tail in the stream.

She watched a moment longer at the point where the fox had disappeared and then she shook the ideas out of her head. She should get back to the party. The next adventure could wait another day at least.

About The Author

Richard Pratt has been a teacher for over thirty years in a career split roughly equally between Britain and China. He is presently Principal of an international school in Beijing. When school business allows, his enthusiasms include music and poetry, stories that make you think, and attending football games featuring his local team, Beijing Guo'an.